THE
DUKE OF
ASH AVENUE

GARRETT STACK

CATAMOUNT
PRESS

an imprint of Sunbury Press, Inc.
Mechanicsburg, PA USA

CATAMOUNT PRESS

an imprint of Sunbury Press, Inc.
Mechanicsburg, PA USA

For information about special discounts for bulk purchases, please contact Sunbury Press Orders Dept. at (855) 338-8359 or orders@sunburypress.com.

To request one of our authors for speaking engagements or book signings, please contact Sunbury Press Publicity Dept. at publicity@sunburypress.com.

FIRST CATAMOUNT PRESS EDITION: September 2024

Set in Adobe Garamond | Interior design by Crystal Devine | Cover by Sarah Chapman | Edited by Lawrence Knorr.

Publisher's Cataloging-in-Publication Data
Names: Stack, Garrett, author.
Title: The Duke of Ash Avenue / Garrett Stack.
Description: First trade paperback edition. | Mechanicsburg, PA : Catamount Press, 2024.
Summary: With its shuttered mills and seldom-empty barstools, the Appalachian town of Lowland, Pennsylvania is ripe for change. So is its prodigal antihero, Elbridge—Elby—Corvallis, a hockey star deciding what to grieve first: his recently deceased mother or his career, cut short by injury. Or, of late, the sanity of his father, the inscrutable Professor Robert Corvallis of Lowland University who may keep a horse in his garage, may get himself elected mayor, and may or may not be the elusive, famed Duke of Ash Avenue.
Identifiers: ISBN : 979-8-88819-233-7 (paperback).
Subjects: FICTION / Literary | FICTION / Small Town & Rural | FICTION / Humorous / General.

Designed in the USA
0 1 1 2 3 5 8 13 21 34 55

For the Love of Books!

For you, Ma

"'My mother,' answered Telemachus, 'tells me I am son to Ulysses, but it is a wise child that knows his own father.'"

—*The Odyssey*, Book 1

CHAPTER 1

Soon, I'm going to tell you how it all went off the rails. But first, I think I owe an explanation.

I should start with the funeral.

I'm not starting with the funeral.

I can hear you say, "But catharsis!" and I might agree if I were the hero of this story. Well, I'm not, and I believe that grief takes its own sweet time. Here are the details for the record, just so we're straight: Mom gets sick. I come home. Mom dies. We bury Mom.

The whole thing was so hasty and batshit that I still don't really know what to say. People kept coming up to me to shake my hand, take a look at me, to get a little piece. Local celebrity comes home or whatever. All these faces that I remember and I don't at the same time. I could hear the whispers. I can still hear the whispers.

And Dad was less than worthless. Just sat there in a folding chair, staring at the coffin like a dog waiting by the front door. And then he goes and tries to kill us. On the way home FROM THE FUNERAL. I got my arm ripped off by a semi-truck (not literally, but almost literally and definitely metaphorically) while Dad, the driver and "party at fault" according to the Western Pennsylvania Insurance Co., was fine (not metaphorically at all, but physically, and sort of literally). The semi had a dented fender.

We good? Good.

Next up, Lowland. The town I managed to escape from. The town that sucked me back in. Lowland is the kind of place that serves as a cautionary reference only. What happens when you build a single-purpose town and the owner of said single purpose decides it's no longer cost-productive to operate there? Poverty, mostly. Identity crisis too, and also a general sense of fuck it. A black lung town, hacking and lumbering toward the grave. There was no "Visit Lowland!" campaign because there was nothing to visit unless you have a yearning to experience upper Appalachia and don't care much for the yinzers in Pittsburgh or are dropping in on your kids at the college. When the rolling mill started furloughing, so did Lowland. You ever watched a town die? I have.

And if you think Lowland University was capable of saving the town, you'd be mistaken. The college was up the hill, symbolically and geographically. The kids did most of their dining and partying on campus because of the sad-sack nature and general meanness of the townies closer to sea level. Add in the general decline of a liberal arts education and an athletics program closer to nonexistent than irrelevant, and you get what Low U administrators generously called an "enrollment dip." Some brand of rose-tinted glasses there. They must have also been Pirates fans.

Speak of the college, and you speak of my father, Professor Robert Corvallis. He was 62 when he decided to go crazy. It was a Sunday.

Now, you may suggest that he decided to go crazy much earlier. For instance, that he may have departed company with his sanity at some unseen rest stop on the long, strung-out highway that was Mom's chemo. Or, it could have been when he tried to kill us both by steering into the path of that oncoming semi. He still insists it was an accident, while I still insist he's a filthy liar. So, we'll settle for Sunday, August 4, 1996, pending further proof.

When I came to visit him on that fateful Sunday, almost six months to the day after my mother went into the ground, Robert Corvallis looked the hermetic part. After my third long lean on the doorbell revealed my old man blinking like the freshly hatched in the wilting summer light, he looked ready to slam the door in my face. He stared up at me like a stranger, smiling blandly in the way of someone confronted unexpectedly by Girl Scouts.

He was wearing an old red sweater and beat khakis. His feet were bare, and he needed a shave. His little white cowlick bobbed like a cattail.

He was either losing his grip, or he just didn't care anymore. It was hard to blame him either way. I figured the day you retired was the day you began to die. To me, it looked like Robert was busy getting down to it, emeritus-style.

"Oh, Elbridge. It's you."

"Hi, Dad."

"Well, come in," he said. "Dinner is almost ready."

The hall was dark and lined with the natural, slightly blurry pastoral scenes Mom was so fond of: cows in a field, trees by a pond, trees by a field, field with a pond, a little town steeple for color, all gently gathering dust, becoming blurrier and eerier with each passing day. Farther on, steam rolled out through the kitchen's big bay windows, thrown open to admit the August breeze and the soft orange light that spilled over the black and white tile. Mom had loved this kitchen, and my father minded it in her stead. It was the epicenter of the house, where we gathered to read and lounge and, in my mother's case, talk. Now it was the eye of the family storm.

"And how are you set for money then?" Robert asked.

"I actually just got the Jacuzzi installed," I said. "Interested in a soak with your son?"

"Ah, so you did invite your friend, sarcasm. And here I was worried I made too much soup."

He was still painfully thin; had been ever since Mom started chemo. His sweater draped off his stirring arm like Spanish moss. His eyebrows were wooly wild. Maybe he was going feral on me.

"Can we just skip to the part where you tell me how I've wasted my life?" I asked.

"Well, surely even you have now begun to consider the possibility of life after sport?"

"Thanks." I sighed, relieved. "It usually takes us so much longer to get here."

Hockey had never been high on his small list of things that mattered, falling just below his students' personal problems and remembering my mother's birthday. He'd taken a dim view of my dropping out of college to play professionally, as he'd taken a dim view of my going to college to play, as he'd taken a dim view of my leaving high school to live with a billet family and play. Dim and dimmer, if you're still with me.

"I will not stand here and listen to you complain when I have offered time and time again to put you in touch with an old colleague of mine at the University. He keeps asking about you."

"No more school."

"I think that if you just heard him out—"

"I said no more school."

"Suit yourself," Robert said and went back to tending the pot with his big wooden spoon.

I sat at the long kitchen table and watched Robert as he puttered around the stove, adding spices and stirring. After attending three different high schools during Junior hockey and one abbreviated year at a small but astonishingly snobby college on the east coast, I came away without any real education to speak of but a contract in-hand to play for a professional team out of Red Lake, Minnesota. I never looked back at higher ed, and if I still had any real agency in my life, that's where I'd be now, freezing my ass off in Red Lake and getting paid to play. But I traded the Bull Elk jersey for a physical therapy table, team meals for Sunday dinner with Dad, seven sharp.

Deciding that it might be a while before the soup met Corvallis standards, I scanned the front page of the newspaper sitting on the end of the table. The headline read, "The Duke of Ash Avenue," and featured a sketch artist's rendering accompanying the full-page story. The drawing showed a man on a rearing horse, waving a hat in the air and gripping the reins. The horseman looked calm and regal, and the title under the picture read, "Artist's conception of the Duke."

"Have you heard about this guy?" I asked, holding the paper aloft.

"Whom?"

I tapped the paper. "This Duke guy."

Robert turned around to squint at the front page before shaking his head. "Dredge. I believe the local rag created him whole cloth." He raised the long spoon to his mouth and smacked his lips loudly.

I skimmed the story. "I guess he wants Lowland to rejoin the British Empire? Is that even still a thing?"

4

"Well, there are certainly a number of countries and disputed territories that owe nominal fealty to the British monarchy. For instance, Grenada—"

"Looks like the Lowlanders really have a thing for this guy," I said, snuffing out the kindling lecture. "He's calling himself the Duke of Ash Avenue. Why not the Duke of Lowland? Better ring to it?"

"The whole ordeal reeks of gimmick," he said. "Old newsies fanning smoke from their dying fire to sell a few more broadsheets."

"Maybe," I said, staring at the picture. He certainly looked heroic, and it made sense that people round here would fall for the guy. They needed *something*. Even before I left, when the last rolling mill was still running, the news was always pretty tame. There was the occasional drowning in the Allegheny, or rumors of the mill reopening under new ownership, or teenagers being teenagers and crashing their cars on the S-curve or setting something on fire, but even those big events hardly produced much in the way of sensationalism. The Duke of Ash Avenue was wholly different prey, and the news hounds at the *Herald Bulletin* sank their dull incisors right in.

"The soup needs another 10 minutes to simmer," Robert said. "Will you go see what that banging is out in the garage? I suspect raccoons have managed to infiltrate and I worry they will make a mess of things."

I dropped the newspaper back onto the table and rose, wondering if the Duke also had to deal with raccoon infestations.

"Excellent," he said. "There's a baseball bat by the backdoor."

I paused halfway out of the kitchen. "Why is there a baseball bat by the backdoor?"

"For just such an occasion."

"And what exactly is this occasion?"

"You know," Robert said, pausing his stirring to lift his spoon and swing it violently. Soup splattered the counter. "For whacking."

"You want me to go in the garage and whack some raccoons?"

"Given your natural proclivity for clubbing, this should be a short ordeal."

I looked up at my father to see if any of the incredulity had registered, but Robert hummed and stirred, apparently finished with the conversation. I waivered for a moment, trying to decide whether I should call him out on all his strangeness or just go look in the goddamn garage.

"Or we could talk more about the job opportunity at the college," Robert said, head wreathed in soup steam like the witch he was.

I opted to keep the peace. As I headed down the hallway that led away from the kitchen to the backdoor, I considered the mental state of a man who would club raccoons. And sure enough, propped up against the wall was my old Louisville Slugger, leaning there like a threat. The handle was still covered in the white tape I'd wrapped it in during fifth grade. I remembered thinking that if hockey sticks needed tape, so did baseball bats. The wood felt strange in my hands, the weight different, the length too stumpy, but my stomach still sunk at the feeling of loss brought on by the simple tactile pleasure of hefting something heavy with purpose.

Back outside, I took a few practice swings to loosen up my sore left arm while looking up at the sky, pondering raccoonicide. Let's clear something up: I had no intention of braining anything, you understand? But if you're entering a dark, indeterminately occupied space, you take such weapons you have to hand. I thought of Mom's friend, Grace, and her words as she hugged me beside the grave, "Without dungeons, the torch makers starve." I doubted she was talking about raccoons, but any water in the desert.

I pulled open the door to the stand-alone garage, felt around for a light switch, and ended up with a handful of cobwebs and no illumination. Of course the light didn't work. That would have made raccoon whacking too easy. I was pissed and already beginning to sweat, and I'd only been at Dad's house for 15 minutes. Strained Sunday at its finest.

I noticed the smell first. Like old men and crappy cars, most garages have a signature musk, something of old newspapers and asthma and 40 years of leaking chemical solvents. But this was uniquely bad, earthier and stronger. Maybe the raccoons had made some sort of nest? Then I heard the thump.

Either the raccoon was the size of wolfhound, or this was no raccoon. I hefted the bat and considered backing out. I could call a professional exterminator, or the cops, or maybe a priest, and get this problem taken care of. But what if it was a raccoon and the cops showed up and laughed at me? Standing there before the waiting door, I tried to psych myself up. *I am not my father. I am a man of action. I stand in front of hundred mile per hour slapshots for Christ's sake. I'm a big tough guy!*

"Hello, raccoon?" I called like a small lost child.

I listened for a response, unsure of what to expect. Was he going to pipe up and say something? "Yes, it's me, the raccoon. I've been waiting for you to come bash in my skull. Shall I lift my little claws in the air to make things easier?"

I advanced slowly into the garage, holding the bat before me, blinking in the darkness, inhaling the earthy stink. From the carport I could hear the noise, a slow, irregular thump that reminded me of something. Something big.

Striding toward the sound, I neared the space where the car should have been. Robert had not bought another car since the accident, and the blank space was a deeper darkness among shadows, a big black hole surrounded by the faintly outlined shapes of wall-hung gardening tools and wrenches.

I was a pace away when my feet got tangled in something and I hit the ground hard. My left shoulder caught fire as I struck the concrete floor, and old-timey flash bulbs erupted behind my eyes as the old break threatened to become a new break. As I struck, I heard a shriek like a train whistle, then something smacked the ground, once, twice. I felt the concrete rumble as I lay prone on the floor, totally immobilized by pain and terror, trying to think my way through the dark.

I was in trouble, and I knew it. But I didn't know what to do, because I was trapped in a garage with something big and scary and my arm hurt and what I really needed was my mommy and maybe a popsicle. But as whatever it was struck the ground again, near enough to my head this time to stir my hair, all I could come up with was one jolt of activity, ancient neurons booting into action, the remnants of instincts no longer useful. I rolled.

And kept rolling until I was under a workbench. Spider webs attached themselves to my face and I sputtered in the underbelly of the old wooden frame. I turned my head just a fraction, holding my breath as my heart hammered at its cage. And as my eyes adjusted to the gloom, I saw the exact moment when something thumped down in the space my face had just been occupying. My shoulder screamed, my brain swam, my eyes watered. But all I could do was watch as the object that had almost ended me moved up and down slowly. I lay quietly, letting the pain recede, working through my thoughts. *I wonder if the shoulder is re-broken? How come spider webs taste like nothing at all? Why is there a big fucking hoof in the garage?*

• . • :

"What the hell?" I was back in the kitchen, dusty, sore, and pissed.

"What?" Robert asked, looking up from the soup in alarm. "Did raccoons give you so much trouble? I remember hearing that they were intelligent creatures, but surely, they were no match for you and your bat."

"You're fucking with me."

"Excuse me?" Robert turned away from his soup to look at me. He clutched his spoon to his chest with both hands.

"You're fucking with me with this raccoon shit. There's a horse in your garage."

"Impossible."

"You're trying to tell me you had no idea there's a horse in your garage?"

"That is precisely what I am saying," Robert said. Despite my righteous anger, I thought that he looked genuinely surprised to hear the news, which did nothing to make me less hateful.

"I almost got my goddamn head smashed in."

"Well?" Robert asked, still clutching his spoon like a rope.

"Well, what?" I asked.

"Did you take care of it?"

"The horse? Take care of it how? Like take it to a stable?"

"No, no, I just thought you could, you know . . ." He gestured with the spoon again, a short striking motion.

"What did you want me to do? Brain it with the bat?"

"Horse, raccoon, a beast is a beast, Elbridge," he said conversationally. "All subject to man."

"You're not suggesting I go in there and beat a horse to death with a Louisville Slugger, are you?"

"Well, it's not so very different than your previous occupation, I should say. I fail to grasp your sudden squeamishness."

"My God. You know for such a bright guy, you're a fucking idiot."

Robert stood there, blinking again, and for a moment I thought I'd actually hurt the batty old buzzard's feelings. Robert looked lost again, just as he had when he answered the door, and I felt sorry for losing my temper with this sad, small man. But not sorry enough to apologize, because of, you know, the horse.

So, I went to the bathroom to clean up. I turned on the sink and took off my shirt to brush away the dust that had collected after my tuck and roll. In the mirror, I flexed the left shoulder and was amazed at all the pain that could go on inside the body without any external physical signs of damage. Sure, there was the scar where they had cut in to repair the muscle and tissue that had been ripped away from the bone, but that was just a fat purple worm against pale skin. That line, like a child's wayward crayon stroke, spoke nothing of the hot shivering agony that I felt now, or the malignant, ever-present ache that escorted me to sleep every night and waited patiently to greet me each morning. *"Hello! Welcome back to consciousness. Shall we resume?"*

I stared into my eyes, at the broken nose and slightly off-colored false incisor, the scars on my hands and chest and face, at the creases and the tightness and the wear that gradually accumulated from a life spent in graffiti-covered locker rooms, in dirty forgotten towns and flat gray Canadian wastelands where the wind never quit, in heatless motel rooms and greasy diners and greyhound bus seats. And after all of that? Here I was, back in Lowland, rehabbing a shoulder so mangled the doctor nearly had to take off the whole arm, still clinging to the slim hope that I could get back my range of motion, get back to the game, get the hell out of Lowland, PA.

But without that hope of putting on a Bull Elk jersey again, I was done, and I knew it. I'd start my Oldsmobile and keep driving until I found a nice steep overpass. The police report would say my foot slipped. That I lost control. That I was tired. It could say what it wanted.

I wouldn't be in any condition to care. I splashed some cold water on my face and tried to stop lingering on my own demise.

You might be tempted to assume that this is where normal families would probably apologize. Well, normal as a horse-in-the-garage kind of family can be. But Robert never looked up as I walked across the black and white tiles and retook my seat at the table. The silence wasn't awkward. It had been awkward at first after Mom died, but repetitive Strained Sundays had eventually borne awkwardness away and replaced it with some other feeling. Sometimes it felt like regret. Sometimes it felt like loss. Right now, it felt like hate.

Eventually, Robert decided the soup was finished and ladled out two bowls, which he carried to the table. He sat down, and without a word, began eating. Taking a cue, I shoveled some into my own mouth and immediately spit it back into the bowl, my tongue ferociously scalded. I shouldn't have been angry. Soup was hot. It was not Robert's fault that I didn't test it first. But those thoughts didn't occur until later.

"What the fuck?" I was screaming, slamming the spoon down so hard the thick wooden table shook, rattling the bowls and standing so quickly my chair spilled over backwards.

"What?" Robert looked shocked, grasping his bowl with both hands, leaning over it, sheltering it with his body like a mother duck.

"What the fuck is a horse doing in your garage? Why did you send me out there with a baseball bat? Why didn't you tell me the soup was a million goddamn degrees?"

"I didn't know."

"That's a load! You've been stirring for an hour."

"Not the soup," he said. "The horse. I didn't know."

"So, I'm supposed to believe that someone randomly opened your garage and stashed a horse in there?"

"I don't . . . I can't—"

"Can't what, you crazy bastard?" I stood in disgust, staring down at my father as he cringed over his steaming bowl. "Christ! Only you would send your son into a garage to beat a horse to death. What is wrong with you?"

"There is nothing wrong with me!" He shouted so loud that his voice raised an octave.

If I could have seen myself through your eyes, looming over this scared old man, I might have said something else, or said nothing at all. I didn't, of course, do either.

"You tried to kill us all on the same day. One big happy family picnic in hell. Shame. It would have been easier to bury you both and be done with it."

I said it, and it hung in the air between us like the privacy screen around Mom's hospital bed. For a second, we were right back in the room, the beeping EKG and the fluorescent lighting and the smell of antiseptic and death, and I watched my father through the shifting curtains of my words, unable to move or speak as he rose and walked from the kitchen.

I let myself out the front door. I didn't see Robert Corvallis again for 28 days.

CHAPTER 2

I was beginning to suspect that my physical therapist was a sadist. In fact, I'd reached the conclusion that everyone in the rehabilitation profession was indecently attracted to misery and pain. As a consequence, I spent a lot of time imagining techniques I might use on the blandly handsome torturers who smiled, contorted, smiled, twisted, smiled. Today, I was paired with a new one, Susie, who was peppy and blonde, and fluctuated between goddess and ghoul with each turn of her slender but shockingly firm hands.

"How does that feel?" Susie asked as she pulled my arm up over my head.

"Ugh," was all the response she got. I was currently focused on what a stupid name Susie was. *Susie. Suuuuusie.*

"That doesn't answer my question, Elbridge."

"You know how it feels when you light a firecracker and then hold it in your armpit until it explodes?"

"No."

"You could try it sometime."

"On a scale of 1-10?" she asked.

"How comfortable are you with exponents?"

"Okay, smart guy, just 30 more seconds."

"Mhmm," I said, wheezing a little. "Do me a favor though?"

"Sure," she said. I was sitting on the padded table so we were level, her face close to my neck as she lifted my arm by the elbow. Her breath tickled, though insufficiently to distract me from the pain, which was immense and inescapable as an avalanche.

"Make sure that when my arm comes off after I pass out, you hold on to it for me."

"I thought you hockey players were supposed to be tough?"

"I thought so too," I sighed. Seven months out from the accident and I still had trouble torquing open a beer bottle, a motion I found myself needing to perform regularly. Without the structure of my previous life, eat-workout-tape-eat-nap-practice-eat-sleep, I drifted. Part of the problem was that the 139 consecutive days spent in Lowland marked the longest time I'd been continuously in one place since I had tried on my first pair of skates at 4-years-old. As physical therapy sessions crawled by, producing more pain than increased flexibility, I was becoming doubtful about my chances of escape. I needed to skate again, but Doctor Connor, the fancy surgeon from the hospital in Pittsburgh, warned me after the operation that a hard fall could undo the fragile tissue graft. I weighed this risk alongside the other, equally tangible threat that if I stopped skating entirely, I would probably kill myself.

So, I let Susie count to 30 while I fantasized about body checking her through a sheet of Plexiglas. I imagined standing over her as she struggled to stand up and say, "Now on a scale of 1-10 . . ."

"See?" she asked. "That wasn't so bad. You were almost smiling there towards the end. What were you thinking about?"

"Hockey." What? Don't judge me. It was mostly the truth.

"That's why I like working with you, Elbridge. You're goal oriented. Everyone else just comes in here looking to *maintain*." Susie emphasized the last word and fluttered her free hand to let me know what she thought about maintainers. She let my arm go and told me to lie on my stomach. Then she took a new grip on the arm, one hand braced on my shoulder, the other wrapped tightly around my wrist, and lifted the arm slowly into the air. She had hands like a golem.

I grunted as the new muscle strained, the tenuous bundled fibers threatening to unravel before my eyes that were suddenly full of tears.

"How's that feel?" she asked.

I moaned the long, low cat-in-heat moan of a man on the edge of consciousness.

"Tut-tut, Elbridge. Use your words."

I would have preferred to remain silent, and to hell with Susie, but I figured talking was better than passing out. "Call me Elby. Everyone else does."

"Except for your father, who—"

"Is truly one of a kind," I finished for her.

"He doesn't talk much when he comes in," she said.

"Yeah, he's a private guy. How's his ankle coming along?"

"Oh, he's maintaining quite nicely."

Now that was funny. I even briefly forgot I hated her.

"There's the real smile," she said. "I wondered what it might look like. It's nice."

I didn't know what to say, which turned out to be a mistake, because Susie was more than willing to fill the silence.

"Just 30 more seconds."

·, · ● ·

"You remind me of him," Susie said as we finished our session.

I raised an eyebrow.

"I mean you're both so quiet."

"Well, I can't speak for my father, because nobody currently living can, but I guess I just don't have much to say."

"You're talking right now."

"That's because you're making me."

"I think it's probably a good thing for someone to make you talk occasionally," she said. "Don't you have any friends in town? Didn't you grow up here?"

"Sort of," I said, shrugging as well as I could. "But not really. I spent my whole life on the road or with host families. I didn't even go to high school here past freshman year."

"So, who do you talk to?"

"No real friends to speak of. Nobody really remembers me. It's just me and Dad, I guess. And Mary of course."

"Who's Mary? Your girlfriend?"

I couldn't help but smile at the thought of my gray-maned landlady as my girlfriend. Then I thought about what it would be like to see her

14

naked, maybe writhe around on her crocheted bedspread in the recesses of that cat-hole apartment, and the smile soured.

"No, just the landlady. Her husband passed away a few years ago and she didn't need the space, so she rents me the top two floors."

"Oh," she said, and sighed as if she were tired. "Are you on good terms with your father?"

"Eh."

"Tut-tut LB. Use your words."

She pronounced it L.B., like initials, which was subtly wrong and completely uncorrectable without looking like a psychopath. I ground my teeth and thought of the SAT: L.B. is to Elby as teeth grinding is to _____? A: smiling. B: sneering. C: frowning. D: none of the above.

"We've never been very close," I said. "My mother was the one who drove me to practices and tournaments because Dad had classes to teach and books to write and that other academicky bullshit."

"Well, you must still be close to your mother then, right?"

"You're not from around here, are you?"

"No, actually," she said. "Just moved this year. Why do you ask?"

"Because everyone from Lowland already knows. She was the librarian. Until the cancer got bad. Strangers came up to me for months, shaking my hand, hugging, the whole nine."

"Oh L.B.," she said. "I'm so sorry. I had no idea."

"It's alright. That's why I came back. Because she passed. And then there was the accident, and so here I am. Stuck until you clear me to play again."

"Not me. It's the surgeon that clears you if you can pass the strength and stability tests. But I'll let you in on a little secret."

"What's that?" I asked.

"I'll bet I hate this town even more than you do," she said. "So, I'm going to do everything I can to help you get out of here."

"And what's in it for you?"

"I'd do anything for my only non-maintainer," she said and smiled straight white teeth. She turned away for a moment to write something in my chart, so I took the opportunity to hop off the table and retreat towards the lobby.

"Hey," she called as I neared the doors. She motioned me back and ripped a strip of paper from the bottom of my chart as I approached.

"What's this?" I asked warily.

"My phone number," she said as she flipped the chart closed. "In case you need anything."

I folded the paper and slipped it into my pocket.

"No one should be alone," she said. "Especially in a place like this."

· · ● ·

I rolled up to the curb in front of my apartment at a crawl. Golden Thunder, my '91 Cutlass Supreme, preferred it that way. The car, like my body, had seen better days, but it had been my companion for so long that, even if I could afford a better car, I wouldn't have had the heart to replace it. The back doors no longer opened from the outside, and only the front passenger side window rolled down without sticking. Years spent on winter-salted back roads left rust spots over the wheel wells that seemed to spread outwards with the stately grace of glacial floes. Both side mirrors had been bashed off by an angry fan after a game, and the front windshield was cracked so thoroughly that when it rained it was easier to see by sticking your head out the window. But the old armchair seats felt like driving on a throne, and while I drove with my good arm lazily draped over the steering wheel, I was king of the rattling, rusting kingdom.

As I hoisted myself from the car, I saw Mary puttering around the front yard. She stood in a nightgown holding a Virginia Slim in one hand and a garden hose in the other. The hose was at full blast and so was the cigarette that raised smoke the same color as her clumpy hair. She saw me and waved her hose hand vigorously, spraying water all over the front of the house and sidewalk.

"How's it going, dear?" she asked.

"Can't complain," I said. "How are you, Ms. Mary? Looking lovely this morning, as usual."

"Don't be a shithead. I look like refried hell. But I know that it pisses Mrs. Johnstone off when I'm outside in my skivvies, so I thought I'd water the flowers." She looked down at the dying shrubs and brown earth, then amended. "Well, water the grass anyways. Goddamn hydrangeas are giving me fits, and this lawn could use a mowing." She waggled gray eyebrows at me suggestively.

"I'll get the mower from Dad next time I go over for dinner," I said. What I didn't say was that it had been almost a month since the last dinner and we didn't have another one in the books until redemption day.

"Oh, you're a dear. It's a wonder I can even charge you rent." She paused to scratch her forehead with a dirty finger, leaving a great brown smudge down the side of her face. The hose continued to flood the lawn; the cigarette continued to burn.

"That does remind me rent was due yesterday," she said.

"I'll leave the cash in your mailbox."

"Why don't you stop in and have a drink? We could play some pinochle, see where the night takes us."

"I've actually got plans this evening. I'm meeting some old friends later."

"Hmm, thought you didn't have any friends left?"

"Turns out that I do," I said, trying to dig my way out of this hole.

"You settling in okay up there?"

"Definitely. Quite comfortable. More space than I need, even."

That part was true at least. Ms. Mary had converted the top two floors of her three-story home into an apartment after her husband died. And since the house was paid off, I was effectively funding her retirement with this off-the-books tenancy. But the arrangement suited us both nicely, despite the inconvenience of paying in cash, as I had no desire for a lease. A lease would mean permanence, my name in ink like cement. And though I had no doubt that rehab would continue for some time, even month-to-month still felt like a steep commitment.

I waved goodbye and headed up the steep concrete steps, stopping to grab my mail from the box. Then it was up another flight of stairs to the flimsy interior door that was my only protection from Ms. Mary and her wandering eyes. I unlocked the door, paused, then relocked it behind me (you can never be too cautious round Mary) before tossing the keys on the kitchen table and punching play on the answering machine.

"You have two new messages," the machine said. "First message."

"Elbridge, this is your father." Then there was a long pause as Robert Corvallis decided what to say next.

"Robert."

I chuckled. I hope your parents aren't nearly so awkward.

"I'm calling to see if you have availability for dinner tomorrow evening? Say, 7." Pause. "We will be having lamb." Pause. "Good day."

Then there was a minute of muffled noises and beeps as Robert searched around for the off button, which he eventually found, and the machine clicked over.

"Next message," the robot voice said, and every single hair on my body stood to attention as the new voice bounced from the machine.

"Elbridge, it's Coach LeDeux. We need to talk. Call me."

That was it. No hint of what it was about, just ten short words delivered in the same clipped monotone that was his trademark when dealing with the press, the players, even his own wife for all I knew.

I began to sweat earnestly. I was listed on the injured reserve roster for the Bull Elk, and as far as I knew, that hadn't changed. My agent hadn't called in a month, the prick, so I wondered why it was LeDeux and not Johnny Canada from Sports Agents Ltd. who had reached out to me first. His real name, so far as I knew, wasn't actually Johnny Canada, but that's what everyone called him and that's what he called himself, so who was I to argue? Then I remembered the mail, and slowly flipped through the junk to the letter that I knew was waiting for me at the back of the pile.

It was a small white envelope. The postmark was from Toronto, and it had several stamps bearing loons. It seemed odd to me that such a small, seemingly insignificant parcel held my fate as surely as a judge. As I tore open the seal, I imagined I was witnessing the end of my career in miniature, and when the one thin sheet of paper slid out of the envelope, I didn't need any of the clean typeface to read the verdict.

But I read anyway. Phrases swam at me. "Unable to continue contract." "Breach of terms." "Unlikely to return to sport professionally." And worst of all, "Best of luck." I thought it would have been simpler just to come straight out and say what they really meant: Fuck off.

I crumpled the letter and threw it away, then grabbed a beer from the fridge and wrenched it open with my good arm. After the second beer, I retrieved the letter from the trashcan, smoothed it out, and read it slowly. Twice. After the third beer I threw the letter away again and sat with my back to the fridge, clenching and unclenching my left fist, feeling the pain shoot up my arm, enjoying it, wrapping it around me like a thick comforter. After the fourth beer I got the letter back out of the trash can again and started to read through it a fourth time, thought better of it, and reached for the matches I kept in the drawer next to the sink.

I slid down the fridge again and resumed my position on the floor. I struck one match and held it before my eyes while I watched it burn itself out. Slowly the flame ate all the way up to my fingers, but I continued to grip it tightly as the fire licked my fingertips. I did not shake. I did not drop the match. I simply waited until the flame ran out of food.

Casting aside the blackened sliver, I struck another match, then lifted my ex-agent's letter over it until a corner caught flame. I laid the letter down between my outstretched legs on the kitchen's linoleum floor and listened as Johnny Canada's soft-mouthed apologies crackled and shadows grinded across the walls while the sun set through the window. As the letter burned out, so did I. What was I going to do now? Confusion on the ice meant one of two things. Either you should hit someone or go ask the coach. Since there was no one around to punch, I opted for the latter.

For the second time, I slid back up the fridge to an unsteady standing position and went into the living room to begin fumbling around amongst cardboard boxes full of playbooks and game tape until I found the list of team numbers. Coach LeDeux's was at the bottom, next to the words "FOR EMERGENCIES ONLY." I figured this counted.

I opened another beer and slid back onto the kitchen floor, phone in hand. The phone cord extended across the kitchen to the wall by the door, its red curls making infinity signs in midair that jiggled as I punched in the number. As I dialed, I thought of the last and only other time I'd spoken to Coach on the phone. I was in the middle of my sophomore year after a summer transfer had forced me to sit out for a season. I'd been playing well, the team had an outside shot at making the NCAA playoffs, and for the first time I was finally starting to gel with the team and the coach and even with the waspy college environment, though we still gave each other the side-eye. Then LeDeux called.

"This is Martin LeDeux of the Red Lake Bull Elk. We need a center. I've watched you play. You've got jump. You've got hands. You've got potential. You want the spot?"

I didn't hesitate. "Yes."

"Get your ass to Minnesota. Tomorrow. The team will recoup your expenses."

"Okay." My mouth was so dry I could have licked an electrical socket and come away unsinged. I was officially a professional hockey player. I'd done it. I'd fucking done it.

This time around, though, I was doing the calling. I might have been just as nervous if I wasn't already sure how this conversation would go. That and, you know, the five beers. The phone rang several times, and I imagined the little electrical bead humming its way through Pennsylvania and New York, around Lake Erie, through Toronto and Lake Huron, and speeding its way through Ontario and the great nothingness of Central Canada. There it would find Regina, and LeDeux's modest ranch home, cutting through the walls to the only phone in the house. I imagined the little kitchen phone ringing in its cradle, Mrs. LeDeux cleaning up the remains of a pot roast in her flowery apron, Coach smoking a pipe in his armchair and reviewing statistics and scouting reports for the upcoming game against Des Moines.

"Hello?" a female voice said. I could hear the sink running in the background.

"Hi Mrs. LeDeux. I was hoping to speak with Coach."

"May I ask who is calling?" she said, sounding wary.

"Yes, ma'am. It's Elbridge Corvallis. From the Elk. I'm returning his call."

"Oh, you poor thing. I was so sorry to hear about everything. How are you bearing up?"

"Honestly," I said, taking a long swig from my beer. "I've been better."

"Well of course you have. I've been keeping you in my prayers, dear."

"I'm glad someone's got the big man looking out for me," I said, wondering if I'd been referring to God or LeDeux. Then I wondered if there was a difference at the moment.

"I'll go fetch Martin."

"Thanks, Mrs. LeDeux."

"Oh, and Elbridge?" she said, lowering her voice.

"Yes, ma'am?"

"Try to remember that there *is* a world outside of hockey."

"Sure thing, Mrs. LeDeux," I said, and decided I was officially fucked.

I took another long pull from the bottle as I listened to the sounds of shuffling and the tap of the receiver being laid down on something firm, a low boy perhaps, as Mrs. LeDeux went to fetch her husband. The next voice on the line was the clipped, sonorous voice of Martin LeDeux.

"Corvallis."

"Hey, Coach."

"How's the arm?"

"Getting better," I said, flexing my hand and feeling the beer-numbed jolts course from hand to shoulder and back in a lightning roundtrip.

"How much better?"

"No word from the doctors yet, but the range of motion improves every day."

This was not exactly a lie, as Susie and her fellow sadists continued to stretch the shoulder further and further. I just couldn't do any of it on my own. Yet. The line was silent for a second, and I imagined I could hear Coach sucking on his pipe.

"I assume you heard from your agent?"

"Got the letter right here." I glanced at the charred remains and took another swig.

"So," LeDeux said, and paused.

I teetered on the brink between giggling and passing out. My entire future rode on the heels of such a simple word.

"I obviously can't hold a roster spot for you. Not with your future uncertain."

I polished off the beer and stared down the bottle neck like a kaleidoscope. The kitchen seemed to spin around, the 70's-patterned linoleum dancing in the brown glass.

"But you're welcome at camp next season if you get cleared," LeDeux said.

"Thanks, Coach." I moved to set the phone down but heard him clear his throat.

"Corvallis?"

"Yeah, Coach?"

"You're a good player. I was looking forward to seeing how high you'd climb."

I could only swallow.

"Sorry, kid," LeDeux said before the line went dead.

The empty bottle slid from my slack hands and rolled across the kitchen floor. And, for the first time since the night my mother died, I cried.

CHAPTER 3

The Crow Bar was not a classy establishment. I sat alone on a stool on the far end, drinking my eleventh beer, well into the *What are you lookin at?* phase of the evening. The neon lights in the windows and on the walls made me feel like I was inside a piñata, and we were all just waiting for some giant to take a big swing of the bat and spill us out into the street like little drunk candies. I had left the house because I was afraid to be alone and because I had told Miss Mary I was going to meet friends. I was both unhappy at the necessity to be in public and glad to be some-place other than my kitchen floor.

When I entered, I retreated to the interior where the lights were dim-mer and the bar stools more plentiful. The bartender, a rangy guy with a thin mustache and not much to do but twist the caps off light beers and watch a Pirates game on the one working TV, never gave me a second look. He did keep a steady eye on the level in each bottle on the bar though, and he replaced each one as it neared the fate of its predecessor, withdrawing single dollars from my dwindling stack each time. I was making steady progress.

The place wasn't too crowded for a Saturday night, filled mostly with men who looked down: down on their mortgages, down on their pros-pects, down on their luck. Denim stretched as far as the eye could see and those who weren't currently smoking looked either ready to reach for another cigarette or sported the ringed outlines of chewing tobacco tins worn nearly though their back pockets in perfect, faded circles. Country music played on a jukebox that no one was feeding quarters into.

Directly across the bar, near the front door, four men laughed loudly and knocked their bottles around for emphasis. I watched as the shortest one turned, mostly bald with teamster's shoulders, to meet my eye. His eyebrow quirked up and he turned and said a quiet word to his grinning friends, who all jerked their heads towards me as if they were hooked to the same line. Two of the men shook their heads, but a third nodded and prodded the short fellow with his beer. The short man, who I decided closely resembled a keg with a head, turned back to face me and sauntered across the bar.

I couldn't help but laugh, several inches into beer number 12, at the idea of a keg sauntering. Like something from a Disney movie, there would be an eye hole in the bung, and it would hiccup, occasionally but loudly, rattling the lid. I thought about how much more fun those college parties would have been out East if the keg got up and strutted around like this little guy. The man saw me laughing and returned a smile of his own. He waved two fingers at the bartender who promptly delivered two Rolling Rocks before retreating.

"Corvallis?" he asked, his voice like a big shoe on gravel.

"In the flesh," I said, spreading my arms. My numb shoulder hardly registered pain, suggesting, as alcohol usually does, that more beer was the solution.

"Remember me?"

"Nope." My memory, faulty as it was at the moment, would not have benefited too much from sobriety. I had spent so little time here, and what memories I did take with me had either been from my relatively placid pre-teen years or whitewashed into obscurity.

"Rob Dillon," he prompted. "Low High? We had algebra and geography together freshman year."

"Sure we did," I said, saluting him with the fresh beer.

Rob grunted and shrugged. "You been gone for a while."

"Not long enough," I said, and laughed.

"What, you too good for us now?" He smiled, elbow on the bar and palm on the side of his face. He was just tall enough that his arm rested flat on the bar top.

I answered by taking a long drink and returning a shrug.

"What are you doing back here?" Rob asked.

"Circumstances beyond my control."

"Heard about your ma. Sucks." He watched me carefully from under thick, brown eyebrows. "My ma got it too. The cancer. Wonder if it's something in the water."

"No surprise there," I said, gesturing around the bar expansively with my beer. "Shithole."

Rob frowned. "I heard you were some hotshot now."

"Was," I said.

"What happened?"

"Burned out."

"How's that?" Rob asked, eyebrows drawing down towards his nose.

I fished the matchbook out of my pocket. "I'm the match," I said, and striking it alight, held it aloft and let it burn.

We both stared as flame licked its way down to my fingers. Rob, for his part, opened his mouth, either to warn me or tell me that I was being a champion dumbass, but no sound came out. When the match finally got to my fingers, there was the brief smell of burning flesh, then the richer smell of smoke as the light went out.

"Get it?" I asked.

He stared at my reddened fingers and shook his horrified head.

"Too obscure?" I asked.

"You okay, man?" To his credit, he looked genuinely concerned.

"Never worse," I said, finishing my beer in two long swallows. "You got a cigarette?"

"Yep." Rob pulled a pack from his flannel shirt pocket. He tapped one out and offered it to me.

I lit the cigarette and watched the match burn down again, but before it could reach my dull, throbbing fingertips, Rob reached across and snuffed it with a pinch. I looked up and met his eyes again as I inhaled deeply. Then the wave of nausea struck.

I coughed the smoke out and my most recent beer tried to follow it up from my esophagus back into the world. I covered my mouth and slid off the stool, then stumbled towards the door. I burst into the parking lot sucking one cool breath of night air into my lungs before puking against the wall of the Crow Bar. I could hear the faint sounds of laughter from inside.

I think we can all agree it was an inglorious but fitting end to the day. A fitting end to a career, so much the better. I wondered at the irony that in taking such care of my body, a single drag from a cigarette could knock me on my ass. I sat slumped against the wall and stared down Ash Avenue as it sloped downhill past Al's Tire Mart and Electronics and one of the three Methodist churches, past Center Park and its ominously creaking playground equipment, past the courthouse's dim exterior lighting, past the high school and grade school and their matching chain-link fences, past the two rows of storefronts either closed for the night or closed for good, until it ended at the dreaded S-curve and beyond, out of sight but not mind, was Robert Corvallis and the house formerly known as home.

Time passed slowly as I considered my next move. I figured I should get up, but I didn't seem to have the energy. Going back into the bar was out of the question, but then walking home also seemed like a tall order when standing presented this much of a hurdle. I wondered if I would get picked up for vagrancy if I just laid down here and slept. Then the door swung open and the sound of Rob and his mates making their way to their pick-ups broke my reverie.

"Hey," I said. "Little help?" I wiped my right hand on my shirtfront and extended it in supplication.

Rob turned, saw me sorry and supine, and made his way back across the parking lot. He grasped the not-entirely clean hand and pulled, hoisting me back to my feet, looking at me for a quiet stretch before speaking.

"If you don't mind me saying so, you should get your shit together man," he said. "I know you probably aren't real happy to be back in Lowland, but it's not so bad. If you're looking for some work, we could always use the help over at Dillon Bros."

Rob Dillon, gentleman and entrepreneur, who had extended his literal hand to me in friendship, surely did not expect the uppercut that I threw next. I balled my left fist and threw the punch that would end this fight and each of the next three fights together before they even got started. It was truly a thing of beauty as it left my left hip like a SKUD, destination: Dillon.

Now, I can see what you're thinking here: *How unsporting!* Well, it wasn't until after I let the punch go that the small shred of my brain not boiled in beer and impotent rage reminded me of the cost of such a maneuver. Too late, too late. Pain exploded across my body like I'd been hit in the shoulder by a cannonball. My fist clipped Rob lightly on the cheek, but I was already sinking back to the ground, screaming and cradling my arm, fighting to stay conscious.

Later, much later, I decided it might have been best to pass out then. It would have been nice not to have the clearest memory of the evening be three pairs of steel toed boots descending on my face, neck, and chest. Before I passed out, I thought I heard Rob yelling "Stop!" over the thudding impacts, but his buddies didn't care as much for his words as they did his besmirched honor. My last vision was the sole of a size 12, mud daubed around the tread and framed by a gauzy spread of evening stars, falling towards my face like fate.

· . • .

I woke up to the beeping of an EKG machine and the unmistakable feeling of being pantsless. Then the pain returned. To my shoulder first, always first, my dear old friend wouldn't miss this opportunity to greet my return to consciousness like a faithful dog, who bites, hard. Then the rest of my body thundered for attention, and I gritted my teeth to keep from either screaming or puking. Both probably. But the beeping machine's cadence sped up alarmingly and I forced myself to stay conscious and calm down.

A nurse poked her head through the lit doorway, saw that I was awake, and turned on her heel. She reentered a few moments later with a white-coated doctor in tow. I recognized his face from my previous stint at St. Anthony Hospital. Dr. Shafar, I thought, then confirmed with a glance at his badge. I felt a rush of relief, strangely at odds with the rest of my pain-wracked body, that my brain wasn't completely destroyed too.

"Hello, Elbridge," the doctor said. "I was hoping I wouldn't be seeing you again so soon."

I tried to respond but my jaw clenched in fresh agony. My tongue searched but discovered no new gaps where teeth should have been.

"Yeah," Dr. Shafar said, nodding sympathetically. "That jaw is banged up, and I'll bet those ribs feel broken, but believe it or not you're nothing but one gigantic bruise."

"How bad?" I managed to gasp out while pointing at my bad shoulder with the good arm.

"I *think*." He paused to remove the spectacles from the tip of his nose. "That you haven't done any lasting damage to the wound site. God knows you've had enough surgery this year."

"Go—home—please?" I begged, taking a breath after each word to steady myself.

"Yes, if there's someone to come get you at this hour. We tried to call your father, but no one answered at home."

"Time?" I asked.

"It's 3 a.m. You've been out since the paramedics brought you in around 11. I'd ask if you want me to alert the police so you can press charges, but something tells me you won't want to do that."

I paused for a beat, remembering the boots coming down and the circling stars. Any rage I still felt had been diluted by the saline solution dripping into my arm and leaked out through my very discomfiting catheter. I shook my head, confirming Dr. Shafar's suspicions. What I deserved was probably less than what I'd gotten, and I knew it, even if I wasn't particularly grateful.

He nodded. "Who would you like to call?"

I was stumped. Miss Mary? No, I'd never hear the end of it. Where in the hell was Dad anyway? There was Grace, my mother's best friend, but she kept librarians' hours and went to bed with a mint tea and bourbon at 8:30, dead to the world. Would they let me call a cab? Follow-up question: Did Lowland have any cabs? Then I remembered the number Susie had given me that morning, along with instructions to call if I needed anything. Well.

"Note," I said, gesturing to the pants I saw hanging from a coat rack in the corner. "Pocket."

·   • ● ·

Of course she drove a LeBaron. It was maroon and sleek and convertible, and I had to admit that she looked good behind the wheel. Her hair was tousled, which could have been explained by being rudely awakened from a deep sleep by a needy, friendless client, or if you are feeling more generous, by a windy trip down a moonlit Ash Avenue to rescue a hand-some it bedraggled stranger. Given the smile that played on her lips as she screeched to a stop at St. Anthony's front entrance, she certainly appeared generous to me.

If only I had been more game, I would have enjoyed watching her drive. She kept two hands on the wheel unless she was reaching to turn up the radio, which she did when Whitney Houston came on, and then again, louder, when Madonna came on next. She weaved through the deserted, darkened streets of Lowland, completely exhilarated and free. I, in contrast, was slumped in the passenger seat like a bag of spuds, doped up on pain medication but still managing to enjoy the sensation of the wind blowing through my hair. When Bob Segar came on, he was swiftly turned down to a soft hum from the old speakers, and Susie's head swiv-eled from the road to me and back.

"You know," she said. "When I gave you my number, I was hoping you'd call today. But this is not quite what I had in mind."

I looked over at her, trying to focus through the fog of pain medica-tion and tight turns at 2G. The intermittent orange streetlights softened her angular features at intervals, and I realized she was lovely, like a fox, or an ermine? Mink? Anyway, you know what I mean. She looked back at me and smiled sympathetically. Her teeth were neat little pills.

"Sorry," I mumbled, though I didn't feel sorry. I did feel like I was in a spaceship, though, which I thought would be neat minus the inevitable violent puking. I'd had enough of that tonight. And then, unexpectedly, I felt that I was back with my mother, sitting in the passenger seat of the old Jeep driving home down the turnpike from a tournament in Philly. My mother liked to drive fast, but I never worried. How warm I'd felt then, how safe.

"Oh, it's alright," Susie said. "I'm sure you'll make it up to me." She winked then turned back to the road and gasped.

"Look!" she screamed, pointing through the windshield at a shadowy patch of lawn. "It's that crazy guy! The Duke!"

I sat up as best I could to peer through the windshield, failing to see anything other than a big brownstone with fake candles in its windows. I was just about to resume my slump when I saw something emerge from the shadow of a tree. Except the thing emerging was too large to be human, not to mention the wrong shape.

"NO WAY! He's riding a HORSE!" And sure enough, there was a horse trotting down the sidewalk underneath a row of shadowy oaks, heading in the same direction as the LeBaron.

As we leveled with the rider, Susie slowed down and I stared, trying to get a look at the rider's face through the gloom. But the combination of tree shadow and a tricorn hat kept his features hidden. Susie began to laugh and revved the engine.

The rider, apparently game, urged his horse into a gallop and yelled "AWAY!" which I thought was something that people said in movies rather than in real life, but here we were, in real life, and a man on a horse just yelled *away*. I decided maybe I had had enough drugs for the evening.

"You're crazy," Susie screamed back, laughing and stepping on the gas pedal to pull the LeBaron ahead and away from the screaming horseman.

I poked my head out over the door, and just as the car turned a corner, the horseman halted and reared his mount. Powerful hooves slashed and the rider pumped a single fist before they were both swallowed by the suburban night.

CHAPTER 4

I like to think of a clean sheet of ice as a blank page. Each time I lace up, another opportunity to say something new. It doesn't always work out that way, but I feel it puts me in the right frame of mind. And if I fail to produce Shakespeare? Well, don't we all? Just rip it up and wait for the Zamboni to insert a fresh sheet. But not skating at all was something else entirely. I was tired of writer's block.

I'd gone down to the Red Horner Memorial Ice Arena—just "The Horner" to the Lowlanders—with the vague notion of seeing about some ice time to get my legs going again. When I finally made the decision to return to my birth rink, I sat in Golden Thunder with my hand on the shifter, adding various weights to the complicated measurement. There was my still-miserable shoulder to consider (left scale), alongside my return to professional play (right scale), and my mental health (both scales), alongside the unweighable context and baggage. In the end, I put the car in park.

When I approached the front of the Horner's monstrous, rotting brick corpse, there was Lou Varney unlocking the doors. I walked up to the old rink manager and my ex-coach with a wave. The cool morning air saw both of us in jackets, and I smiled to see Lou still wearing the maroon nylon windbreaker he'd worn since my childhood, "Highland Raiders AAA" hand-stitched over his breast.

"Mr. Varney," I said as he came across the parking lot. "You probably won't remember me, but I used to play here awhile back."

Lou lowered one woolly gray eyebrow at me before he returned to rattling his ring of keys in the lock of the sheet metal door. "92 points at 15 years young. I don't forget a player like you. Hello, Mr. Corvallis."

I scuffed an embarrassed tennis shoe on the gravel parking lot like the kid he remembered.

"It's still the club record," Lou said. "Probably never get broken. Especially seeing as how the goalies keep getting bigger."

The door finally unlocked with a *thunk* and opened, but only after Lou put his shoulder into it. The blast of frigid air that wafted out smelled like my childhood.

"Some kids got speed," Lou said. "Some kids got hands. Some kids got brains. The lucky ones got two of three. You got the trifecta."

"Well, I've got you to thank for the hands," I said. "I should have come back sooner, but I was still sore from all the welts."

Lou smiled. He'd lost a few teeth to pucks and high sticks over the years and never bothered to replace them. Thankfully, he worked in just about the only place on earth where a missing incisor added professional credibility.

"Tennis balls don't leave welts, Corvallis. That's why I use 'em."

I followed Lou inside as he turned on the lights, making his way back across the spongy skate-proof lobby to the manager's office, which was tucked away behind the concession stand and upwind from the stinky hallway of locker rooms. The office was tidily imploding, and though I couldn't discern an organizational system amongst the stacks and reams of mismatched documents, I bet Lou would notice a single missing sheet. The computer in one corner looked like it hadn't been turned on since I scored my 92nd point.

"Have a seat." Lou indicated a beat-up lime green folding chair as he made his way around to the other side of the desk. "I was real sorry to hear about your ma. She was—" He cupped his hands as if trying to catch the fluorescent light in the wrinkled bowl of his palms. "—something special."

I looked down at my tennis shoes again as the grief rose and fell buoy-like in my throat. "Thanks."

"I don't need to ask why you're home," Lou said. "But I am curious about why you're *here*."

I thought about my reasons for coming by, about the withered arm and withering legs, my recent termination and dim prospects, conflicting yet mutually rising senses of panic and apathy.

"I need to skate," I said simply.

"I heard your skating days were maybe done."

"Maybe," I agreed. "But I'd like to think they're not."

"Well, there's a beer league that plays Wednesday nights that's pretty quick. It's mostly a bunch of your old teammates and a few of the younger kids who haven't figured out a way to get the hell out of Lowland yet. But it would still be better than nothing."

I thought with pleasure about hanging a few goals on my assailants from the Crow Bar, but a twinge in my shoulder reminded me that there would probably be a fair number of elbows traded, and I grimaced at the ghost of future pain.

"I'm not sure I'm up for that yet. I was thinking—" But I had no clear picture of what I was thinking. Just that if I didn't start skating again soon, I would probably kill myself.

"I don't blame you," Lou said. "There's a bench clearing brawl at least once a month out there. Christ, last week the goalies beat each other up so bad the teams had to play with two empty nets for half a game. Hard to blame 'em for wanting to come out on the ice and let off some steam, but some of the fellas come in here just looking to fight. I tell you what, Mr. Corvallis. Everybody in this town seems to get angrier every year and there's nothing they can do about it. Just a whole population, walking around mean."

I didn't know what to say so I sat and watched Lou stare out at the still dimmed rink through his wide office window. Or maybe he was staring at Lowland beyond the walls. Either way, he looked disappointed. He brought himself back to the office with a nod.

"What are you doing for work?" he asked.

"Still working on work."

"Unfortunately, I don't need any help around here." He glanced again through his office window at the darkened ice surface as if willing it to disgorge a sack of cash. "But if you're free in the mornings, I'd be happy to let you have the sheet. First skaters don't come in until 8."

I smiled. It felt strange on my face. I thought maybe it was the first time I'd *really* used those muscles since before the cancer ward.

"I'd be grateful," I said. "And I'm happy to help out around the rink for your trouble."

Lou waved it away. "Not much to do around here but drive the Zamboni and fill the popcorn machine. But, for what it's worth, I'll keep an ear out for anyone looking for help."

"One handed help," I said, raising my left arm weakly.

"I'd take an honest, one-handed man over most of the peckerheads round here any day. You wouldn't believe the state of this town." He looked down at his desk, where a copy of the Herald Bulletin showed a grainy photo of a man, a horse, and a tricorn hat.

• • ●

Shaking the rust off and the sweet burn of skating again were medicinal ecstasy. I sat, comfortably soaked and rapidly cooling, breathing the same Horner air that filled the lungs of every important childhood memory. I felt nostalgic and optimistic and, admittedly, maybe even a little happy. With my first faltering steps on the ice again now safely cleared away by the Zamboni, I was watching the next set of players warm up for a pick-up game when the creaking of the bleachers alerted me to the presence of another spectator. Looking up, I made eye contact with the stranger, who raised a hand and a questioning eyebrow. I nodded at the empty stretch of bleacher and returned my attention to the game just getting under way.

With no referee, a black-jerseyed geriatric took the liberty of dumping the puck down into one end of the rink to get the game officially started. Despite my seat 20 feet above the ice, I could swear I heard the collective creaking of knee joints as players lumbered into motion. Though it was hardly what I'd call must-see athleticism, I felt incredibly calmed by the familiar sounds of chopping ice and slapping lumber, the smack and thud of the puck as it made its way from blade to blade, skittering off plexiglass and polyethylene dasher boards. Combined with my already pleasantly aching hamstrings and the lingering scent of Zamboni propane, I was teetering on the edge of enlightenment.

Meanwhile, the stranger eased himself into the indicated seat on my left and let out his own contented sigh. He smelled like cigarettes, and if he had not left a gap in between, his khaki trenchcoated bulk would have spilled into my lap. His brown hair ringed around the back of his skull like a half-eaten doughnut, leaving behind a shiny forehead and a clear view of sharp little eyes. He extended one heavy hand across the intervening seat which I shook warmly, still floating in the grace of my post-workout trance.

"Now let me guess," the stranger said, his voice deep and scratchy. "You must be Clara's kid."

"In the sweaty flesh," I said, smiling.

"Dick Newport. *Herald Bulletin*."

"Elbridge. Glad to meet you."

We sat quietly for a moment as the puck slowly made its way out of the black jerseys' zone and meandered unhurriedly in the direction of the white jerseys' goalie. A burst of speed from an old-timer in a mustard yellow helmet brought him clear of the last defenseman, but an errant stride dumped him on his ass. Laughter rippled up from both benches.

"What brings you back to the Horner this morning, Elbridge?"

"I was looking from some ice time. I'm rehabbing the wing." I shrugged the shoulder, which was sorer than usual, but not unpleasantly so. "How about you?"

"Two things," Dick said, thrusting up the corresponding fingers. "One is a profile piece I'm writing on the Silver Foxes here."

"Really?" I asked.

"Observe the magnificence." Dick gestured like Caesar toward the colosseum, where yellow helmet was unsteadily climbing back to his feet holding onto his stick like the third leg of a tripod. Nearly on his feet, a passerby's errant skate jarred the stick, and he went tumbling back to the ice.

I laughed, but not as loud as mustard helmet himself, who lay like an overturned turtle shaking with mirth.

"Honestly, I think it's going to be a great story. You know the starting age to qualify for the Silver Foxes is 60? And that's the minimum. Arnie there is 78 this year." He indicated mustard helmet, who had now successfully risen and made his way back to the bench, where he was being liberally brushed free of snow by his teammates.

I raised my eyebrows at that, reappraising the situation. Sure, the old boys weren't flying out there, but everyone was ambulatory and a few of them still had jump. As I watched, a white jersey—white in inspiration if not in actual hue—dragged the puck around a giant of a defenseman and skated his way in alone on the goalie. A dip of the shoulders and a flick of the wrist, and the puck snapped past the goalie's head into the back of the net. My smile widened. I knew that snap shot. And sure enough, it was Lou Varney who hoisted his stick in celebration.

"Of course, you know Lou," Dick said. "But we've got a couple of almost-famouses and cup-of-coffee-pros here in Lowland. And then there's the medical miracles." He indicated the goalie in black. "Jim over there has beaten cancer three separate times. And Lonnie's arm is mostly prosthetic."

"Really?" I looked closer at the giant defenseman Lou had just skated so easily around, who was now shaking his head and apologizing loudly to the goalie.

"Mhmm. Free operation. The Vietcong kindly removed it for him."

"You can't even tell."

"It's the left one." Dick grabbed his own left arm just below the elbow and flapped his hand loosely. "It's actually attached to the stick. He calls it his 'hockey arm.' The glove is purely ornamental. I think it's a nice touch, though."

I nodded my approval absently, thinking selfishly of my own situation and feeling no small measure of shame. My new companion seemed to sense the discomfort.

"Puts things in focus, doesn't it?" Dick said. "That's why I want to write their story. Lot of Lowlanders who could use a little perspective these days."

We let the quiet stretch. Dick seemed comfortable and I appreciated the company while I tried to resettle my perspective. I felt that some measure of self-pity was warranted, given the hand I'd been dealt here over the last year. But given my still-healthy legs aching under me and the long view that, however remote, shoulder rehabilitation was possible, I felt I was coming around to the uncomfortable conclusion that I didn't have too much room to bitch. As the shame swelled, threatening to shatter my post-workout transcendence, I hurriedly changed the subject.

"What was the second thing?" I asked.

"Hmm?"

"The second reason you were here."

"Oh, right. That's the fortuitous bit. I was hoping to ask Lou how I could get in touch with *you*."

"Me?" I asked. "Why?"

"You're kidding, right?" he said, turning to face me. "Aside from this Duke business, you're the biggest thing in this little town."

"Come on," I protested. "I'm currently, though hopefully not permanently, a washed-up athlete."

"Yes, but you're *our* athlete. People want to know your story."

"But I haven't been back to Lowland since, what, 1990?"

"Elbridge, for most folks round here, the nineties would best be forgotten. So, what you managed to pull off here in the interim was to light a little candle in a dark decade."

"But—"

"Plus, there's the legacy angle," Dick said.

"Legacy?" I rolled my eyes. "Dad never did squat outside a college classroom. He once told me that he retired because writing on the chalkboard was becoming too strenuous."

Dick laughed and shook his head. "No, no, though your father's involvement with Low U might make for a good town-and-gown angle." He stroked his thick mustache and jowls thoughtfully for a second as he watched the Silver Foxes ramble around.

"Anyway, I was talking about your mother, of course," Dick said.

"My mother? You mean because of the library? Or because I'm a fifth generation Lowlander or something on her side?"

For the first time since he initially approached me, Dick turned and made direct eye contact. I thought the look on his face was equal parts skeptical and opportunistic, but you know as well as I do that anyone who claims they can read emotions like "opportunistic" on someone's face is a goddamn liar.

"The skating?" Dick said. "The speed skating?"

"What speed skating?" I said, genuinely puzzled.

"It can't be. You can't *not* know."

"Can't not know what?" I was feeling rather good for the first time in a long time, so I was actively trying not get frustrated with the portly newsman.

Dick again seemed keenly aware of his subject's mood and rose immediately from his seat with a rustle of his nylon trench coat.

"Come with me and I'll show you," he said.

Confused but game, I followed Dick down from the bleachers and back into the lobby towards a set of identical gray doors. I knew the door on the right was the pro shop, because it was where I'd purchased every piece of equipment I'd ever owned until I turned sixteen and left Lowland for good. It was dark now, but I could see a stack of skates in a range of sizes resting on the counter, and I knew that Lou would be warming up the sharpener and grinding away at blades for the better part of the afternoon. I had never been through the left door though, had never even noticed it as far as I could remember. With the lure of new gear and popcorn so close at hand, why bother?

Dick reached for the second door handle and yanked it open without hesitation. There was a rustling as he searched for a light switch and a grunt as he found it followed by a flicker and a hum. Looking over Dick's shoulder, I saw the walls were lined with wooden, glass-fronted cases, and I realized we were looking into what was apparently the Horner's trophy room.

Dick glanced back over his shoulder and registered the naked surprise on my face.

"You really didn't know?"

I shook my head, but he was already moving to the nearest wall case which held the first artifacts in the chronology of Lowland hockey history. Yellow press clippings were tacked up and slowly disintegrating inside plastic sleeves. Black and white photos of skinny boys in leather skates loosely arrayed in front of ponds were plastered up around a maroon sweater, faded and clearly hand-knitted, with a big cream-colored R sewn on the breast. "Lowland Raiders" was hand-painted on signs and placards in nearly every picture. Apparently, this town used to have some pride. Who knew?

The next wall held the case containing the odds and ends celebrating the construction of the Red Horner Ice Arena. There were pictures of smiling men shaking hands in front of the recently cleared forest, of the pit and ancient excavation equipment, of the construction as the bleak brick behemoth rose from the ground with the help of twenty sweating masons, even of Red Horner himself: bald, suited, sternly pleased. The ceremonial shovel used in the groundbreaking ceremony leaned rusting in the case's corner.

The third case, immediately opposite the door, held the actual trophies. 50-plus years of garish plastic pillars topped by faux-gold skaters ranging in height from inches to yards stood on ranks of shelves. Plaques, ribbons, and cut-glass awards were glued or pinned or sat resting in nooks around the trophies, all celebrating forgotten Raiders' championships, individual scoring records, state finals appearances, MVPs, and every other conceivable merit that may be bestowed on an amateur in exchange for sweat. On closer inspection, I saw with a certain twinge of silly pride that the tallest trophy was from my final year with the Raiders, when we'd gone to a AAA tourney in Philly and surprised just about everyone, including ourselves, by winning it all. That was the tournament where the Junior scouts had first noticed me, and the last time I'd ever worn a Raiders jersey. I bent to stare at the shiny little player on top, trying to read something of my own past in its smooth, blank face.

Rousing myself, I turned to look at Dick who stood before the fourth and final case, staring intently with his arms crossed behind his back like a patron at an art gallery. I sidled up beside him to share the view and was greeted by a huge but grainy photo of a speed skater in a skintight suit with a hood pulled tight around her face. Ringing the photo were countless medals cast from the three customary ores, but I noticed the vast majority were gold. There were also newspaper clippings, primarily from the *Herald Bulletin* but also a few from the Pittsburgh *Post-Gazette* and the Philadelphia *Enquirer*. She must have been something, I thought, to bring the east and west poles of Pennsylvania together here in the Lowlands. And sure enough, on a few medals and plaques and certificates, I noticed the five intertwining Olympic rings marking victories in the trial tournaments winnowing the field to see who would compete in the Games.

I returned my focus to the picture in the middle. The eyes were squinted but determined and stared right into the camera, the nostrils flared with exertion, the mouth part grimace and part smirk that spoke of danger for whoever she was chasing just beyond the photo's edge. And I realized they were features I knew well, from singing while fixing sandwiches in the kitchen to cheering "L-B-L-B" from the stands to shining with fresher sweat and fester in chemo-pain. From across the plains of time and death, I was reintroduced to my mother.

CHAPTER 5

"Knock knock!"

I woke in the living room lying on the third-hand couch where I'd been napping since my morning skate in a shaft of sun. The couch, which I'd recently acquired from a curb, was both comfortable and unnervingly tangy, both in smell and taste (don't ask).

"Knock knoooock!" I heard the door handle rattle then the sound of a key sliding into the lock, and a person was suddenly standing in the small entryway to my second-floor apartment.

"Knock!" the voice sounded next from the kitchen, where I heard the fridge door open—pause—close.

"Knock," I heard a drawer in the bedroom slide out and the sound of soft rustling as something, I guessed my underwear, was shifted around.

"Knock," the voice said, more quietly, as it moved to the bathroom and pulled the shower curtain aside setting the little iron rings jingling.

I remained prone as the voice grew closer, strangely at peace with the intrusion. The shuffling steps came into the living room and sat in the bay window chair I'd acquired from my father's porch when Robert was out running an errand. It creaked as the intruder gave it a test rock. I could hear the intruder muttering "knock, knock, knock" as the chair eased back and forth.

When the creaking stopped, and the shuffling footsteps came toward the couch, I was ready. When Miss Mary's head popped over the back of the couch to find me smiling up at her lying with my fingers intertwined behind my head, the landlord screamed.

"You scared me," she said accusingly. Her hair, which had previously been a frizzy gray dome, had been lopped off and died the rank yellow of dirty snow.

"Welcome to my living room," I said, still lying prone.

"I said *knock knock*," Miss Mary offered by way of explanation.

"Yes, I heard that. What I didn't hear was any actual knocking."

"Well, the door was open, and I was worried."

"And here I could have sworn the door was locked and that I heard you use the key you've got there in your hand."

"You must be slipping in your old age," Miss Mary said, though she had the grace to look guilty. She did, however, lack the other kind of grace that would have prevented her from giving me a long once-over as I lay shirtless and still a little sweaty from my workout and sunny nap.

I covered my nipples with my hands, feeling absurd.

"Why don't you come downstairs for a cup of coffee, and I can apologize properly." Her eyes narrowed and traveled unsettlingly back down towards my midsection.

"Oh, sorry I can't. I have to—" and I sat up to buy a little time as I searched for an activity, any activity, that would keep me away from the first-floor apartment. "—go help Dad with something."

"Oh good," Miss Mary said. "You can pick up that lawnmower like you promised."

Which meant a trip to my father's house for the lawnmower and the end of the radio silence that replaced Sunday Dinners. To top it all off, by being the party to give in first, I was tacitly admitting guilt after the dust-up of a month prior. I might have preferred to bite the bullet and have coffee with the batty widower.

"You can keep the shirt off when you mow. It's still awfully hot out there for November."

I changed my mind about the coffee.

· ·•·

Golden Thunder sat two houses down from Dad's place with its engine running, while I sat inside, sizing the place up like a bad daytime burglar. The old foursquare house with its wraparound porch looked a little more dilapidated than it was under my mother's tenure. Some of the amber terracotta roof tiles were missing, and the brick badly needed some work with a power washer, but overall, it was still a pretty impressive end piece to Ash Avenue. Behind the sparsely wooded lot, I could just make out the old swing set tucked onto the last remaining bit of flat land before the hill sloped down to the river. I considered that somebody, not me you understand, but somebody else, should take that swing set down before some kid fell off the top and broke his neck and his parents sued Robert into the poor house. But as I stirred through the loose change with a finger, trying not to think about how the Oldsmobile's cup holder held most of my liquid net worth, Robert's fate wasn't my primary problem. I wondered what it would be like to have the kind of money to know that whatever happened, I could afford to fix it.

I quit stalling and killed the engine, hauled the door open, and made my way around the side of the house to the detached garage. I was a little worried that I'd find a live horse in there again, or worse, a very smelly and very heavy dead horse. But as I hauled the unlocked garage open, I found it empty of equine. There was no trace of tack or bridle, hay, or dung. It smelled refreshingly like old gasoline and mold. I wondered briefly if I'd imagined the whole thing. I also wondered if I could just take the lawnmower and run. I decided negatively towards both and went instead to the backdoor to eat crow.

I knocked and waited and knocked and waited before deciding to take a page from Miss Mary's playbook and tried the latch. As the door swung open, I called, "Knock knock?" Closing the door behind me, I walked down the hallway towards the kitchen. I opened the fridge, just to see if there might be lunch in the offing, when the doorbell rang.

Feeling a little nostalgic, I walked back down the hallway to answer my ancestral front door for the first time in a decade.

"Hello?" I said, trailing off as the déjà vu melted away in the face of the bell ringer, who was three feet tall, wearing a tricorn hat, and holding a scroll.

"Hear ye! Hear ye!" the little reedy voice piped. "I bear glad tidings and a proclamation from the Duke of Ash Avenue!"

"Oh, Jesus, no."

"OH YES!" the boy yelled, grinning like a maniac.

"Well," I said, giving him the *out with it* hand motion.

"You are cordially invited to a festival this evening celebrating the day which shall never be forgotten wherein the traitor, Guy, failed, and the glorious empire triumphed."

"Which guy?" I asked.

"EXACTLY!" the boy yelled. "Merrymaking will abound, lie-bay-shuns will be served, and the Duke himself will commence the festivities. All residents of the Duke's realm are welcome."

"Huh. Which realm might that be?"

"ASH AVENUE," the boy yelled. "Stupid," he muttered.

"What was that last bit, kid?" I took a menacing step through the front door.

The boy turned and ran, holding his hat with one hand and the flapping scroll with the other. "7 o'clock! Ash Park! The Duke is expecting YOU!"

"Wait!" I called after the retreating figure. "Who's the Duke?"

"Come see for yourself," the boy called from halfway across the wide front lawn. "Expect MIRACLES!"

．　･●･

The little neighborhood park was sandwiched between two homes and abutted on either side by Ash Avenue and the same Allegheny River that ate my father's backyard, respectively. As I rolled down the street, I was surprised by the number of people flowing past me on both sidewalks. I parked a few blocks down from the park and walked around the hood to hold the door open for Susie, who unfolded herself spryly from the passenger seat.

Earlier in the day, after cutting the grass (in a sweatshirt, despite the heat, because this is my life now), I'd taken a cold shower and mulled attending this so-called "festival." In the two weeks since my trip to the hospital, I'd been trying to come up with a plausible first date to take Susie on to thank her for bailing me out of that tight spot at the hospital. The problem, like all problems in the main, was money. I would be damned to hell before I'd ask my father for money, and I'd been combing through the yellow pages, but unsurprisingly, my complete lack of college and job experience seemed to be detrimental towards actually getting a job. I wasn't shocked, but I was poor. As I lathered up, though, I remembered the little punk kid had said something about libations, and I figured what the hell? Plus, I was genuinely curious about this Duke despite my best efforts not to get sucked in, and now, given the crowd filtering into the park as the sun set towards seven, I discovered that I wasn't the only one.

I led Susie through the little wrought iron portal and down the brick path and its flowery border into the park. People were gathered in a loose ring around a tall stack of wooden pallets where a scarecrow perched on top, looking a little ominous in an old black suit and tilting drunkenly on a wooden frame. I scanned the crowd for familiar faces and saw many of my old neighbors from youth, looking grayer for the intervening years, but clearly excited about the festivities. I noticed a couple of cops standing at the back of the crowd, trying hard not to look like they were looking everywhere, and I wondered for the first time about the legality of declaring independence from the United States. I also wondered, and *not* for the first time, if it was possible that my father was behind all this silliness, but Robert didn't appear anywhere in the crowd.

I was just trying to decide whether or not to start introducing Susie—and reintroducing myself—to my old neighbors when I heard someone in the crowd call my name. I looked up to find Dick Newport waving at me from over by the monkey bars.

"Hey, Dick," I said as he walked up, and I shook the man's firm hand. "This is Susie Carter, my therapist."

When Dick raised an eyebrow, Susie laughed.

"His *physical* therapist," she said, grabbing my sore shoulder a little painfully. "And his occasional rescuer. And tonight, apparently, his date."

"Pleased to meet you, Susie," Dick said and shook her hand. "You ready for the show?"

"I'm just thrilled," Susie said, rocking on the balls of her feet in excitement. "Did Elbridge tell you we saw him two weeks ago riding around town in the middle of the night?"

"He did not." Dick looked at me curiously.

"Never came up," I said, shrugging. "How'd you hear about this shindig, Dick? You live around here?"

"I was just going to ask you the same question," Dick said. "For my part, a little town crier walked right into the *Bulletin*. Hat, scroll, the whole nine."

"Same story. My father lives at the end of the street," I said, answering his unasked question by pointing toward the setting sun.

"Say, where is your father?" Susie said, looking around. "I'd like to say hi."

When Dick raised the eyebrow again, I clarified. "He's also Susie's client."

"Yes, I'm fond of all the Corvallis men," she said, smiling.

"He doesn't seem to be around," I said to cover my embarrassment.

"Maybe he'll reveal himself as this Duke." Dick was smiling, but I couldn't tell if he was fishing for information or not.

"If he is, this is the first I've heard of it," I said. "But if you ask me, I just don't think he has all of *this* in him." I gestured around at all the excited, chatting people, the stack of pallets, the scarecrow. I omitted the horse in the garage.

"I have to agree with Elbridge there," Susie said. "He doesn't seem like much of a showman."

"I guess we'll see soon enough." Dick pointed north towards the back of the park where it dipped sharply into the ravine.

At first, all I could see was a round blob of color at the top of the trees. Slowly, the shape resolved out of the pink evening light into a ball, and then as it moved closer, I finally realized what I was looking at: a balloon.

As the hot air balloon inched closer to the park, I saw it was styled after the British union jack flag, navy behind the red and white crosses. The rest of the crowd had noticed it too, and they collectively gasped as it cleared the trees and entered the park's airspace.

"Welcome!" a voice issued through a bullhorn from the suspended basket. "Welcome, one and all. Enjoy the bounties of the Duke of Ash Avenue!"

I saw the speaker, face shadowed by a tricorn hat and wearing the same red coat I had seen on the rider that night in Susie's LeBaron, a night that now felt so long ago. As I watched, the figure swept his arm out over the side of the basket again and again, and as he did, little parachutes began opening one after another, trailing behind the balloon and floating gently to the ground. Children ran screaming to catch the falling objects as they settled gently towards earth. The balloon was directly over the swing set as I reached up to catch one of the hundred falling objects.

It was a jug, cold and slick with beaded moisture. Susie reached up and caught another object, this one a little basket that held a bundle of caramel apples. Dick intercepted his own falling basket, which held popcorn balls, of all things. I cracked the seal and sniffed. Dick and Susie looked at me expectantly. So, shrugging, I took a long quaff.

"Cider," I said. And I laughed. It started deep in my belly and rumbled up through my chest and out my throat and I couldn't stop it even if I wanted to. I handed the jug to Susie who took her own swallow before passing it to Dick and then they were all joining me, laughing like we were kids again at the novelty of it all.

Susie handed me an apple and I crunched into it still laughing like a fool. It was delicious, all of it, and as I looked around through bleary eyes, I saw laughter on all the faces of the denizens of Ash Avenue as they ate and drank and watched the stately passage of the balloon as it hovered over the pile of pallets. Then the bullhorn sounded again.

"Tonight, we remember Guy Fawkes!" the Duke cried. "That traitor to the crown! We burn his effigy in remembrance."

A spark, a flash, and suddenly a torch glowed in the basket of the balloon.

"Long live the Queen!" the Duke shouted. Then he dropped the torch.

It fell slowly, tipping end over end, before disappearing into the apparently hollow middle of the pile. The crowd hushed expectantly. I had time to briefly wonder at the anticlimax before a whump shook the air, and then the pallets all ignited simultaneously in a shimmering burst of heat and light.

The crowd gasped for the second time and hurriedly stepped back from the pyre as the Guy Fawkes effigy caught fire. It burned in silence for one held breath, and then the crowd in Ash Park burst into cheering applause. I stared, mouth hanging open, still bubbling with laughter at the spectacle, and made eye contact with Dick, who shrugged then hoisted the jug of cider into the air.

"Long live the Duke of Ash Avenue!" he shouted. "Duke of Ash! Duke of Ash! Duke of Ash!"

Then the crowd picked up the chant, and the park rang with cheers as the Duke sailed out over his dominion and on into the evening.

• . • • .

Susie and I walked down the moonlit sidewalk, holding hands and smiling, still.

"I thought the car was the other way?" she asked.

"It is. I just want to check something."

I was thinking about the Duke, about my father, and about the possibility that they were the same man. But I couldn't square my thoughts. Stacked against the evidence of my father's absence from the party and his unknown whereabouts the night of my hospitalization, not to mention the fucking *horse*, were the demonstrable facts I knew from my long history with Robert, including but not limited to his complacency, timidity, and general do-nothing scholarliness. So, with the Duke securely ensconced in a balloon drifting somewhere south of Lowland and in slow but persistent pursuit by one of Lowland's four squad cars for the presumptive crime of helium aviation without a license, I felt compelled to see what my father was up to.

As we neared the end of Ash Avenue, I saw lights glowing in Robert's house. I led Susie down the driveway and toward the back door where I could see the kitchen lit up against the cooling dark night. Still holding Susie's hand, not sure what to expect, I knocked. We waited in a silence still redolent with the park's heavy magic.

Then the door creaked open to reveal Robert's face, surprised but pleased.

"Well, hello there, Elbridge," he said. "Have you come to return my mower?"

"Uh," I said, feeling surprised despite my self-conviction.

"And who do we have here? It can't be the lovely if firm-handed Susie Carter?"

"Oh, you," Susie said, obviously pleased.

"Come in, come in. I just made soup." He held the door open and stepped out of the way. "I should warn you in advance, though."

I looked up into my father's eyes, and as I saw them sparkle, the incredulousness of the whole night washed over me. I had no idea what to expect as my father opened his smiling mouth.

"The soup is very hot."

CHAPTER 6

I discovered the hardwood floors in my apartment under the same auspices in which a small boy encounters the corpse of a giant horned bug: completely by accident and immediately enthralled. I was leaving the kitchen with a glass of water when my foot snagged on the awkward transition from green linoleum to once-white hallway carpet. The water went flying and I curled to protect my shoulder from the impact, which left my face to take the brunt of the landing.

As I lay stunned, inhaling the scent of ancient nylon pile and drifting dust, I noticed the carpet had ripped away from the faux-gold door sweep. I crawled back to investigate and saw just a hint of lustrous brown in the midmorning light. I peeled back the carpet, sending staples ricocheting off the walls and clattering along the kitchen floor, to reveal a foot of original flooring. Flawless, it was not, but to me, the slight warping and striated chestnut color added charm. Combined with the sun nudging past my shoulder from the kitchen window, it really did glow. I felt possessed.

I moved across the short landing and into the living room where I searched for another loose seam. I found one over by the brick fireplace that probably hadn't felt smoke since well before my birth and ripped with my good arm. I found the same rich wood, and though I was no expert, I assumed it was oak by the dark color and firmness and general oakiness of the thing. I also didn't know that many other types of tree, and it definitely wasn't cherry or white pine, so it was oak by my idiot process of elimination. It was nowhere pretty, but the roughness felt earned, a time toll paid, and still standing for it. Generations of steel families had learned to crawl and walk and run and hobble and finally come to rest all on my same floor. I could almost hear the hobnailed heels of the men scoring the floor as they rose in the predawn dark to walk downhill to the mills that used to populate the waterfront.

I sat wondering for a while what the floor looked like without the acre of shitty carpet. Then I wondered if Miss Mary even knew about the floor. Then I decided to quit being chicken shit and just go ask. She answered her first-floor apartment door after the fourth knock. I was relieved to see she was atypically fully clothed.

"You have the worst timing," she said. "Here I am all dressed up to go to the bank and you finally come knocking."

Per usual, I was incapable of participating in flirting with a woman even my father would have deemed "too seasoned." Some people just put you off your footing, you know? Mary was my conversational kryptonite. So, I spluttered the only thing on my mind that wasn't Miss Mary's frankly undignified neckline. "Floors."

"Tell me you didn't flood the place?" she asked, glancing up at the ceiling in search of leaks.

"No," I said, finding my footing. "Underneath the carpet, there's wood."

"Yes, dear. Houses tend to be made of the stuff."

"Pretty wood, though," I said, feeling ridiculous.

"I installed that carpet for a reason, you know? To add *value* to the place."

"How long ago did you install that carpet anyway?"

I noticed my landlord's eyes narrow as she caught the drift of the conversation. "No new carpet."

"I don't want new carpet. I want the old wood."

"And what will that cost me? Carpentry ain't cheap."

"I'll do it," I offered, without taking the single lucid moment required to properly consider the ramifications of my offer.

"Like I said, what will that cost me?"

I studied her thickly mascaraed eyes and weighed my chances before taking the plunge. "Rent until I'm finished, and you find me a, whadd'ya call it, big wood smoother?"

"That would be a drum sander, dear. And you get one month."

"I get 'til the end of the year, since this month is already half gone," I said, trying to buy some time to find a job so I wouldn't finish the floors of an apartment I couldn't then afford to rent.

"Deal," she said, extending a hand.

I shook and did my best to ignore the nails that caressed the back of my hand as I considered my wondrous stroke of luck.

"I'll get you that sander. In the meantime, you might want to rest up," she said, and shimmied past me into the hallway and towards the front door. "You've got a big job ahead of you."

The grin on her face as she closed the door made me wonder if perhaps I'd made a mistake.

*   *   *

I had made a mistake. I should have checked under *all* the carpet. Some idiot, I presumed Mary's dead husband, Bob, had painted the hardwood red. Mary had referred to it as "the style at the time" when she dropped off the monstrous drum sander, one pair of goggles, one pair of pliers, and some plastic sheeting. To me, the style at the time looked like someone had been murdered there, long ago, and the blood had dried and congealed into cracks and corners, puddled and pooled in dips and crevices, until it generally resembled an abattoir. I was now attempting to drum sand the killing floor.

It had taken the better part of a week just to get the carpet removed and the staples plucked. Some other idiot, I presumed probably also Bob, had tired of the style at the time and decided to make sure that the carpet he put down would never ever come up ever again. Ever. I decided that only a McCarthy era kid would worry about carpet shifting during an atomic blast. Ream upon ream of staples had been plunged into the hardwood, and time had shifted the boards and rusted the staples until they were virtually indistinguishable. Where one staple slid out slick as ice, the next took two minutes of yanking and prying and swearing.

So, when the time finally came to use the giant drum sander, I was ready to get some real work done, fast. Until I hit my first missed staple, and the noise and sparks startled me into letting go of the machine which swung crazily away from my outstretched hands with me in hot pursuit.

After the fourth staple sent sparks up my shins, I put the sander away, put on my hockey shin pads, and spent two more days re-removing staples.

But after two honest weeks of work, I had to admit I was proud of myself. My fingers were bloody raw, my second-best pair of jeans were now far and away my worst pair of jeans, and there was sawdust lodged in every conceivable place on my body. But as I showered at the end of each day and the tub turned the vicious brown-red of a battlefield after rain, I was proud of myself for the first time in a long time.

As I luxuriated in the shower, scrubbing the final day of sanding off me, I thought back to the same time last year, late November, when I'd cracked the league's top scoring list for the first time and Coach LeDeux had taken me aside after practice to let me know that *people* were starting to notice. Then the AHL and NHL scouts started to call, to take me aside after games and ask me about my future which seemed to roll straight out in front of me like a bowling lane. But the strike never came, just a phone call from my father, a dead mother, and a funeral and a car accident on the same day. Pain after pain upon pain, and just look at me now, cleaning sawdust from my ass crack in Lowland, PA. Behold, my glory.

My thoughts wandered back down the path that had become so well worn over the last few weeks, to training again, to the Horner, and inevitably to my mother. How many times had Clara walked past the trophy room, the literal shrine to her own accomplishments, without a second glance? How many of my hockey bags and sticks had she toted through the Horner's lobby to give me the same chance that she had passed on? Like the skate sharpener in the next room, was its presence a grinding force on her mind, honing her regret with each successive glance? Or, like all the other almost-made-its before her, did she sour on the experience and try to leave it in the past where she felt it belonged?

I shoved the last thought down as it struck a little too close to home right now and tried to understand why the information bothered me so much. Ever since I'd seen her picture, I had a rat-gnaw feeling in my guts that I couldn't explain. If I had to put it into words, I'd describe the feeling as abandonment.

I couldn't grasp why she didn't tell me about her own triumphs on the rink, the very thing that could have made us closer as I moved further and further from Lowland. All those pay phone and motel room calls after big games, all the long road trips in the old Jeep for tournaments, all the time at the dinner table where we sat talking about everything but hockey because of Robert's indifference, and never one mention of speed skating. And then she died, and it was too late. She got sick and gave up and left me with Robert, the hapless academic, who couldn't help me through this or any crisis of injury or money or spirit.

Then the phone rang, and I hustled to turn off the shower and the stream of self-pity. I wrapped myself in a towel and padded, dripping into the kitchen.

"Hello?"

"Elbridge, it's Mary. Did I catch you at a bad time?"

"Just taking a shower."

"Are you wearing a towel?"

"Mary," I sighed. "Is there something I can help you with?"

"You may have noticed my absence, which I'm told makes the heart—"

"Yes," I cut her off. "Where have you been?"

"At my sister's place in Hanover. Can't abide the noise you're making up there. Tinnitus, you know?"

"Is that so?"

"Too many years on the back of Bob's hog. Oh, but we did have some fun. There's a roadhouse outside Lancaster where if you take your top off, they'll give you free drinks for the whole night. And it's in Amish country! Can you believe that?"

"Again, something I can do for you?"

"Right, well first, water my begonias. They'll die and we need to keep up the curb appeal. That's my retirement you're lathering up in."

"Check." Water was pooling uncomfortably around my feet. "If that's all?"

"One more thing. Carl, down at the hardware store, has a palm sander for you. You'll need it to get into those tight corners. I want that floor to feel so smooth you could sit on it naked and not get any splinters in that bony butt."

"Carl. Palm sander. Got it."

"Speaking of that bony butt," she said.

I hung up the phone.

• .• ● .•

I coasted down Ash Avenue in Golden Thunder wondering where I would find the money to refill the Oldsmobile when this tank gave out. I'd never been particularly foolish with money, but they'd taken care of my room and board on the Bull Elk and instructing at a series of elite summer hockey camps took care of the rest. Needless to say, I was pretty shocked to learn how much rent actually cost. Combine that with the alarming price of food that wasn't canned, flash fried, or microwave ready, and I was about one bag of apples away from poverty. I eased up on the throttle.

Ash Avenue looked about as abject as I felt. Half of the shop fronts were boarded up or for sale. MVP Sports, where I'd bought the baseball bat still leaning by my father's door, was closed, though the adjacent Toy World was still kicking. Mom used to let me spend one dollar for every A on my report card and for every goal I scored. When I was twelve, the goals added up to a new BB gun, the A's a fistful of rock candy. A well-meaning real estate window advertised picture after picture of enormous, downtrodden homes terribly like the cannibalized Tudor I now occupied, not to mention my father's lovely but aging foursquare. Everywhere I looked, I could see the whole town's band playing the same final fading note.

The hardware store was at the end of the line, diagonal to the wearily majestic red brick courthouse. In case there was any doubt I was at the right place, the freshly painted sign above the store read "Carl's Hardware." Unsurprisingly, I found convenient street parking and bypassed the meter, assuming if Lowland could afford meter maids, they could afford a little small business stimulus. The shop bell jingled as I pushed open the door.

A few gray hairs looked up from a low conversation in the Nuts and Bolts aisle, but resumed talking with a nod when they didn't recognize me. I proceeded down a central aisle to the back counter where a hefty bald man in a green smock and name tag, "CARL," was helping a customer. I stood a respectful distance away and perused the shelves, wondering how a store this small could contain all the things necessary to build an entire house. I was pondering the placement of the hoses—next to the shovels, as opposed to what I considered a more natural choice, next to the sprinkler heads—when pieces of Carl's conversation interrupted my reverie. And though their discussion wasn't loud, and I tried to mind my own business, I successfully eavesdropped all the same.

". . . just quit showing up," the customer said.

"I'm sorry. I would have never of sent him your way if I'd known," Carl said.

"I know it. It is what it is. Just a goddamn waste. Now I'm a man short."

"He needed the money, too," Carl said. "Told me he might lose the house. And after Beth left n'at."

"I can overlook the drinking. But my gut says he was into something a little heavier than Iron City Light."

"Well, Rob, if I come across anyone else, I'll send 'em your way. Want me to start checking for track marks first?"

The customer laughed, and I finally slotted in the last piece of the puzzle. Then, for the second time in a month, I screwed up my confidence to take a chance and butted into their conversation. "You said you need a man?"

The customer turned and his eyes widened when he recognized me, but to his credit, Rob Dillon didn't take a step back or a step forward. Then my unwilling assailant from the Crow Bar extended his hand.

"I been meaning to look you up," he said. "I owe you an apology."

I coughed in surprise and shook the hand, which was rough and warm.

"What do you need to apologize for?" I asked. "I took the first swing, like a moron, and I paid for it, also like a moron. I am real sorry about that. As far as bad nights go, it was a Hall of Famer."

Rob had a good-natured chuckle and a natural smile. I felt seen when he turned them both on me.

"Hope the boys didn't work you over too bad. I reigned 'em in too late, unfortunately. Dropped you off at the hospital, though you probably don't remember that?"

I shook my head, slotting a few missing pieces of the night back into place.

"Sorry I didn't stick around," he said. "But two of those boys have priors, and I didn't feel like lying to the cops."

"No worries," I said, feeling ashamed. "Like I said, my fault. Thanks for sparing my face."

"Wouldn't want to bust up the moneymaker of the most famous guy in town." Rob smiled to take the heat off.

"All the good that does me. I got a quarter tank of gas and a borrowed sander to my name. And a fortune in cutting edge hockey gear that's perfectly useless."

"So, you're serious about needing work?" Rob asked.

"Yep. I'm doing a refinishing job for my landlord right now, but I've got another month to tie that up and it's mostly a labor of love."

"You know much about carpentry?" He eyed my dusty jeans and carved-up hands, and I had never been happier that I'd failed to change clothes or apply bandages.

"Honestly?" I said, discarding the six lies that crawled across my tongue before spitting out the truth. "I sure don't. But I work hard and learn quick, and I don't do drugs or really drink for that matter since I'm still in PT and training to get back on the ice."

When Rob raised a skeptical eyebrow, I could only shrug. "Like I said, Hall of Famer of a night."

Rob rubbed his jaw thoughtfully and Carl chose the perfect moment to offer, "He did come here to pick up a palm sander."

"Shit, what am I even thinking about? Meet us tomorrow morning over at number 331. We're putting in a new kitchen. We start at nine."

When I blanched at the address cattycorner to my father's house, Rob frowned.

"Nine going to be a problem for you?"

"No, no," I said. "I'm up for my workout at five. No problem at all."

"Well don't wear yourself out before work. You're going to have to put out twice as hard until you learn the ropes."

"Thanks," I said, extending my hand. "I can't tell you how much I appreciate it."

"You're welcome," Rob said, and shook again before making his way up the aisle. "Elbridge, I'll see you tomorrow. Carl, I hope I don't see you for a few days."

Carl laughed and rubbed his shiny head. "Who else is going to pay for my haircuts?" he called to Rob's retreating back before turning to me. "He really is a good guy. You may even learn to love the trade. Lots of us have after starting life with different dreams."

When I looked skeptical, Carl shrugged and smiled. "Here's that sander. My best to Mary."

As the door jingled behind me, I noticed a small sheet of yellow paper flutter under my windshield wiper. I swore, snatching up the ticket and searching right and left for any sign of the parking enforcement vehicle, but Ash Avenue remained deserted. I hefted the palm sander in one hand and the citation in the other and exhaled a long breath into the cool afternoon.

I looked up at the sky, wondering what my mother would think of this pit stop in my career. Then I noticed an old red plane circling low above Lowland, and watched as the plane, too, began to exhale. And I was still watching rapt when the plane finished smoking and flew off over the eastern skyline, leaving behind a perfectly white cursive script, hanging hugely in the blue bowl of afternoon.

"God save the Queen."

CHAPTER 7

I hate college. I hate it the way other people hate crowded freeways or the smell of patchouli or cats. It's an abstract hate, a discomfort that stems from a few bad personal experiences, and stoked by a lifetime of lingering dread. For my father, the college campus is a "bastion of civility and properly aligned high mindedness." For me, it's all my personal insecurities bundled into an ivy-wrapped box and labeled, "Are you supposed to be here?"

Though Robert had worked at Lowland University for more than three decades, I had only set foot on campus a handful of times. In a literal town-gown divide, Robert kept his campus life separate from his family life, such as it was. Our home was surprisingly bare of the stacks of books you might expect to find in a history professor's abode. Robert preferred to work from campus, and even now, as an emeritus faculty member, he maintained an office that he still travelled to almost daily. Or he had been traveling to until the accident. But, after another out-of-the-blue, "Elbridge, it's your father, Robert," phone call, here I was, lurking on the third floor of Boyd Hall at Low U, searching for my father's office like the lost boy that I was.

Beyond the row of hallway windows, I could see the green quad and its X of sidewalks, boxed in on all sides by Wealthy Donor Halls, and dominated in the center by the alleged but unofficial oldest oak tree in Pennsylvania. It was a pretty campus, as these things go. A local limestone quarry supplied the stone for every building so that even the maintenance sheds looked like small grottos of learning. It wasn't a large college, even in the booming mill days, but enrollment had dropped perilously low in the eighties before flattening out as it found its niche as a haven for Pittsburgh and Philly kids who weren't bright enough for Penn, but too rich for State. Standing there in the quiet hallway with the sun on my face on a pretty winter day, I could see how my relationship with college might have been different had I been a different person, with a different family, living in a different town. So, you know, not me in any conceivable way. I wondered if my father had stood here and enjoyed the same view before returning to his cozy office to read in peace.

"Can I help you?"

I jerked and twisted and immediately felt ashamed for jerking and twisting. I'd been caught enjoying myself for a minute and here college was to sneak up and remind me that I didn't belong. But the apologetic look on the man's face was so sincere that I thought he might start weeping.

"I'm sorry," we both said at the same time, and that cleared the air a bit.

He smiled, and I smiled too, and he offered his hand.

"Bruce Bartlett."

"Elbridge Corvallis."

His smile widened at that, and he gave me a lightning once over from behind perfectly round spectacles. Then he turned and walked down the hallway without another word, beckoning me to follow with a hand waved back over his shoulder. With panic-stricken flight left as my only other option, I followed.

Bruce was the only black man I'd seen so far at Low U, though the winter campus was admittedly pretty deserted, the students holed up cramming for finals or drinking their sorrows or just staying out of the freezing wind. Bruce was tall and broad and overweight in a maroon sweater vest that strained at his shoulders, neck, and belly. He had a neat gray goatee and just enough hair to cover the back of his head, and he strode along the hallway in soft brown shoes that helped to explain how he had been able to sneak up on me so effectively. I caught up quickly enough.

"I take it you know my father?" I asked.

"Oh, yes," Bruce said. Out of the side of my eye I could see he was still smiling. "I knew your mother too, though obviously not quite as well, and sadly for too brief a time."

"Really? We never came up to the college much."

"True, too true. But there was a time before you were around where your mother was around quite often. She was a student here, after all."

"Of course," I said, trying to cover for my lapse. "I just thought that might have been before your time."

"That's kind of you to say," he said, and ran a hand through the gray fuzz still clinging to the back of his scalp. "But no. I've been here for the better part of three decades. In fact, I taught your mother Shakespeare in 1971."

"Get out of here."

Bruce's smile deepened at my evident pleasure in this discovery. "It's true. Though, *attempted* to teach her Shakespeare would be more appropriate. I'm afraid she didn't take very well to it."

"Was she a bad student?" I asked. She wasn't stupid, far from it, but she never sat still, and the thought of her suffering through a semester of lectures on Shakespeare was hard to picture. When she worked at the library, she was always roaming the shelves, helping patrons find books or work the computers, acting out stories for children's read-alongs, even hosting after-hours yoga. During all those long years watching me play hockey, she would never be in one place for long, and I used to enjoy trying to find her like a "Where's Waldo?" book while I caught my breath on the bench between shifts.

"Oh no, not at all," Bruce said. "She was probably one of the most naturally intelligent students in her year. But Clara liked practical things, chemistry and math, and particularly ecology if memory serves. Though she never came right out and said it, I got the impression she thought the bard took too many words to say too little."

We turned a corner and Bruce came to a slow stop in front of an unmarked office door. Up and down the hallway, I could see nameplates and office numbers adorning all the doors. In fact, I'd walked down this hallway already right past this unmarked door.

Bruce saw my grimace and looked sheepish again.

"Hmm," Bruce said in a huff of air, rubbing his forehead with one big hand. "He chiseled off the name and number when he retired. Students kept coming to ask advising questions and he got sick of doing the same job without the pay. He likely forgot to tell you that."

"He did," I said and sighed, but I could feel my anger slipping away. "That sounds very much like my father."

Bruce smiled again, delighted to once again be on more pleasant turf.

"That's me right across the hall." He pointed to the adjacent and clearly marked door.

"So, you must have known him for a while?"

"Oh yes," he said fondly. "Longer than anyone still here, that's certain."

"Were you," I said, searching for a way to ask a question that would not require the man to admit my father was the longest lingering pain in his ass.

"Friends?" Bruce offered, helping me out. "Oh, yes, or at least, I like to think we are. He is a brilliant man, and funny."

He laughed when he saw the skepticism on my face. "Honest. I can prove it," he said, gesturing to the door. "Open her up."

I slid the key in and cranked the ill-maintained lock. The office wasn't dusty, though I was fairly certain he hadn't visited in months, so I guessed the custodians must clean all the offices at night. As I entered, I was struck by a powerful, familiar sensation that I couldn't put a name too, other than to say that I had never been in a room that so clearly embodied personal space. It looked like a 15 by 15-foot piece of my father's mind. It even smelled like him, or maybe he smelled like this room. Either way, the room was Robert.

Dark wooden bookshelves lined both walls, which were crammed and ill-organized and scattered throughout with knickknacks and small reproductions of historical scenes: continental congresses in fierce debate, musket smoke over open fields, tall ships at sea. A bust of George Washington sat on top of one shelf. On top of another bookcase was a very brown plant, the tendrils of which had crept around the edges of the shelf and were heading sneakily for the top row of books. On the far wall was a desk overflowing with papers beside an old leather armchair and a reading lamp backed by a large window that looked out not onto a parking lot as I had expected, but onto an arboretum. It was quite a sight.

I walked over to flick on the stand lamp while Bruce rustled around on the desk. As I lowered myself into the shockingly comfortable chair,

Bruce snatched up a laminated sheet and chuckled in triumph. He handed it over and I read in the soft yellow glow of his reading lamp:

I have retired to greener pastures.
If you're wondering why I am still sitting here,
please consider your role
in the browning of my previous pastures.

I laughed, a snort that turned into the second belly laugh of my year, and Bruce joined in freely until he collapsed into the desk chair with a squeak of wheels.

"He started hanging it from the door after the first poor student found his office despite its conspicuous lack of signage. When he was the department chair, he used to change all of the stationery so the school motto said, 'Rise to Mediocrity' in Latin."

"Stop," I pleaded, wheezing.

"I told you he was funny."

"I had no idea," I said as the laughter ran its course. "He's been so distant since Mom died, and it wasn't like we were close before that."

"I pieced together as much. I never had kids myself. For a number of reasons," he added quickly, holding up a hand to bat away any questions. "If I did, I sure would have wanted to show them off. But he never brought you around, or your mother for that matter, though the latter is a little more obvious."

"Obvious how?"

"Well, primarily in how they met. It's not forbidden for students and faculty to have relationships, so long as they're not current students, but the rumors do run regardless of timing."

"Mom was his student?" I asked, astonished. I felt unexpectedly flushed by the information, like I was the byproduct of some lurid affair.

"Naturally. How else would they have encountered one another? But surely, they told you?" he said, and then a look of shame swept onto his face again as he realized he had just aired a friend and colleague's long-held secret to his one and only son. His eyes welled.

"I should go," he said and squeaked up out of the chair with surprising agility.

"Bruce, no." I rose to catch his arm. "I like hearing about her. About them."

He turned to look at me, his eyes still glassy through his round steel frames.

"Please?" I asked, letting some honest desperation slip in.

"Fine. But like Robert Corvallis, it never leaves this office."

⁘

Apparent to everyone but me, apparently, Robert Corvallis was a firebrand. A marcher for civil rights, a conscientious objector, a thundering Libertarian, a thorn in the administration's side. My father was a campus demagogue.

According to Bruce, there was a clique of students, mostly young men, who enrolled in all his classes, then followed him around the quad after lectures while he talked over his shoulder on his way here and there. When the clique aged out and launched forth into the world armed with the twin grenades of personal freedom and strict constitutionalism, ready to pull the pins on the Senate floor and the SEC, a younger cohort took their place. Clara was not one of these men. But her boyfriend was. Sam Blotke was something of a big man back when Low U still had a football team and an endowment to speak of. He was big, literally, and not stupid, but earnest and amenable, and Robert had allowed him to tag along mostly to use as a straw man. Bruce actually did a fairly good Robert Corvallis impression, just so you know.

"Sam," he would say, "Why are you here?"

The rest of the clique would grin in anticipation.

Sam, knowing a trap lurked, would try to take the easy way out.

"Because I want to learn."

"No, Sam, why are you here at Lowland? Here in Pennsylvania? Standing here, in America, with your sneakers and your pig skin and not over there in the jungle fighting for your country?"

"Well, they haven't called my number yet."

"And when they do call, Sam, will you go?"

"Well, sure."

"Because you believe in the cause?"

Sam had spent enough time around Robert to know that patriotism was a slippery concept for the history professor, like freedom or property or Lyndon B. Johnson.

"Not as such. I just expect I'll have to is all."

"Why?"

"Well, they make you, don't they? You have no choice." Sam would look at his comrades here, but they weren't about to throw him a rope in front of the captain.

"So, you're saying the government can take away your choices?"

"Well, there isn't another option besides jail."

"You could flee. You could resist. You could fight."

"You can't just fight your own government," Sam would say.

"Which brings us home. How do you think you're standing here? At Lowland, in Pennsylvania, in these United States, if your ancestors didn't fight their own government?"

Then the clique would crow and strut and leave poor Sam standing in their wake under the Oldest Oak Tree in Pennsylvania while *Why are you here?* probably floated around in his head. You can understand why I empathized with the poor bastard.

Apparently, after a while these little demonstrations started to chip away at Sam's rock-solid belief in America, democracy, Ford automobiles, a just tax system, and hamburgers until he began to doubt even his own athletic prowess. When he blew the big game against the rival Catholic college in Pittsburgh and broke up with Clara to "figure himself out," Clara made up her mind to see what all the fuss was about.

Though Bruce was willing to admit to some nosiness, even he didn't know the details of their romance. What he did know was that Clara enrolled in his introductory history course and was later seen occasionally in his presence around campus.

"*After* the class had ended!" Bruce maintained over and over.

But it didn't matter. The quarterback's girlfriend (not to mention the sharpest student in her year) and the hellion history professor having coffee was just too juicy to resist. When the couple got married shortly after Clara's graduation in '72, the scuttlebutt mostly died away. Bruce was one of the few faculty invited to the small wedding, held not in the campus chapel as so many students, recent graduates, and even faculty often did, but in a small park in town.

"It changed him," Bruce said. "Either the wedding or marriage or the gossip or the end of Vietnam took something out of him. Or maybe it just redirected the flow of spirit elsewhere. But whatever the reason and result, he returned to teaching in the fall of 73 a changed man. He ditched the clique, kept his lectures focused on the tangibles, finally accepted tenure. And then you came along."

"And ruined everything," I said. It was a kneejerk reaction and I immediately regretted it, but Bruce grimaced with empathy.

"It wasn't you, Elbridge. As I said, he was already a changed man. And you've got your name to prove he wanted you."

This time Bruce had the grace to look less aghast at my puzzled expression. He turned back towards Robert's desk and, shifting a pile of papers to the side, unearthed a book that he passed to me.

"His magnum opus," Bruce said.

The book was called *Elbridge Gerry: A Definitive History.*

*, . • .

By the time Bruce finished spilling his guts, he had filled in a shocking amount of my family history, and the sky through the office window was beginning to dim. He helped me find the books on my father's list scattered amongst the shelves and desk, and one that he sheepishly admitted was in his own office.

I slid the copy of *Elbridge Gerry* into a plastic bag along with the rest of the books and followed Bruce into the hallway. As I turned to lock the door, I thought I saw one vine on the neglected plant twitch in the fading light. I felt bad for it, and knowing it was doomed if I turned my back on it, went back in and rescued the pot from the top of the bookcase. When I hesitated in the hallway, burdened and clearly befuddled, Bruce once again took pity on me.

"Let me grab my coat," he said. "This day is just about shot anyway."

"I'm sorry for that."

"For what?" He returned from his much tidier office wearing a thick navy pea coat.

"For stealing your afternoon."

"You're kidding me. This is the most fun I've had in this hallway in twenty literal years. I should have guessed it would be a Corvallis that made me laugh again." He pulled a sheet of paper from his pocket and handed it over.

I opened it to see two phone numbers, carefully written and labeled "home" and "office."

"Just in case you'd like to continue our chat."

"Be careful," I said, waving the paper at him. "The last person to give me their number had to pick me up from the ER in the middle of the night."

"Goodness. Are all you Corvallis men so interesting? Must be the French blood."

I followed Bruce down a flight of steps that I would have otherwise passed right by, and we emerged out onto the quad with the last light. It felt like snow, and our breath puffed as we stood adjusting to the real world. Across the quad, I saw students spilling from a building and forming untidy rows on either side of a door. As I watched, they flowed out in a stream until there was a crowd of almost 50 people standing identically angled towards the doors.

"A proud Low U finals tradition," Bruce said. He seemed somehow both delighted and resigned. "You'll want to see this. I hope you're not squeamish."

We watched in silence as the last few students trickled out to join the end of the long lines. There was a hush, and then a low rumble as all the students bent and began patting their knees in uneven cadence. Then the cheering started.

It was low, like crowd noise just before kickoff, building in pitch until I was sure they would all just collapse. Then the front doors blew open with a bang and out sprinted three pale figures.

The crowd exploded with noise as the sprinters moved quickly through the tunnel of spectators and headed towards the oak tree. As they emerged, I could see that they were two men and a woman, and all three were stark naked. As they neared the oak tree, I saw that the lead boy was holding something like a pole aloft in one ghostly arm.

The crowd continued to roar, and as they made their first circuit around the oak tree, the object trailing from the pole caught the wind and unfurled in their wake. It was the Union Jack, streaming proudly, and as the crowd caught sight of the flag, their incoherent screaming changed and syncopated until with one voice they chanted, "Dukes! Dukes! Dukes!"

The trio continued to run circuits around Pennsylvania's Oldest Oak Tree until a campus squad car rolled to a stop and the lights and sirens came on.

Without hesitation, the streakers bolted in three different directions in what was clearly a premeditated scatter. The squad car inched forward, then stopped, and its siren and lights went dead.

"Truly effective police force we have here," Bruce said.

I stared at him incredulously, looking for another answer after a day of truths.

Bruce just shook his head and shrugged his great shoulders. "Rise to mediocrity."

CHAPTER 8

Okay. Stay with me here, because I'm just going to come right out and say it. I don't *like* Susie. I don't have the capacity to tell you why, though, other than to say that I enjoyed the concept of her company more than the reality of her person. I wondered what the difference would be between a date with Susie versus the Guy Fawkes effigy. I'd have a much higher chance of getting the occasional word in, though the heavy petting in the backseat of Golden Thunder would be considerably more awkward. We'd probably get straw everywhere. Anyway, I was certainly on board for her outsider status and general disregard for Lowland and its inhabitants, but a relationship built primarily on shared enmity and physical therapy seemed thin, even to me.

As she stood behind me, observing me fingertip-walk my hand painfully up a wall and chatting about her other clients (all "maintainers"), I thought about how this would probably be the last time I ever set foot in a physical therapist's office. With my Bull Elk insurance officially ending with the calendar year, 1997 was looking real grim before it even got started.

"First, he was all sweet, like 'thank you' and 'yes, right there' and 'you're so good at this, how'd you get such strong hands?'" Susie said. "And I was flattered, but just trying to do my job, you know? And so, I'm working on his hammies, getting in there really good, and guess what?"

My little fingers walk-walk-walked and my brain went fuck-fuck-*fuck* as, inch by inch, my hand ascended past my shoulder, past my forehead. The muscles groaned, I groaned, and the guy getting worked over on the table ten paces down groaned too, in solidarity. I gave him a nod.

"I said, guess what?"

"What?" I asked.

"Guess," she said.

"Guess what?"

"Guess what happened, with the hammies?"

"Hammies?" I asked, confused.

"Ugh. Never mind."

"I'm sorry," I said. "I was trying to push it. You know, for gains?" I knew where her sympathies lay.

"That's okay," she said. "Just 30 more seconds."

"So, what happened," I asked, seeking distraction. "With the hammies?"

"Oh!" she said, excited all over again. "He had a *boner*!"

"Ha."

"Aren't you mad?"

"What for?" I asked.

"Because of the boner," she said.

"Am I mad at the boner?"

"No, aren't you mad at him for getting the boner?"

"Well," I said, contemplating the great mystery of the erection. "They sort of just happen."

"Yeah, I know that," she said, clearly frustrated. "But he was putting it right in my face."

"I thought you were working his hammies?"

"I was," she confirmed.

"So, wasn't your face, sort of, down there anyway?" I asked. "You know? Like an accident?" I reached for a metaphor to help explain and defaulted to what I knew best. "In hockey, when two players are both battling for a loose puck, just going about their business, but they get tangled up and fall down or whatever, we call it incidental contact."

"You're calling a boner stuck in my face 'incidental contact'?" she said, dead pan.

"No, no," I said. You can supply your own "toing the edge of a cliff" metaphor here if you want. "I'm sorry, that's gross."

I turned to look at her, but she'd crossed her arms and turned away to survey the rest of the therapy space. I watched her as she smiled and waved at a tall fellow across the open cavern of a room. He was working with a kid on the Astroturf section they used for ACL tears, helping him balance on an exercise ball. When he saw Susie waving, he let go of the kid to wave back. The kid, suddenly released, toppled silently to the ground. I gasped, but Susie and the tall guy both started laughing while he bent to offer the kid a hand.

I considered telling her it was over, either the PT sessions or whatever you'd call this weird relationship, or both. But when she turned back, she was still smiling, and my nerve failed me.

"So, got any plans for the holidays?" she asked, leaning in and placing an arm on my uninjured shoulder.

"I have to go see Dad."

"Oh," she said, taking her hand off my shoulder. "That's fine. I guess I'm going up to Slippery Rock to see my parents. Now."

"Can I stop this?" I asked, gesturing with my chin up toward my still crawling hand.

"30 more seconds."

Lowland looked its best at Christmas time. They hung lights and red ribbons from all the lamp posts, they decorated the band shell in the park, and the stores that were still open tried their best to look happy and festive. If you blurred the lens and shifted the focus just a little bit, it might even be pretty.

As I made my way down Ash Avenue headed for the grocery store, I glanced at the window to my left and read, "Christmas: it's great for loners!"

I shook my head and looked again at the travel agent's window display.

"Christmas: it's great for lovers!"

They were hawking beach vacations and ski chalets, optimistic in Lowland even in better days, but you couldn't blame them for trying. Neither could you blame the folks walking by on the sidewalk who stopped to consider that window display and daydream, resisting the tug of errands or work or impatient children, at least for a little while. Indulging in a little escapism was just about the only thing to do for free around here. That and sex, I guess, which explained all the tugging children, and why people hadn't quit Lowland altogether yet. There wasn't a cheaper place in Pennsylvania to raise a child and the schools weren't half bad, though if things continued, it wouldn't stay that way. The grade school and high school, the library and the ice rink, the parks department and the road crews, they were all manned by folks like my mother who were aging out or dying off or giving up, and there were no young feet willing to fill those dirty old shoes.

And could you blame them? Pittsburgh was just up the river, far enough away to be out from under the thumb, but close enough that you could still come back and do your laundry. There was nightlife there, more than three restaurants and a movie theater. At night, it seemed you could almost see the city in the dark, hear the laughing voices floating down the Allegheny, smell the new opportunities. I can hear you asking, why not you too? Well.

At the travel agency, after my Freudian incident, I saw an advertisement for a "Romantic river cruise along the majestic Monongahela River through Pittsburgh, the City of Bridges." Stepping closer, I inspected the text.

"Did you know Pittsburgh has the most bridges of any city in the United States?" the sign said.

"I did not," I said.

"And second in the world only to Venice, Italy, in Europe?" it asked.

"I didn't know that, either" I said. "And thank you for pointing out the Venice-is-in-Europe connection. I might have missed it."

"You're welcome," the sign said.

Okay, it didn't say that last bit, but you get the flavor of my state of mind better this way. At this point in time, I was the kind of guy who talked to signs. I was drifting, stalling, hanging around for no good reason. My previous line of thinking that my father needed help felt increasingly legless. Aside from Sunday Dinners, I hardly saw him. In fact, he had called me just that morning, on Christmas Eve, to tell me he wouldn't be able to have me over, as he was feeling "most unwell." When your own father disinvites you for Christmas, it makes you take a hard look in the mirror. Or in my case, the grubby reflection cast by a travel agency window.

I went next door to the Screaming Eagle grocery store, where I was intending to buy a turkey, still thinking about Pittsburgh. I got a shopping cart, not because I thought I'd need it, but because I wanted something to lean on, and squeaked my way back towards the freezer section. They probably had fresh birds, but aside from the cost discrepancy, I was dreading having to tell the man at the meat counter that I needed a turkey that could comfortably feed one. So, I cruised the aisles, arms and chin resting on the cart like a crutch.

Pittsburgh, or Philly for that matter, would both have more options for me. Though with no degree or discernable skills, those cities simply widened the field of shitty options. I could wait tables, or find a job on a line, or do the exact same thing I was doing here except without the benefits of Rob Dillon's company and his under-the-table-overtime cash. There would be more young people, ostensibly to make friends with, but I was quickly discovering that making friends outside of a locker room was hard. What was I supposed to do? Go down to the bar and pick up some friends? "Hey, bud, you look like a nice guy. Want to hang out sometime? I mean, someplace other than here?" I'd had my ass kicked in enough parking lots for one lifetime, thanks.

I found the turkeys in a long, open-air freezer, and just my luck, the little ones had already been gobbled up (ugh, I know, it's terrible but I already wrote it down). I was weighing two birds, one in each hand, and trying to decide just how many times I could eat turkey on white bread with American cheese before I died of food boredom, when something nudged me from behind.

I turned to find a half-full shopping cart but no pusher. I looked around for the mother whom the cart had surely rolled away from while she scolded a child or reached for something on the top shelf, but there were no mothers in evidence, or children, or people at all for that matter. I was trying not to think about ghost carts and getting murdered in the Screaming Eagle when hands descended over my eyes.

"Okay, buddy," someone said from behind me. "Put the turkeys down, real slowly now."

I lowered the birds into the freezer, trying to place the husky voice.

"Now, answer me these riddles three."

I smiled now, the tension running out my neck and shoulders and back as I relaxed into the gentle but firm grip of my assailant. "Is it a man? A block of ice? And you take the sheep first, then go get the cheetah, then bring the sheep back with you and switch it for the grain?"

"We, as a species, need to come up with some new riddles," Grace said as she turned me around and pulled me into a hug. Her voice had turned singsong and quietly mocking, which was as unchanged as the rest of my mother's coworker, though Clara's death meant she was now head librarian. Her dark hair was still free of gray and there was no stoop to her tall frame, though I noticed she had upgraded her old, enormous glasses for a smaller, more tasteful pair. At a neat six feet, we were eye to eye, and she bowed her head to whisper in my ear, "I can guess why you haven't come to visit me, but it still stings."

"I'm sorry." I hugged her back and thought of all the happier times she'd given me hugs just like this one, and I was suddenly fighting back tears. "I was working through some stuff."

"So," she said. "You're back?"

"That's what everyone keeps telling me."

"But not for good?"

"Not sure about that part yet."

"Then you're here for a period of convalescence?"

I nodded. I liked the sound of that.

"And the turkey helps you convalesce?" she asked.

"Well," I said. "Chicken soup for the soul, etc."

She smiled. "God those books are awful. I hope they die soon."

I smiled back. I hadn't realized how much I missed her until she was standing before me, shifting from one white sneaker to the other, probably anxious to tell me something that she would never say unless I asked. I tried to ask.

"Grace," I said, trying to pick a question like a participant in a magic trick who is offered the whole deck of cards to choose from. "What are you doing for dinner tomorrow?"

Her smile widened. "Dinner for one, chez Grace."

"Would you like to come over?" I asked, then completely invented, "I'm having a few people over and I'd love to catch up."

"Your father?" she asked, raising a skeptical eyebrow.

"No, he's feeling 'unwell'."

"Well, I'd be delighted."

I gave her my address and she hugged me again, pushing her cart off down the aisle with a few quick strides and then, not entirely to my surprise, she hopped up onto the back, her long skirt billowing out behind her like a sail. She turned the cart with a pivot, and as she disappeared down aisle 12, I could hear her calling, "Wheeeeee!"

I looked back down at the turkeys I'd been weighing. I got the big one out.

Here's a new riddle for you: how do you host a Christmas dinner with no dinner table?

After inviting Grace, I'd returned home, got the turkey thawing in the sink, and called Bruce who said he would be "dee-lighted" to attend. That settled (I was actually dusting my hands off), I turned to regard my kitchen and realized that I didn't have a table. Or chairs. I'd been eating my sad sandwiches in the rocking chair because it was nicer to look out the window at my street than it was to look inward, where both my apartment and its lonely occupant left something to be desired.

I panicked a little. I didn't have the money to go buy a dining room set, and anyway, who sold a dining room set in Lowland on Christmas Eve? I considered breaking into my father's house to steal his furniture, but that seemed a little too Grinch-like even for me. Plus, I didn't have the helpful little dog sidekick. It was going to be a real sad affair if everyone had to squeeze onto the couch and eat turkey off their laps. And just as the panic sweats were starting to sink in, I heard the house's front door open and shut, a long chesty cough, and the sound of a key in a lock. Unfortunately, I had my solution.

When I knocked on Mary's door, I could hear her TV thumping. *Wheel of Fortune* was on, and Sajak was excited about the prizes.

"What?" she called, declining to turn the volume down.

"IT'S A STATE OF THE ART WASHER AND DRYER!"

"Miss Mary, I was hoping to borrow a table and some chairs."

"Why?" she called.

"IT'S A TRIP TO CANCUN, STAY FIVE DAYS, FOUR NIGHTS IN THE LAP OF LUXURY!"

"I'm having some folks over for Christmas dinner tomorrow."

"So?" she called.

"IT'S A NEW CARRRRR!"

I'd been tempted to avoid what came next, but figured it was unavoidable. There was also that it was the right thing to do, spirit of Christmas, blah blah. I sighed.

"I was wondering, if you're not doing anything, if you'd like to come too?"

The TV clicked off abruptly and the door swung open.

"Who's coming?" she asked, peering up at me from bangs that were fading from yellow back to gray, again. "Your father? I'd like to get know *him* a little better." Her eyebrows waggled.

"Just a few friends," I said. "Nothing special."

She squinted up at me suspiciously.

"I got a big turkey?" I added.

Whatever her reservations, apparently they were no match for the offer of a free meal cooked by someone else.

"Well, my daughter was supposed to come by," she said. "But she never stays long."

"Terrific," I said.

"What time, then?"

"7?"

"Fine."

"And the table?" I asked.

"Oh, there's a card table and folding chairs in the basement," she said. "I could have sworn I told you to take them the day you moved in. Guess not, huh?"

I shook my head, doing my best to look thankful and not like I was ready to chew rocks.

"My mistake," she said, smiling. "All yours now, big fella."

•. • • •.

Somehow, against all the laws of man and nature, dinner wasn't a disaster. Bruce and Grace seemed to hit it off right away, and Miss Mary was surprisingly knowledgeable about Lowland history and gossip, which we all ate up along with my turkey and the side dishes and wine contributed by my guests. By the time dinner was over, no one wanted the party to end, and Mary disappeared downstairs for a minute to reemerge with a two-liter bottle of Sprite.

She grinned her devil's grin as she held it aloft, the green sleeves of her velvet dress falling down her wrists. The dress covered everything from neck to ankle except for a shoe-boxed size hold cut out over the tops of her breasts. I tried not to watch the jiggling as she rattled the bottle in triumph.

"Sprite?" I asked.

"SLIVOVITZ!"

"What is sleevo-visk?" Bruce asked, trying to wrap his mouth around the word.

"What? You never had slivo?" Mary asked, flabbergasted. "Then you've never lived. Serbian lightning, they call it. Bill used to make it in the garage." This answered both the question of what a slivovitz was and why I wasn't allowed to park in the detached garage.

"His still is still in there," she added, then she chuckled at her own pun before pouring us all a measure into some plastic cups she fished out of my cupboards.

We stood in a loose circle in my ugly kitchen, staring at one another nervously, except for Mary who licked her lips. Then we raised our glasses.

"To Elbridge," Bruce said, breaking the ice. "For gathering up all the lonely souls and welcoming them here for such an excellent and much needed dinner party."

"To the turkey," Grace said. "Which was probably a good bird, since he tasted so good. May his leftovers honor his little bird memory."

"To the Duke," Mary said. "Because why the hell not."

We drank. Then choked. Then coughed. Then gasped. Then laughed. Well, all of us except Mary, who tossed it back like it was nothing, then watched us, shaking her head in bemusement at our suffering.

When she offered another round, Bruce and Grace both politely declined simultaneously and started shuffling toward their coats. We left my apartment together, walking down the stairs and out onto the front porch where we stood hugging and puffing in the chilly air. As we said our goodbyes, I watched Mary bend to retrieve something resting on the top step.

"What is it?" I asked.

She held up a little box, neatly wrapped in blue paper and tied with red ribbon, which fit right in her palm. She looked up at us and shrugged.

"Well?" Bruce asked.

"Yes, open it!" Grace said. "Open it! Open it!"

Mary, true to her nature, ripped the bow and paper off in one harsh jerk. Then she pried the box open and tipped the contents into her hand, holding up a note and a coin.

"Why, it's a British pound coin," Bruce said, leaning closer to inspect it.

"What's that worth?" Mary asked quickly, clutching the coin a little closer to her chest.

"About a dollar twenty-five," he said. "Give or take current exchange rates."

"What's the note say?" Grace asked as Mary's face fell in disappointment.

She read the slip of paper in her other hand.

"Happy Boxing Day!

—Warmest regards, The Duke of Ash Avenue"

CHAPTER 9

Who carpets a bathroom? The answer, apparently, was Ms. Noreen Nash of 655 Ash Avenue, recently deceased. The current job was already well underway courtesy of Ms. Nash's son, who was as eager to unload the groaning Victorian as Dillon Bros. Renovation was to take his money. Despite this knowledge, I still didn't understand *why* you'd carpet a bathroom. So, I asked Rob.

"Never seen it before," he said.

"Never?"

"Never. And I've seen some shit."

"I'll bet you have," I said, not exactly trying to suck up, but as our relationship started so badly, I had spent my first few months on the job aiming for model employee. Plus, I was beginning to enjoy the work, at least some of the time, which I figured was about the best that I could hope for, or deserved, come to think of it.

"Yeah, there was this crawlspace one time," Rob said. "I guess the owner had been illegally shooting squirrels and stuffing their little corpses down there. Anyway, we opened that sucker up and a mountain of little bones comes spilling out. I lost two guys right on the spot. Went out to the yard to puke and never came back."

"Woof," I said. "What else?"

His walkie talkie beeped, and he held up one "hold" finger while he clipped it off his belt.

"Yeah?" he said.

"Rob, it's Ron. Over."

"Ron, I know it's you. We only got the two radios. You don't have to say it's you every time."

Rob rolled his eyes at me, and I chuckled honestly, thinking of Dad and his customary telephone introduction, *Elbridge, it's your father, Robert.*

"Noted. Over."

"What do you want?"

"You've got some inquiry calls, and Bill Watkins finally showed up. Over."

"That piece of shit," Rob said. "Tell him to go home and kill himself."

"Well, he's sitting right here." Ron's voice grew quieter as he distinctly lifted the mouthpiece away from his face and, still holding the button, said, "No I'm sure he didn't mean that, Bill. Please don't cry." Then his voice grew louder once again as he lifted the radio back to his mouth. "I really think you should come back here, maybe. Over."

Rob sighed and held the walkie to his forehead while he collected himself. I felt bad for him. His brother had a soft touch and carried around a sack of second chances. I hadn't worked for the Dillon brothers for too long, but even I could guess Rob was just now thinking how easy it would be to get rid of the "Bros." bit and save himself a lot of hassle. Except everyone knew that Ron was the real brains behind the business, and he ran the accounting and customer side of things, so unless Rob wanted to go get a degree and start being a whole lot nicer to a whole lot more people, he needed his kind-hearted brother.

So, when the walkie talkie, still pressed to Rob's face, whispered, "*Please.* Over," he relented.

"Be back in ten," Rob said, and clipped the radio back onto his belt.

He looked at me and I tried to give him my best *Family, man, what can you do?* shrug.

"I gotta go bitch out a deadbeat. You gonna be alright here?"

"Yep," I said.

He poked his head into the bathroom. "Get rid of it."

"Even the, uh?" I asked, gesturing generally towards the sink and its affiliated cabinetry.

"Vanity," he supplied. "Yes. All of it."

"Check." I shuffled past him to get to work.

"Elbridge," he said, stopping me with an arm on my shoulder. "Make sure you turn the water off first."

"I knew that," I called after him as he headed down the stairs. It wasn't a lie per se, because I *would* have figured it out. Eventually. As his footsteps receded and the front door slammed, I tried not to think about how the room wasn't that much bigger than a coffin.

. . .

It didn't take long to discover why Noreen Nash carpeted her half-bath. Underneath the navy shag was the ugliest set of tiles I have ever seen. In the worst vein of 70's enthusiasm, the pattern was asymmetrically checkered in mustard and mahogany. I knelt, once again, amidst floating carpet dust, and considered the kind of universe where people intentionally tile their bathrooms in yellow and brown.

With the carpet safely removed to the hallway and the tile chiseled out, I felt that I was starting to find my rhythm at this handyman game. So, of course, that's when I hit my first snag. How do you get rid of toilet water?

I got the rusty bolts off the base and the water line unhooked, but there was still a half tank of liquid that lingered beneath the pump. I eyed the narrow window and was considering trying to hoist the tank up for a tip into the backyard, but a tentative heft proved that my shoulder, while stronger daily, was not up to the task of deadlifting that much porcelain. I considered trying to use the hose as a siphon, but the thought of putting my lips on any piece of toilet equipment was above my pay grade.

So, I sat there, knees on either side of my shiny white enemy, idly rifling through my loaner toolbox, looking for anything that might help, preferably something with a neat label like "toilet emptier," reassessing my competence as a handyman. I had grim visions of Rob returning, probably with shameful but competent toilet-emptier Bill in tow, to find me as I was, sitting there defeated by six inches of toilet water. I thought I heard a creak and peeked into the hallway, preparing to look busy, when my eyes fell on the pile of discarded navy carpet. The solution to emptying a toilet, it turns out, is to fill the tank with shag.

An hour later, I had the room emptied into the dumpster parked in the driveway and was feeling the same pleasantly exhausted sensation I got after a good skate. It was a little strange to associate the feeling with something other than hockey, but the happy little chemicals zipping around my brain were the same and didn't seem to care what caused their release, so neither did I. Without the god-awful tile and shag, the fading-to-yellow toilet, and the chipboard vanity, the half-bath was starting to show the same potential as a fresh sheet of ice. You never think about it, but possibility is contagious.

I was considering what to do next and leaning towards lunch when I noticed the little plastic ring. Six inches around and stained orange, it once separated the plywood floor from the base of the toilet. Now it was my only obstacle to a job well done. I considered leaving it, because surely the new toilet would need something similar, but even after two short weeks on the job, I knew "similar" was not the same as "the same." Plus, Rob had said, "All of it." I sighed and fetched a screwdriver.

Then I fetched a bigger screwdriver, then a hammer, then what I assume is referred to as a mallet by professionals but which I called the "super hammer." And it was all for nothing. Despite my efforts to pry, chip, and smash, the little ring wouldn't budge. Somehow, a quarter decade of overflowing toilet water had melded the plastic with the wood to form some kind of unholy, unbreakable uber material. I lay there on the floor, sweating and swearing and hammering, harder and louder with each unsuccessful minute. I really wanted to have the bathroom empty when Rob returned, and I wasn't going to let a little piece of plastic stop me.

I redoubled my efforts. Wielding the super hammer with my good arm from a kneeling position, I bore down on the ring with everything I had. I felt like a blacksmith, and the hammer ricocheted around crazily with each swing. The room started to heat up around me with my effort, the thumping rhythm became hypnotic, and I lost myself in it until suddenly I was back on the ice with Coach LeDeux, exactly one year before, on a Monday when he'd taken the pucks away.

It was LeDeux's way of punishing the team, to take the pucks away. Oh, he'd leave them in a bucket out in the middle of the ice where everyone could see them, like a highly visible but tantalizingly distant cookie jar. He'd line us up, let us get a good look at the puck bucket, and then smile. "Pucks are for winners, and I don't see any of those around here," he'd say. Or "We're giving the goalies a break today because you hung them out to dry yesterday." Or maybe just "We're skating 'til you puke."

Then the whistle would blow, and it was chop chop chop—stop—chop chop chop—stop until Charlie Landers vomited. It was always Charlie, and we loved him for it. But between that first whistle and Charlie giving his breakfast back to the earth, there was the pounding. Scattered at first, we eventually fell into the same cadence, like soldiers marching, so no one fell behind are got too far ahead, both of which made LeDeux madder for no apparent reason. The drumming percussion, the low moan of over-exertion, the heat building up inside the nest of padding, it was like I was home again inside the half-bath. I was lost in the hammering, waiting for the sound of Charlie's first choking retch and Coach LeDeux's whistle, when a voice sounded from the hallway and jarred me from the zone. I looked up to see a face, eyes wide with shock, and recognition struck me at precisely the same time as the rebounding hammer.

• . • • .

"Elby," a voice called.

"Oh, Elbyyy," again, a drawn-out song.

I hadn't passed out, exactly, but my brain had a way of resetting after a heavy collision where my vision went yellow and all I could hear was the sound of an old radio being tuned to a clear signal. It never lasted long, and it wasn't traumatic for me, but I had been told before that the experience was a little alarming to witness. The radio stopped tuning and settled on the "present" frequency, and my vision cleared to reveal a woman kneeling over me, looking not overly concerned but perhaps a little relieved that my eyes were focusing properly on her again.

"That," she said, "was something to see."

I struggled to sit up and regain some composure. My head was pulsing in pain. "Am I dead?"

She shook her head and looked more relieved, perhaps because by speaking I had cleared her of criminal charges related to brain damage.

"Elby Corvallis," she said, smiling.

"Abbey Winthers." I spread my arms weakly. "How impressive do I look?"

Abbey laughed. "You've looked worse. The last time I saw you was the last day of ninth grade and your hair was dyed piss blonde."

"Sun-In: a truly regrettable life decision. You look," I said, and stopped to take her in. Kneeling between my outstretched legs, she looked like what her ninth-grade self must have hoped she would look like in ten years. But I couldn't say that, so instead I said, "Great."

We both realized at the same time how close we were sitting in the small bathroom, and I had the insane urge to kiss her, which I resisted on the basis that she would very probably scream. She stood lithely in the way former athletes or yoga practitioners do and offered me her hand, which I took gratefully.

Vertical, I felt much dizzier, and my head throbbed more intensely. I stumbled a step before Abbey's firm hand pulled me upright again.

"Careful there." She looked at me with real concern while she brushed some of the carpet fabric and tile dust off my t-shirt. "Maybe we should go get some fresh air."

I was reluctant to leave the tight confines of the warm bathroom, where the closeness of Abbey's spearmint breath and kind hands were doing more for my general spirits than I thought naked February would, but she gave my hand one more squeeze and walked out. So, I followed, of course.

We sat on the concrete steps leading down from the front door, and though it was a mild day, I instantly regretted forgetting my jacket when the air hit my damp skin.

"Wanna go get your coat?" she asked, reading my mind.

"No," I lied.

"Suit yourself," she said, but slid a little closer.

We sat in silence for a while, and I had to admit the air was helping clear the angry pulsing pain. Winter birds bounced from oak to oak down the long line of Ash Avenue, where I knew four blocks to the south my father would be sitting at home doing whatever he filled his retirement with, most likely reading, which seemed a whole lot like what he filled his pre-retirement with. I thought about how sad that was. Then I thought, if I retired from hockey, wouldn't I want to keep playing just like all the old Silver Foxes? I decided to withhold judgment pending further wisdom.

"What the hell are you doing here, Elby?"

"Gutting a half-bath."

"Yeah, I got that much. I meant here," and she pointed at Ash Avenue, aorta of Lowland.

"Rehabbing."

"I heard about the arm. But can't you do that, like, anywhere else?" She sounded a little bit pissed, and I couldn't figure out why.

"Where should I go?"

"How about your team in Nebraska, for starters?"

"Minnesota."

"Whatever."

"I got cut."

"Oh," she said, and looked down chagrined at her sensible hiking boots. "I guess they don't need a one-armed forward?"

"Guess not."

"Sorry about your ma." She put a hand on my knee, like she used to in ninth grade when she wanted to see me squirm. "I liked her."

I nodded and looked down at my own, less sensible gym shoes. "What about you?" I asked, steering the conversation away from my pathetic life. "What brings you to my construction sight?"

"Well. As you know, ever since I was a little girl, I've always been interested in zoning enforcement."

"Yes, of course. I do remember you going on and on about permits."

"And don't forget the site inspections," she said, and peeked over her shoulder at 655 Ash Ave. which loomed behind us like a chaperoning parent.

"I suppose you're looking for Rob, then?" I asked, and she nodded. "He went back to the office to bail out Ron."

"I'm glad you fell in with them. The Dillons do good work, unlike some of the other shoddy outfits around here I could mention."

"That's the Dillon Brothers for you. No corners cut, unless you want them to cut your corners."

"Or at least they did until they hired you."

"I've got to be honest with you here, Abs. I have no clue what I'm doing." I realized after it was out of my mouth that I'd called her by her kid name, now surely long dead, but she didn't seem to mind.

"I could see that. You know? From when you hit yourself in the head with the hammer?"

I laughed, and so did she, and I realized my head didn't hurt so badly anymore. I had forgotten she was funny. I had forgotten a lot of things about Lowland, apparently. I *had* remembered how her mouth looked when she laughed though, wide and uncaringly toothy, and that was still the same.

"I hear you're seeing Susie."

"Susie who?" I asked.

Her mouth dropped open a little bit and after a startlingly long time I figured out why.

"Oh, that Susie! Yes, I'm seeing Susie. Well, sort of. How are we defining 'seeing' these days?" I looked up from my shoes to gauge her reaction and couldn't get a clear signal. "Sorry, I was recently struck on the head."

"Can I give you a piece of advice?" she asked.

"Definitely."

"You need to make up your mind about that one."

"Okay?"

"Susie's a friend, and I know for a fact she's not hesitating over the answer to that question. How do you think I found out you were still in town?" Then she looked me right in the eyes, as she always used to do when she was serious. "Strange way to find out, by the way."

"Sorry," I said, apologizing entirely for not calling Abbey when I got back to town rather than for forgetting my sort-of girlfriend's name.

"I forgive you," she said, which seemed like a general benediction, and I thought I still had a lot of work to do before actual forgiveness was bestowed. She got up and dusted her hands off, then descended two stairs until she was staring at me eye-to-eye.

"It's good to see you again, Elby." She turned to go, and the thought of her walking away without a concrete plan to see her again seemed stupid.

"Do you want to grab a beer sometime?" I called to her retreating back.

She stopped and turned back to stare me down beneath one lifted eyebrow.

"You know, to catch up?" I added. "I want to hear about how all your zoning dreams finally came true."

She smiled again and tilted her head. "You know what? Let's do a double date on Saturday. You can bring *Susie*," she said, putting extra emphasis on the name. "And I'll bring John. You might like him. Or you might not."

I flinched at the boyfriend being named so blatantly, and you can say that I'm a whiner and a narcissist and definitely an idiot, but I dare you to call me a coward. At least when I'm not down on my luck, or injured, or having a glum day. Okay, you can call me a coward.

"I'll have to check my calendar," I said, gesturing back at the creaking Victorian. "Pretty full these days."

"I can see that. Speaking of which, can I give you another piece of advice?"

"Definitely," I said, nervous this time.

"Get a flathead wedged under the lip, *then* whack it with the hammer. It may take a minute, but leverage is more important than strength when you're dealing with these old places."

She was right, of course.

CHAPTER 10

"The special is cheesy wings."

"Come again?" I asked.

"Cheesy wings," the waitress said. "You know, like regular wings, but with cheese."

"Are we talking cheese sauce here? Or like cheese melted over the top."

"Look." She patted her notepad threateningly against her palm. "The special is cheesy wings. If you need more time, I'll come back." She stared at me through red cat-eye glasses while I pondered the versatility of cheese at Jumbo's Diner.

"I'll think I'll just have a salad." I wondered just how far off my playing weight I was given I didn't own a scale and had been living off Bimbo bread and Kraft singles for months.

She scribbled my order with a roll of her eyes. "Comes with French fries."

"Of course it does," I said.

"Do you want more water?" she asked, omitting the "time waster" she probably wanted to tack on the end.

"Whenever you get a chance."

"Of course you do," she said, and smirked as she turned away.

I watched her walk away from my window seat into the interior of Jumbo's, which was low slung and narrow, with a Formica countertop and bar stools running down one wall and a row of black tables down the other. She split the difference, patting patrons' backs at stool and table alike, bantering good-naturedly. I thought it was funny how you could be sitting warm inside a place and still feel like you were a stranger peeping in through the window.

I chewed some ice from my empty glass and fidgeted with the ad-covered paper placemat, waiting for Dick Newport to show. He'd called to set up the interview, and despite my continued protests about my lack of newsworthiness, we'd found a time to meet on a Friday for lunch. Dick sealed the deal when he offered to buy, and my stomach rumbled in anticipation of my first meal since soup with my father that didn't feature American cheese.

I had been a bad son lately. I knew Dad was alone, just like me, but I used my morning workouts and the job and sporadic dates with Susie as my excuses. Plus, I was still mad at him for bagging on Christmas, and you know, the car accident, the horse, my general state of affairs. All those cuts would probably never seal up completely. Getting back to the Bull Elk, or at least getting the hell out of Lowland, would be a good start to mending the wounds, but that wasn't going to happen until summer at the earliest. And if I'm being completely honest, it was more of a lingering strangeness that kept me away from Dad than anything else. He was so much more *fatherly* than he had ever been, and frankly, it gave me the creeps. He'd been calling more often, and though we hadn't resumed Sunday Dinners regularly, it felt less like pulling teeth every time we had a conversation. The irony of distancing myself from him when he was very clearly trying to step up his parenting game was not lost on me, but that still didn't make me aim for his driveway.

I was staring at a placemat ad for Big Ed's Concrete, complete with a cartoonish, grinning mixing truck, when a knock on Jumbo's big front window made me jump. I looked over to see Dick, waving and chuckling at my surprise. He walked away and I heard the bell over the door jingle, then Dick was sliding his bulk awkwardly onto the opposing bench seat.

Before we had a chance to say hello, the cat-eyed waitress reappeared at the booth. I expected more snark and was dead wrong.

"Hey there, Dick. Where have you been hiding?" She kneaded his shoulder affectionately with long, crimson fingernails.

"Hey Deb," he said. "Sorry, but you know how the news game goes. This Duke is great for business, but he keeps me running."

"Any new bits?" she asked, the anticipation clear in her voice.

"Promise you'll still buy a paper?"

"Cross my heart," she said, and did just that with her notepad.

"Well, you remember that hubbub with that hot air balloon?"

She rolled her eyes. "You really asking me that? It's the most interesting thing that's happened here since that parade for Gerry Ford."

"Ah yes, the unforgettable day of the Ford motorcade visit," Dick said. He looked at me. "They spent three weeks hanging red, white, and blue bunting from every building and streetlight. They closed all the streets and moved the bleachers out from the high school gym to Ash Avenue so everyone could get a look. Then the bastard never stopped the car."

I laughed and Deb looked at the ceiling, her shoulders shaking with mirth.

"Some folks still say they saw him wave out the window," Deb said.

"Errant Republicanism, never confirmed," Dick said. "And yet it remains our claim to fame. Lowland: Where Gerald Ford allegedly gesticulated through a crack in the window in 1976."

"Until the Duke, you mean," Deb said. "Folks just can't stop talking about him. Half are pretty sure he's nuts, and the other half think he's on to something."

"What do you think?" Dick asked.

"I think he's a regular Donkey Hooty," she said. "Crazy as a loon."

"Can I quote you on that?" Dick asked, getting out his own notepad.

"You bet."

"And you said he was a regular . . . ?" he paused, black Bic poised over his yellow reporter's steno.

"Donkey Hooty. That's D-O-N-K-E-Y-H-O-O—"

"Got it," Dick said, and against all reason he managed to keep the smile off of his face.

"Anyway, what were you saying?" she said. "About the balloon?"

"Right, well." Dick leaned closer to us conspiratorially. "The cops finally tracked down the balloon owner. I guess on the night in question they followed beneath the thing for miles until they lost it in the darkness when it floated out over the state forest. Well, according to said balloon owner, it wasn't even the Duke riding in the balloon."

Deb gasped, and my eyebrows lifted along with my heartbeat. There but for the grace of God went my father's alibi.

"Then who?" Deb whispered.

"It was the balloon owner himself!" Dick slapped the table with his pad.

"Get out!" Deb said.

"Cross my heart," Dick said, waving his own pad over his trench-coated chest. "Interviewed him myself."

"How do you know he's not the Duke, then?" she asked.

"Well, for starters, he had some pretty consistent paperwork for the order, instructions, requested route and time, etcetera. He showed me all of it."

"Couldn't they be faked?" I said involuntarily and a little too defensively, but I thought Dick was enjoying his story too much to notice.

"I've spent a long time in newspapers," he said. "I've gotten pretty good at spotting a phony when I see one. I don't think this guy has the imagination for all this—" and he twirled his notepad towards the window, indicating with a simple gesture all the midnight horse rides, declarations of re-dependence, sky writers, spontaneous Guy Fawkes Day celebrations, and other general Duke-ness that had consumed Lowland for nearly a year.

"Plus, he only has one leg," Dick said.

Deb arched her back and hee-hawed with laughter, and Dick and I shared a smile.

"I think we would have heard if our Duke was a tripod," Deb said, and hawed again.

"So, did the cops arrest this one-legged balloon man?" I asked.

"Nope," Dick said. "Turns out most of what he did was strictly legal, or at least too gray to bring charges against. The best they could drum up was disturbing the peace, to the tune of a $200 fine. And you'll never guess how he paid it."

"How?" Deb asked, literally quivering in anticipation.

"Delivered to our balloonist's mailbox the day after the flight was an unmarked envelope containing exactly $200 in loose bills and a note that read, 'For services rendered to her Majesty, the Queen.'"

"Hoooo!" Deb said. "Yinz gotta admit it. Our Donkey's got *balls*."

•. •●.·

"So, tell me about your mother," Dick said.

I had finished my French fry covered "salad" and Dick had made a cheeseburger disappear with alarming speed, and now we were sitting over continually topped-off cups of coffee while Dick got down to business.

"What would you like to know?" I asked. "It seems like everyone around here knew her better than I did."

"Tell me what everyone around here doesn't know."

I sighed and thought of all the million small things that added up to a mother. "I don't know where to start."

"Why don't you tell me a story?"

I stared out the window at the opposing row of grimy houses and thought of a lifetime of hockey trips, countless ice rinks, hotels, gas stations, and diners just like this one, and their one constant.

"My mother," I said, pausing to look into my mug and clear my throat. "My mother only asked for one thing in return for the thousands of miles and dollars she spent on hockey. I remember a game in Detroit. It was this big showcase tournament, and we were the first team ever from Pennsylvania to play. It was my fifteenth birthday, and I stayed up too late, juiced on fudge brownie sundaes and Dr. Pepper, watching R-rated movies on HBO in the hotel room after Mom went to sleep. And the next day, I played like dog shit."

I paused, forgetting I was on the record, but Dick waved for me to continue without looking up from his notepad. "We can fix it later. What does playing like dog shit look like for you?"

"I shy away from hits. I'm a step slow. My feet and hands aren't in sync. It's still like that when I have a bad night. Anyway, in the third, I missed a check that led to a breakaway goal and we got sent home early."

"How did that make you feel?" Dick asked.

I looked at him over the rim of my coffee cup and waited until he stopped writing to look up at me. Then I shook my head slowly at him.

"Sorry," he said. "Force of habit."

I stared for another second then sighed. "You have to understand, Mom was like an air conditioner."

When Dick raised an eyebrow, I tried to explain.

"When she was smiling, or even thinking of smiling, everyone seemed to breathe easier just for being around her. But when she got mad, her whole face, personality, aura, whatever, it all changed. Everything got sharp and cold, and you felt like you were just holding your breath."

"And that's how she was after you lost the game?" Dick asked.

"Yep. Mom points the old Jeep Cherokee south and doesn't say a single word for fifty miles." I shook my head at the memory. "Just stared straight ahead. No radio. I could actually hear her jaw moving, clenching and unclenching, like she was grinding up flour with her molars. I remember watching all these exit signs rolling past, wondering what it would be like to jump out and run off to live in a new town. To have a different kind of life, you know? One where I could wake up to a morning where my biggest concern was unfinished algebra instead of remembering the weak side lock or staring down the barrel of another 7 a.m. practice. Anyway, after a while I couldn't take the silence anymore, so I told her, 'I tried.' And she says, 'Did you, Elbridge?' which she only called me when she was really pissed."

"What did she usually call you?" Dick said.

"Elby. Like everyone else."

"What else did she say?"

"She said, 'Can you honestly look at me and tell me that you did your very best?' And she stares straight at me for what must have been a mile. Doesn't look up at the road once. Just making eye contact with me in the middle of the highway like a lunatic. Anyone ever done that to you?" Dick peeked up from his notes and shook his head, his second chin shaking rhythmically. "It's incredibly unnerving. So, of course, I just caved."

I didn't mention how, sitting there in the safety of Jumbo's, I could still feel the seat coils digging into my spine, the lightheadedness brought on by the gas-tinged heat blasting from the vents, the exhaustion from playing three games in two days, the no-sleep-burnt-out-generally-just-being-fifteen-ishness of it all. And suddenly I couldn't tell if my legs were still long enough to reach the floor under the diner table or if they were swinging in teenage petulance.

"So, you're saying she was what?" Dick said, bringing me back to the moment at hand. "Tough? Obsessed? A rage-filled housewife living out her own failed sporting dreams through her only child?"

I laughed, and Dick smiled at me as he eased up from his notes. I had to hand it to him, he knew how to run an interview, when to push and when to back off.

"Tough for sure," I said. "But obsessed? No. And that last option is for her and a heavenly therapist to sort out. But that's not the point I was trying to make."

Dick made the go-on motion with his Bic.

"So, I'm sort of huddled in my little seat of shame, replaying the game in my head, probably crying—that's off the record, by the way," I said, and watched as Dick pretended to scratch out his last line. "Then she looks over at me again and, I'm sure this isn't exactly right, but she says something like, 'All I ask is that you do your best. I don't care if you win, because sometimes you just can't win no matter how hard you try. But it's not worth showing up if you don't give it your all.' Then we stopped at a gas station, and she bought me a candy bar."

I still felt a little dizzy, like I was back in the Cherokee somewhere outside of Cleveland, like Mom was still alive and so was my future. "I don't know why I remember all that. Or why I'm telling you now."

"When did you leave home?"

"A year later. I went to live with my first host family in Des Moines. You know, I don't even remember saying goodbye to her before I left for good. Or what I thought was for good. But I remember that car like yesterday."

"It's funny how memory works," Dick said. "The ATM chews up three of my credit cards a year because I can't remember my pin number, but I will be able to recount this conversation almost word-for-word a month from now."

"Then what's with the notes?"

"It's for effect," he said, and winked at me. Then he flipped back a few pages and pretend-squinted at his handwriting. "I pulled your stat sheets. You were—*are*—really something."

He peeked up again, a little sheepishly, and I waved it away. It was hard to blame other people for slipping up when I thought the same thing five times an hour.

"I was playing my best hockey," I said. "I finally felt ready to make the jump."

"But you weren't drafted when you turned 18," he continued. "Do you know why?"

"I can't speak for the scouts. But I think a lot of it had to do with how far away I was born from Toronto."

"Ah, another Lowland blessing," he said.

"Appalachia in general," I said, but silently agreed. "I was actually approached by a few scouts last season, kicking the tires on free agency. But then, you know, *everything* happened, and now I'm sitting in a diner talking to you."

"Speaking of *everything*," he said. "Do you remember much about the accident?"

"Nope." When Dick looked skeptical, I added, "Honestly. I remember coming home from the funeral with Dad at the steering wheel, and then a honking semi, and waking up in the ER getting prepped for surgery number one."

"So, tell me about how things stand with your father," he said.

"No," I said, and stared back at him.

He nodded and moved on seamlessly. "So how does your contract stand with Red Lake?"

"It doesn't. But they did offer me a tryout for next season."

"So, you're rehabbing. Anything else?"

I thought about lying and saying something earnest and false about "remaining focused on my goal of returning to professional sport" but went with the truth instead. "I'm working for Dillon Brothers, trying to learn carpentry, dry wall, plumbing."

"Really?" Dick asked, making a note.

"Gotta stay busy," I said, then thought that either Rob or Ron might actually read the story and hastily added, "I'm really enjoying it. They're great guys to work for." And I found I was being honest here too.

"That they are," Dick said.

"Any more barn burners?"

"Just one. The Duke suspiciously started his activities just after your return to our charming hamlet." My stomach dropped and for just a moment I thought that maybe Dick had sleuthed out my suspicions about my father. Maybe he saw something on my face when I found out about the balloon. My palms started to sweat on the table.

"So, our readers want to know," he said, leaning across the table. "Are you the Duke?"

"Ha!" My laugh was the sound of pure relief exiting a body.

"A laugh of guilt?" Dick asked, grinning.

"You know the night Susie and I saw him riding around?" I asked. "I was getting my ass kicked, literally, in the parking lot of the Crow Bar two hours before."

"Oof. Rough way to secure an alibi."

"You're telling me," I said, rubbing ribs that still occasionally ached from the ghostly memory of three pairs of size 12 work boots.

I felt a hand on my shoulder and looked up to see Deb the waitress leaning on me and giving me the same knead she'd given Dick when he arrived. Her nails were sharp but oddly comforting.

"What's this one's story?" she asked, still holding onto my arm but addressing Dick across the booth.

"How rude of me," he said. He had fished his wallet out of his pants but ceased combing through the incredibly dense layers of business cards and receipts to look up at Deb. "Allow me to introduce Elbridge Corvallis, previous and current Lowlander, previous and future professional hockey player, and only son of Clara Corvallis, whom surely to god you knew."

Knew. My stomach always dropped when people talked like that. I wondered if that would ever feel normal. Mom: past tense.

"Well, why didn't you say so?" She addressed me now and gave my shoulder a little shake. "I thought you were a college brat down here slumming." Then she leaned over to grab my chin with her free hand and turned my head gently to stare into my face.

I blushed and she smiled.

"I see the resemblance now. We used to have a knitting circle. Met in the library. Lord could your ma crochet." She held my chin for another long pause then let it go, sighing. "Terrible thing."

"Terrible," Dick said.

"Well, yinz come back soon." She gave my shoulder another squeeze. "Especially you, young gun. Your mother was a favorite around here."

As we stood and shrugged on our coats and chatted our goodbyes, I imagined looking in on myself through the window, at the little scene we made, and realized I was less of an outsider now than when I walked in. I wondered how much could change in an hour. But I guess that's how it goes: slow then sudden. As we turned to leave, I still hadn't decided on which side of the glass I'd rather be standing.

CHAPTER 11

Elbridge Gerry was not a handsome man. According to the lithograph in *Elbridge Gerry: A Definitive History*, the Founding Father had these little poofs of hair that soared from either side of a bald scalp so that his head perfectly resembled half a watermelon. Pair that with a strong nose, a weak chin, and quill jockey shoulders, and you have a clear picture of my namesake. Though, according to Robert Corvallis, there were good things too. Apparently, he was the twentieth signee of the Declaration of Independence, the reason for the term Gerrymander, a shaper of the Constitution, and "A highly important if misunderstood character in America's fight for sovereignty." As I made my way slowly through the monstrous book, it was becoming apparent that my father had a pretty high regard for old Elby, first of my name.

One thing, however, was very clear from my reading: Elbridge Gerry did not care for England. Or kings in general. Or really for centralized government in any form, which was a radical concept to me. Certainly, some civics teacher had once tried to explain what a federalist was at one of my three high schools, but it failed to stick along with such other hits as algebra, economics, and the Beatitudes, that poor nun. Old Elby did like America though, and most particularly some place called Marblehead, which I think we can all agree is just a funny word. The level of detail my father had dredged about a man nearly 200 years in his grave boggled my mind, and yet I wondered if he knew what month my birthday was in.

I may or may not have told you before that I was a reader, but I'd let the muscles weaken after I returned to Lowland. Somehow, the thing that sustained me most in all those coach buses and bleak motel rooms, and which anchored me to my mother and her library and our long trips together, abandoned me when I finally came home. Added to the sluggishness of my reading muscles, the weak winter sun seemed magnified by the bay window, and the old rocking chair felt glorious. Basking in the afterglow of sun and a hard day, Elbridge Gerry's embarrassingly boring snafu with the XYZ Affair was not helping me regain my form, and the back-forth motion of the chair and soothing sun did the rest. The book slid from my lap to slap the floor at the exact moment the phone blared from the kitchen.

I reached for the book first, realized that was stupid only after I'd picked it up, then lumbered into the kitchen on knees stiff from my morning session at the Horner followed by six hours of baseboard work. My feet squeaked on the linoleum as I reached the phone on the last of its eight rings without a second thought to who was calling.

"Hello?"

"Hey." It was a soft voice, tinny and unrecognizable because of my shitty old phone, but definitely female and extra definitely not my father, which was always a plus.

"Hello," I said again, like an idiot.

"It's Abbey."

"*Hello*," I tried a third time, with gravitas. I unconsciously ran a hand through my hair.

"Jesus God." She feigned exasperation but I could hear the laugh in her voice. "Are you ready for this dog and pony show?"

"Which, um, pony show would that be?"

"Don't tell me you forgot," she said, actually exasperated this time.

"No, I didn't forget anything," I said defensively. "I didn't even know about this—dog—whatever."

"We're doing this stupid double date, which was your stupid idea."

I opened my mouth to protest that I had wanted something a little more intimate and much less double, and that it had actually been *her* stupid idea. Then I thought better of it and twiddled the cord with my finger.

"Susie *told* me she told you," Abbey said.

I looked over at the answering machine, where the Messages light flashed 7-7-7-7 and swallowed.

"News to me."

"Well, news travels fast in Lowland, Elby. Hose the filth from your scarred carcass. I'm picking you up in ten."

"No, I uh," I said, and looked down at Elbridge Gerry for inspiration, who grimaced at me from the cover like a man unafraid of facing down redcoats. "I've got some reading to finish."

Abbey didn't have the grace not to laugh, which was hearty and demeaning and attractive.

"Nine minutes now," she said after the laughter had subsided. "Unless you'd rather pick *me* up, but I hear your car is a real piece of shit."

"Don't you speak about Golden Thunder like that. It's a million-of-a-kind perfect piece of American automobile craftsmanship with the added thrill that every ride in it may very well be your last."

"Right, so, eight minutes?"

"Eight minutes," I said. Old Elby shook his head in disappointment from the cover of the *Definitive History* as I shuffled towards the shower in defeat.

*   •   *

Joanie's is what passed for fine dining in Lowland. There were tablecloths (paper), placemats (not paper), and they gave you a glass of water that a nervous teenager kept dangerously full for the entirety of your visit. I was no connoisseur, given my poverty, but being a professional athlete meant a decent amount of experience with steak houses simply by nature of the profession. Fundraisers, banquets, galas, and the occasional big city road game splurge meant that I knew my way around medium rare. Joanie's was a well-done joint, cash only, thanks for comin' in.

When Abbey and I entered, I noticed there were framed pictures of newspaper clippings above the hostess stand which ranged from off-white to piss yellow with age. As the girl and Abbey conversed, I leaned closer to see that the most recent frame held a blurry picture of a man on a horse riding down the sidewalk with Joanie's storefront framed perfectly in the background. Under the picture, which was just beginning to fade, was the caption: "The only known picture of the Duke, seen here riding past local landmark, Joanie's Tavern. Photo by Dick Newport."

The girl saw me looking and smiled. "He's been good for business," she said. "Joanie Jr.'s real pleased. If she could find out who this Duke is, I bet she'd give him free steak for a year."

I nodded solemnly, still staring at the picture. I was continually amazed by the Duke's pervasiveness and general acceptance by the Lowlanders. I leaned in further to get a closer look, but the Duke's face was turned away from the camera as he stood like a jockey in the stirrups. I thought he looked like a pretty athletic guy, though I was about as far from a horseman as one could get, my closest encounter being the time one almost caved my skull in. Horse in the garage: one tally for the "Dad is the Duke" column. General athleticism: one tally for the "Anyone but Robert" column. The ledger remained scrupulously, annoyingly balanced.

"I can show you to your table now," she said, and when I didn't immediately respond, Abbey tugged my arm and brought me back to myself. She left her hand in the crook of my elbow as we rounded the half wall and walked into the dim dining room. As we approached a row of booths cattycorner to the brass railed bar, I saw a few tables were occupied, but only one drew my attention. The couple sat laughing across the candlelit booth at each other. They were clearly having a good time, and in the charm-intended gloom, I thought they made a handsome couple. Then Abbey's fingernails dug into my arm, and I realized what I was missing. The handsome couple was Susie and presumably Abbey's boyfriend, whose name was as lost to me as the Beatitudes.

As they turned to look up at us, Abbey jerked her arm from mine and I felt the loss of contact much more acutely than any jealousy from Susie's obvious happiness, but I let that line of thinking slip away as Susie bounded out of the booth to hug both of us simultaneously.

"You're here!"

"We're here," Abbey said, smiling tightly over Susie's shoulder at the chagrined-looking man unfolding himself from the booth. He was lanky, but muscular in the way of people who work around gyms, and his hair was cut like he was deploying for Kuwait in the morning.

After releasing her grip, Susie introduced John, and we shook hands. He was one of those hard squeeze types and he looked me in the eyes for the overlong duration of the shake, which put us off to a bad start before either of us said a word. He was taller than me by an inch, and his polo shirt showed his biceps to good effect. His smile was broad though, and I wondered if this was one of those shark smiles or if I was just reading too much into the situation. It slowly dawned on me then that I recognized him. He was the physical therapist who let the kid fall to wave at Susie. Small world, eh?

"The famous hockey star," he said. "It's nice to finally get a good look at you. I thought you'd be taller." He laughed as he finally let go of my hand.

"Hoo boy," I said. "You know if this place has cheesy wings?"

∴ ∙ ● ∴

"So, then the guy says, 'Stop or my leg's gonna come off!' and so I said, 'Well, Mr. Roberts, if it comes off, I'll buy you a peg leg and call you Captain.'"

I was still waiting for the rest of the joke when Susie choke-snorted into her glass of wine and I realized the bit had ended. I looked across the table and raised my eyebrows at Abbey, who smiled ambiguously and rolled her eyes slightly. Meanwhile, Susie was laughing so hard that our booth was vibrating.

"Elby said the same thing to me when I first started treating him." Susie patted my sore shoulder firmly.

"There's no tolerance for pain with some people," John said, handing Susie his napkin to wipe the drops of white wine that had spattered her cheeks. I tried not to think about my constantly aching shoulder and was reminded instead of my first instinct about physical therapists and their tendency towards sadism, which I kept to myself, along with all my other thoughts. Dinner was not going well.

Over the course of drinks and an appetizer (not cheesy wings), I learned that John and Susie had worked together at Lowland Physical Therapy for about a year. He worked mostly afternoons and specialized in working with kids, which I thought was a danger to the future of our fair city. They had carpooled over to Joanie's from work, which explained my ride with Abbey, and I wondered if it was odd that I hadn't even questioned why she picked me up instead of Susie. Then I wondered if I was nearing the edge of the Big Trouble Pit, or if I had already stepped willingly into it. I watched Abbey watch John watch Susie, and I couldn't be sure who was actually running the dog and pony show. Safe to say it wasn't me.

When the waiter came to take our order, I was thinking hard about leaving. It had been too long since I'd had to sit and make conversation with normal people, or at least people who I didn't just take a shower with. What John lacked in humor he made up for in self-confidence, and I was having trouble eating much more of his bullshit. Over the salad course, he claimed to have struck out Jeff Bagwell, boxed collegiately but declined to turn pro because the money wasn't right, and rescued a child from an avalanche *on skis*.

"Do you ski, Elbridge?" John asked. The conversation had been going this way all night, like John was playing Ping-Pong against the flipped-up half of the table. "I've gone with the ladies here a time or two." He held up his arms to mime hugging the ladies in one great big John sandwich. I gagged a little on some lettuce.

"Nope," I said, clearing my throat. "I like my slippery surfaces level."

"And speaking of levels, I hear you're in the carpentry game these days?" he asked.

"Carpentry is a stretch," I scratched the back of my head in embarrassment. I didn't give one damn what John thought of my current profession, but I didn't want to pretend that I had any actual skills to speak of. "I'm working on it."

"Do you ever feel—" and he paused to gesture ambiguously with his glass of red wine while he searched for words. "I don't know, like you let yourself down?"

I was temporarily struck dumb by the bluntness of the question. I sat there with my mouth slightly ajar while he stared at me over his wine. The silence might have carried us right on through to dessert if Abbey didn't lose her mind.

"What the fuck is wrong with you?" she asked. He slowly turned to face her in the booth and tried for a disarming smile again.

"What?" he said, leaning back against the wall of the restaurant and creating a little space between Abbey and himself. "I was just curious. I'm sure he doesn't mind, do you, Elbridge?"

He looked over at me where I had just managed to get my mouth closed. I reopened it to say something noncommittal, but watching John get cornered was the first time I'd enjoyed myself all evening. What I wanted to say was, "You say you're a boxer? Better get off the ropes," but Susie leaped on the grenade.

"I'm sure he didn't mean anything by it," Susie said. She looked between the other couple nervously, anxious to get dinner back on track.

"No, Suz, I think he did mean something by it," Abbey said. "So, big guy, what are you trying to say, huh? You like living in your nice little house, don't you? Well, how do you think it got built? Magic!?"

"I didn't mean that," John said, setting his wine down so he could protest with both hands.

"So, what did you mean?" she asked.

"I just—"

I was really enjoying the dinner now. My salad had a renewed crispness, and my water glass actually *was* runneth-ing over. It was like watching a man fall into a bear enclosure at the zoo from the safety of the observation platform. And, from the safety of said platform, hollering, "You got yourself in there pal, now get yourself out."

Then Susie kicked me underneath the table and made a sly, imploring gesture with her eyes to throw the poor bastard a rope. I wavered, thinking a *little* mutilation would be alright, then she kicked me again, harder, right in the shin.

"He meant," I said. "What's it like to fall from grace?"

Abbey turned to look at me, still angry, and quirked one eyebrow. John's face remained carefully blank.

"And I'll tell you, John, it sucks. They're right, you know? The bottom really is covered in rocks, and it hurts when you hit it."

I moved my stiff shoulder in a circle and raised my left hand, palm out. I lifted it slowly, like a shy child answering a teacher's question, and the burning started as my hand reached level with my forehead. I gritted my teeth and kept inching it upward as the tremors became more noticeable. The table watched silently as I finally brought the arm straight up in the air so that my bicep rested against my ear. A sigh hissed between my gritted teeth as I held it there for a moment, then slowly let my hand drop back down to the table.

"All you can do is try to rise."

.   . • .

We were standing around in front of Joanie's while John had a cigarette and Abbey and Susie chatted. The moon was not quite full, but the winter air was warming a bit, and the usually brutal wind was mild, offering just a taste of March. John had quit trying to talk to me after the little dust up, so we loitered under the moon and an orange streetlight in silence. He was looking a little grim, and he kept glancing at his girlfriend and then at my girlfriend and I thought about hitting him just because. And this time I'd remember to use my right hand. I was even thinking about something cool to say as I stood over his unconscious body, something like, "Look who's taller now?" but that felt real lame, and frankly so did hitting the poor dummy who clearly wanted both the soup and the salad.

My thoughts were derailed though by a shout that echoed down Ash Avenue from the direction of the park and courthouse. The noise was passed eave to eave by the old leaning row houses and storefronts down to Joanie's and its quiet stoop.

We turned expectantly as a group, now accustomed to strange happenings at night thanks to our local nutjob, and watched a figure emerge from the shadow of the park and then dip into shadow. It emerged again into the glow of the next streetlamp and then disappeared again. Whoever it was, they were still blocks away, and yet they were yelling one long continuous shout. As the figure neared, still emerging from shadow into light and then back into the sidewalk's darkness, it was clear that it was not a man on horseback, or even a man at all. I was immediately relieved, until the little piping voice got close enough and the shout became clear.

"HEEEAAAARRRRR YEEEEEEE!"

"Oh no," I said.

Then, as he finally made it onto Joanie's block, it became clear it was a boy. A boy on a bicycle. A boy on a bicycle wearing a tri-corner hat.

"Oh, Jesus no," I groaned, and let my head drop into my waiting hands.

"OH, YES!" the town crier said, literally skidding to a halt. Then he saluted. "I have a special missile here for one Elbridge Corvallis."

"Missile?" I asked.

"Yeah, a missile, you know, like an old timey letter?"

"Oh, right."

"Stupid," he muttered, then handed me an honest-to-God scroll sealed with a blob of wax. The paper felt heavy and was tied with a red ribbon.

Everyone stared at me, mouths hanging open, and I realized what a spectacle this whole thing was. I looked from face to shocked face, then looked back at the boy, who stood with his hand outstretched. He cleared his throat loudly in the universal "Tip, please" way.

"You little—" I made a swipe for the hat, but he leaped back on the bike and sped away.

"CHHHEEEEAPPPP ASSSSSSSS!" he called long and fading as he disappeared back towards the park.

I looked at my still astonished party and shrugged. "Well, the pony never made it, but I'd still call this a dog show."

CHAPTER 12

"You have one unheard message."

I moaned as I sunk onto my borrowed brown folding chair. After Christmas, I'd held on to the card table and chairs, shoehorning them into the kitchen across from the fridge (also brown, man did the '70s have a thing for monochrome or what?), and on which now rested the answering machine and the still unopened scroll from the Duke of Ash Avenue.

"First new message."

I was dog tired from weeks of deconstruction and daily workouts and not in the mood for any of the possibilities coming my way via the machine's tinny speaker, including but not limited to: Miss Mary demanding I cut her grass, my father demanding I gopher back to the college, or Rob "asking" me to work some more overtime. My money was on Rob, but then again, what money?

"Hey, L.B., it's Susie."

I groaned again. Another bet lost. And there was L.B. The nickname wasn't short for Lawrence Bernard, so pronouncing the letters like that just didn't make sense. I considered reaching for the delete button, but it was awfully far away. And, as I hadn't had the energy or inclination to call her in the five days since our double date, I felt I could at least listen to the message. I owed her that much, and frankly much more.

"I'm not even super sure you listen to these messages, so this feels a little dumb."

She got me right off the bat. Guilt prickled along my scalp like static, and I felt an honest swoop of regret for not calling after our date. Or before our date. Or really ever for that matter. Our relationship had mostly consisted of some scattered meals and a few private therapy sessions after the new year terminated my health insurance.

"It's been fun getting to know you over the last couple of months. I feel like we have some pretty good chemistry."

I was on the fence there. As I've said, I liked the artist's rendition of Susie more than the flesh and blood version. She brought the same energy to everything, from trying to yank my arm out of its socket to making out in the backseat, but when I was with her, I always felt like I was walking along the edge of a pool and any minute she might just push me in for fun. You can't have a deep conversation with anyone when you're always watching their hands.

"But I'm not sure we're both heading in the same direction. I need someone who's a little more serious about me, about work, about, you know, moving on. It almost seems like you like it here or something."

I think we can all agree that was hurtful. Did she just call me a *maintainer*? My stomach sank a little lower. I'd never had a real girlfriend before, and I wondered if this was what breakups always felt like.

"Anyway, I hope you hear this. You're a good guy, L.B. I hope you find what you're looking for, whatever that even is."

I slumped over until my forehead met the surface of the card table with a soft thump. I realized I was alone again, but it didn't feel any different than it had ten minutes before. I wondered if that meant I had never stopped feeling alone even when I was with Susie, or if whatever I was feeling had nothing to do with loneliness, and Susie was a nonfactor in the equation. It felt a little like math, or psychology, and I was too tired for both.

"Oh, and one more thing," Susie said. "If you try to hook up with Abbey Winthers, I'll blow your whole fucking world up. Buh-bye!"

I got the creepy-crawleys from my hairline to my toes. I'm not going to lie, when the phone rang suddenly from its hook on the wall, I may have peed myself a little.

I weighed my options before deciding that cowardice was not a real option. So, forehead still pressed to the table, I fished blindly along the wall for the phone cord. When my fingers finally made contact with its smooth curly length, I followed the trail up to the cradle and pulled it gingerly down to my ear. The table, with my nose pressed to it, smelled faintly of old Hoyles and spilled Yuengling.

Head still down, praying for release, I answered the phone.

"Yes?"

"Hey, Elby, it's Rob."

"No."

"Now hang on, I just want to know what you were up to tomorrow?"

"No. Don't get me wrong, Rob. I'm grateful for the work. I'm just not having the world's best week."

"Why so glum?"

"I just got dumped."

"Perfect," he said. "I know just the thing to keep you busy. Let's go fishing."

"I can't work, I—wait, what?"

"Ever been fly fishing?"

"No," I said.

"Even better. I'll be there at 5."

"A.m.?"

"Yes."

"No."

"Yes," he said. "You'll like it. Trust me."

"No."

"Okay then," he said. "I'll just let you get started on the Nash basement."

"Also no."

"So lemme get this straight. You got no girlfriend and you're not working and unless you picked up some other friends when I wasn't looking, you're free as a bird. So, I'll see you at 5." Then he hung up.

I listened to the dial tone for a while with my eyes closed and head still pressed to the table. As I reached to hang the phone back up and the old, slow pain rippled down from my shoulder, I remembered that he had said *other* friends. And then I smiled.

•. • • .·

"You ever read that poem?" Rob asked, his voice rolling quietly over the water. "The one about peace?"

"Probably not," I called back. "Why?"

"I think that old hippie made us read it in eighth grade."

"Seems like we read a lot of poems about peace that year."

"Oh, you know she was smoking out in her car during lunch. Remember how she used to park by the baseball field? Me and Mark snuck out into the dugout one time and tried to take a picture of her to blackmail some A's."

"Did it work?" I asked.

"Na," Rob said. "Turns out a joint looks exactly like a cigarette when you take the picture from 30 yards away through a chain link fence."

I focused on making the slow, fluid casts Rob had demonstrated on the bank before handing me waders and slipping into the Little Forks River. The water swirled around our thighs, still chilly in spring despite the layers of neoprene and denim. We were using tiny brown flies made of delicate, spun thread with small splashes of color woven in to lure the fat trout off the murky bottom.

"I can't remember all of it," Rob said. "But I know it was about peace and how it falls down real slow."

"Hmm." I tried to think of Ms. Kepler's class and her march through the Romantics, but eighth grade was increasingly a foggy memory. I blame the concussions, but long poetry recitals and a lack of central air-conditioning probably had more to do with it than blows to the head.

"Something about Scotland maybe?" Rob asked as he effortlessly plunked his fly between the roots of a tree that leaned out over the water.

I was fishing the slightly less technical eastern bank, which was mostly grass and largely devoid of the line snarling tree branches that Rob so enjoyed maneuvering around. I quickly learned untangling your line was both a very specific type of misery and also the first of the many Great Mysteries of fly fishing. When you got into a rhythm, it was a lot like skating, which made a kind of sense. Learning to skate sucked, like presumably learning to walk sucks except we don't remember it. So, this was just another thing that sucked until you got good enough to think about something else instead of the mechanics. I picked it up fairly quickly, which Rob chalked up to general athleticism, and I was finally starting to lose myself in the casting, 10-2-10-2-10-2, watching the line unfurl in graceful swoops and letting the fly near the surface before calling it back and feeding out more line until the great lasso of wet plastic felt almost too long to control, then finally letting it land, without a splash, without a sound. Watch the little brown fly bob, recall the line with the left hand, wait for something to happen, repeat. It was repetitively gratifying, and as my shoulder loosened up nicely, I began to forget about the technicalities of casting and the hazardous dangling branches and Susie and even the Bull Elk. Then Rob hooted.

I turned to watch as he lifted his rod like a maestro, tapped the baton to set the hook, then went to work conducting the fish into his hands. He quickly stripped the line with his left hand so that the reel wined as the green string zipped out into the water, and simultaneously maneuvered the fish with the rod in his right hand. He steered his prey around tree branches and rocks, letting it tire itself out while he slowly took back the slack he had just doled out. He sidestepped left, then right, navigating the treacherous footing on the slimy river rocks without looking down. I could see the point where the line met the water inching closer to Rob, whose rod was bent in a perfect arc from his hand to the surface of the water. Suddenly, he lunged, nearly putting his face into the river, and emerged with a brown trout dangling from his hand.

I'm still trying to decide who was more surprised, me or the trout, whose black eyes bulged and gills flapped and tail swam in the currentless air. Maybe it was my imagination, but when Rob turned to show me the fish, all I could see was the trout's mouth open and close, open and close, as it seemed to silently say, "Well, fuck me."

Rob just chuckled, freed the hook from the gaping mouth, and dropped the trout back into the brown water. Then he reached inside his waders and brought out a towel to dry his hands before pulling out a cigarette, which he lit with great satisfaction, blowing out a long puff of sweet smoke to join the afternoon clouds.

"I think about it a lot," Rob said.

I raised an eyebrow.

"Peace," Rob said.

"What about it?"

"How it seems to fall down real slow."

"How do you mean?"

"Take here in the river," Rob said. "For the first hour, what were you thinking about?"

"Honestly? I mostly worried about why my casting doesn't look like yours and not getting snagged in trees and how come I'm not catching a damn thing. Plus getting dumped, hockey, the goddamn Nash basement. Should I keep going?"

"Exactly. You were all tied up."

"But you weren't?" I asked.

"Sure I was." Rob took a long drag on his cigarette so that the paper crackled. "I was thinking about water conditions and line weight and matching the hatch and putting you on a good fish so that you'd remember this trip and think it was worthwhile when you trot on back to Minnesota and your real life."

We watched our lines swirl in the Little Forks current, and I was touched that Rob cared so much about my opinion. I was trying to think of something to say when he spoke up again, saving me the trouble.

"You know what I was thinking about when that fish hit?"

"What?" I asked.

"Nothing at all."

"Nobody thinks about *nothing*."

"I do," Rob said. "That's my peace. And that old hippie was right. It does come down slow."

"I'll tell you what else Mrs. Kepler was right about. She said that I'd never make it as a pro, that I should focus on my studies. If I wanted out of Lowland so bad, she said an education was the best way to do it."

"Well, she got us there." Rob turned to grin at me. I smiled back, and we stood in silence for a while and listened to the river.

"Do you really think you're done?" Rob asked finally. "Because I've gotta say, and I hate to say it because you're my best worker, your shoulder seems a lot stronger. You don't even make the face anymore when you lift something."

"What face?" I asked, and watched Rob as he made a horrible grimace, mock-hoisting his suddenly heavy rod. I laughed. "God, that's awful."

"It truly is," Rob said. "I've come to rely on that face as your 'I'm stuck here' meter. As the old bag said about all our missing homework, 'Its absence is startling.'" He even did a pretty good old lady impression, and I laughed so hard I slipped on a rock and pinwheeled my arms, trying to keep my balance while I staggered around and scared away every fish within 50 yards. Rob reached out a hand to help me recover my balance, and I wiped my running eyes while we stood silent for another minute.

"I have to go back to the league," I finally said. I thought of my mother, of the hot Jeep heat and her white knuckles on the steering wheel and the taste of Snickers bar mixed with my own tears. "I need to know that I gave it everything."

Rob nodded but kept his peace as the Little Forks made its way past our legs and our floating iridescent lines and on towards West Virginia.

•. •.•.

Stripping off waders may be the best feeling in the world, I decided, especially when Rob's truck was so, well, not wet.

As Rob steered the Ranger back toward Lowland, I could feel the town pulling at me. I thought of it like a black hole, and I was caught in its gravitational field. In my spaceship, I was circling around it, but the pull was not overbearing, and my life support systems were fine. I had food for months, maybe even years if I played my cards right. I could sit on the bridge and relax and do carpentry. Occasionally, I could almost forget that this wasn't just an ordinary quick trip back home. Until I looked out the window and there it was. Awesome and mountainous and inescapable as death, the black hole ate up everything around it. And at its beautiful, terrible center, my mother's frost-covered grave and the oncoming semi headlights glowing brightly, implacably, indifferent to the cosmos it slowly consumed.

"You're gonna dig this place, man," Rob said, jarring me from my captain's chair of despair.

"What place?" I asked. "I thought we were going home."

Rob just smiled and turned off the two-lane highway onto a gravel road. The sky darkened as the truck climbed upwards, although the canopy of branches blotted the view. I inhaled the piney smell into my lungs. I had been doing that all day, inhaling deeply. I did it so often that

Rob asked if I'd gotten a touch of asthma. Occasionally the stars peeked through, but the trees were dense enough that the only notion I had of our location was that we were, technically and exactly, nowhere.

"We're here." Rob turned a corner to coast into a parking lot adjacent to what appeared to be a small, one-story cabin. We parked the truck near a couple other pickups, each and every one caked in dust and mud. Posted over the red doorframe was the only signage I had seen since we left the highway: a hand-painted piece of wood that read, "House Bar."

"Rob, what am I in for here?" I asked.

Rob smiled again and opened the door wide. In front of him, a set of wide stairs led down to a room with a bar on one side, and a fireplace and a long wooden dining table on the other where a few men sat and ate and talked quietly. But on the far wall, opposite the stairs and the porch railing that I clutched to stay upright, was the biggest set of windows I had ever seen, and through them, framed against the pitch-black sky, were all the stars of creation. Everywhere I looked in the great broad glass, some distant sun sat burning.

I felt Rob slide up beside me and speak quietly in my ear, giving me a guided tour of this new solar system.

"The place was built on the peak by a retired astronomer. Built it all himself. Took 10 years, and he had the glass specially shipped from Italy. Word is he flew out there and brought it back himself using some system he designed to keep the monsters from breaking. It's 4 sheets of glass, each 15 by 15, and how he rigged them to fit so tight together I still don't know. Anyway, he died, as you do, and the place went up for sale, but who in their right mind wants to live this far from civilization and clean that much window? So, my friend Alice bought the place at a foreclosure sale and opened up the House Bar. She's the bartender right . . . over . . . there," Rob said, and grabbing me by the ears, angled my head away from the magnificent windows toward the simple wooden bar, where a woman stood drying a pint glass. "Why don't we go say hello?"

I nodded, still feeling a little dumb, and followed my friend down the wide stairs.

"Hello," Rob called to the bartender as he bounded down.

"Well, if it isn't the Fish Man," she said, continuing to wipe down glasses. "And who do we have here?"

"Alice, may I present to you the distinguished professional hockey player turned temporary carpenter, newly competent angler, and generally swell guy, Mr. Elbridge Corvallis." He turned to me. "Elby, this is Alice Mackintosh, owner of this fine establishment."

I approached the bar and extended my hand awkwardly. Alice set her glass down and shook warmly, leaning close and whispering loud enough for Rob to overhear. "Hey stranger. The windows have that effect on most people. Don't be nervous. Be comfortable." She gave me a wink and let my hand go.

I pulled up a stool and Rob sat beside me. At the long dining table behind us, someone got up to feed another log to the fire and the small group laughed loudly and clinked mugs. I continued to stare around wide-eyed, my gaze traveling around the room before returning to the windows, which seemed to magnify the view.

"Lemme guess. Beers and keep 'em coming?" Alice asked. Without waiting for a response, she topped off two pints and placed them on the bar. "I'm sure it'll be burgers too. I'll be in the kitchen. Holler if you need me, and don't let those bastards steal anything." She eyed the far table in mock sternness.

I tore my eyes away from the windows long enough to see her exit through the swinging kitchen doors. My mother would have described her as "backwoods thin," which so far as I could tell, meant she was lean, but a strong wind or a horse nudge wouldn't knock her down. Her brown hair fell to the middle of her back, and she walked like she was comfortable with herself and didn't give a shit if you agreed.

"I'm going to marry her as soon as I can get her to stop calling me the Fish Man," Rob said as the kitchen doors swished shut. "She's a poet too, got her master's and everything from some fancy school out east. Came up here slumming and never left. Watch this." He gulped at his beer, wiped his mouth, and called out towards the kitchen doors. "Hey Al! What's the name of that Scottish poem about peace coming down real slow?"

"It's Irish!" she called from the recesses of the kitchen, where we could hear pans clanking on the stove. "And 'The Lake Isle of Innisfree' is too pretty for your muddy mouth, so keep it off of Mr. Yeats!"

"See?" Rob said. "Amazing."

I nodded and drank my beer, still reeling, and listened as Alice's strong clear voice wafted out from the kitchen above the clatter of pans.

"I will arise and go now, and go to Innisfree,
And a small cabin build there, of clay and wattles made;
Nine bean-rows will I have there, a hive for the honey-bee,
And live alone in the bee-loud glade."

I rose from my stool and, mug in hand, wandered down the long bar. To my left, the group of thick, flannelled men laughed again at a story as the big fireplace roared and warmed the room.

"And I shall have some peace there, for peace comes dropping slow,
Dropping from the veils of the morning to where the cricket sings;
There midnight's all a glimmer, and noon a purple glow,
And evening full of the linnet's wings."

Alice's voice was lovely and seemed to follow me as I approached the gigantic, looming windows. The stars rattled in the dark, as if being so clear made them somehow less real.

"I will arise and go now, for always night and day
I hear lake water lapping with low sounds by the shore;
While I stand on the roadway, or on the pavements gray,
I hear it in the deep heart's core."

I walked over to stand in front of the center window, my breath fogging the magnificent glass. I sipped my beer and wondered why it was so hard to focus on circling the Lowland black hole with this much of the universe staring right back at me.

CHAPTER 13

I should never have opened the goddamned scroll. If I'd just kept it sealed, I wouldn't be sitting in my kitchen, sweating slightly, dwelling on the contents of the beautiful calligraphy: Black tie, string quartet, hors d'oeuvres, gala. I was invited to a party on Saturday. And not just any party, but a fancy party. Hosted by the Duke. With dancing and tuxedos. In Lowland, PA. Can't you just feel my excitement?

The scroll might have remained unopened forever if I hadn't come back from my morning workout to find Miss Mary standing in my kitchen holding the rolled parchment up to the kitchen window. She'd been trying the old "letter to the light" trick, but the thickness of the paper was denying her access. At the sound of the door opening, she turned and dropped the thing, which hit the kitchen linoleum with a clear and ominous crack.

We both stared at the scroll as it wobbled gently towards the fridge and began to unfurl like a dropped roll of toilet paper. She looked up at me, and I knew better than to expect to see guilt or shame on her face despite being caught red-handed in my apartment fondling my possessions, but I didn't expect to see such naked greed.

The scroll settled against the fridge, and I finally broke the stalemate. "Could I have my scroll back, please?"

Miss Mary bent down to retrieve it and her bathrobe opened to reveal, well, everything. Mary straightened with the scroll and used my embarrassment to tilt the momentum back in her direction. She leered and handed me the parchment, saying, "Well?"

I wasn't sure if she was talking about her undergarment-free physique or the contents of the scroll, so I went with the safer option and settled into a folding chair to read. The landlord took up a screwdriver I had failed to notice and reached behind the fridge with it. I could hear her clanking around and so I guessed this was what we were supposed to be pretending was the reason she let herself into my locked apartment.

As I read, my heart sank at the idea of attending any party, let alone this one, but it was buoyed back up by the fact that I could just say no. The Duke may have crawled into the rest of the Lowlanders' heads with his balloons and horses and un-secession, but I wasn't going to play his game. And yet, there was still the lingering doubt, the ever-present whiff of *What if?* concerning my father's involvement. I wondered if it would be better for me to finally answer this question once and for all, or if that was in fact the very best reason to stay the hell away.

Miss Mary finished clanking around behind the perfectly function-ing fridge and emerged, snorting a blonde-gray strand of hair from her face. "It's from that Duke, isn't it?"

I nodded, but held my tongue, still rolling over the idea of attending a lunatic's black-tie gala.

She licked her lips, and for a change she stared at the parchment instead of my thighs. She looked a little wild, and it had nothing to do with the bathrobe she'd forgotten to close or the screwdriver she clutched like a knife.

"Where did he bury it?" she asked.

"Come again?"

"The treasure," she said in a husky whisper. "Where did he bury the treasure?"

"What treasure?"

"They say he's got money, gold bars, coins, doubloons even. How else could he afford all these shenanigans? And those silver dollars he gave to everyone for Boxers Day?"

"Boxing Day," I corrected.

"Right. They say that was just a sliver of his treasure, and that he has all of it buried, and that," she said, pointing with one long yellowed fingernail, "looks like a treasure map."

She looked so eager and serious that I couldn't help it. I started laugh-ing and couldn't stop. Through my tears I could see I was hurting her feelings and so I handed the scroll over and laughed harder as I watched her face crash from frantic to frustrated.

"A party? Well, shit."

My laughter began to ebb as she handed the scroll back and made her way to the door.

"Why don't you go in my place?" I offered. "Maybe you could waltz the Duke into telling you where he's stashed his treasure."

She raised her chin as she finally cinched her bathrobe. "Dancing is just foreplay without the sex."

I shuddered as the door slammed behind her, my glee shriveling as I was forced, once more, to picture Miss Mary mid-coitus. I wanted to talk with someone about this so-called gala, but the idea of asking my father about any personal decision was laughable, let alone in this extremely ludicrous and sticky situation. Rob would listen, of course, but I didn't want him to get the impression I was associated with this Duke character in any real way. I considered Lou and Bruce and Dick and cast them all aside like duplicate baseball cards. It was finally time, I thought, to return to the library.

. . . .

The Carnegie Library on Ash Avenue was the most beautiful building in town, and it wasn't a close contest. Of the complicated legacy old Andrew left in Western PA, you couldn't really argue with the library system, and especially with the Lowland branch. Unlike all the other buildings in town, which were either old red brick or Low U limestone, the library was made entirely of mortared, multicolored river stones. I've always thought of it as a castle, and the boxy, high-windowed design and oak trimming added to the medieval allure. Come to think of it, I was a little surprised the Duke hadn't tried to militarize it yet.

When I approached the solid front door and grasped the iron handle, a wave of nostalgia rolled over me as I remembered the thousand times I'd had to reach up for the same handle I now looked down on. Most days after school I stopped in to visit my mother, do homework, or more often, see if any new stock had come in. While I admit to being an indifferent if not downright shitty student, I loved to read, and I had a habit of putting off schoolwork, which was often assigned reading, in favor of plowing through something more interesting. It made my mother smile. It drove my father nuts.

The air inside was papery, but not stuffy like some libraries, and as usual, it was empty. I peeked at the centrally located reference desk but found it empty too, as I knew it would be. This was an old game and I had to let it run its course. So, I turned right into the fiction section and perused the shelves, fondling the spines on a few favorites and taking down some others that were new to me. Aside from my father's Elbridge Gerry biography, I was still struggling to shift back into the practice of daily reading. There was too much to unpack there. Reading had been my bond with my mother. She had made me read aloud to her on our long hockey road trips to pass the time. I continued the practice after I left home, though I kept the text to myself. Reading was bad enough, but reading out loud would have put me permanently in the bus seat closest to the toilet.

I listened for footsteps as I pulled down a few new-to-me novels, but I got caught up in reading book jackets and first pages and I forgot to listen. I forgot about the game, and forgetting about the game was a bad idea.

It was just for a second, a momentary lapse, but that was all she needed. From the shelf I was leaning against, I felt one hot breath on the back of my neck. I tried to lurch away, but I was too late, and a wet, cold finger slotted right into my ear canal. I shuddered convulsively and automatically sat down hard. Aside from being struck head-on by semi-trucks or size 12 work boots, my ears are my only weakness.

"Graaaaace," I moaned helplessly as the finger continued to wriggle in my ear. "Please."

Finally, the finger withdrew, and I sat awaiting the arrival of my tormentor, who peeped around the side of the aisle, smiling broad as ever.

"Elby," she said. "You really must remember that bookshelves are not walls. They're permeable surfaces."

"Honestly, I thought we'd outgrown wet willies."

Grace looked aghast. "Never."

She offered a long, thin hand that I took, and she pulled me up with an elastic strength and held me in a tight hug honed, I knew, from years of Muay Thai. The lesson here? Librarians: don't go assuming.

"Would you like some tea?" she asked.

I nodded and she ruffled the back of my head fondly before letting me go. I watched her walk towards the backroom and the kitchenette that was tucked away next to the janitorial closet. I knew she was giving me time to get myself put back together and I was grateful for it. I walked over to the reference desk and took the chair that used to be my mother's. It was the same chair where I'd pretended to do math and history while I not-so-secretly paged my way through Tolkien and Dahl and Asimov. I was grateful Grace hadn't gotten rid of it yet.

I pulled open my mother's old drawer, expecting to find all of its contents replaced with Grace's tools of the craft. So, I was shocked when the drawer slid open like a portal to 1985. My heart did a little shamble as I saw my mother's life laid out in miniature: there her crochet needles, here the green fountain pen, a post-it filled copy of *Where the Sidewalk Ends*, her beautiful little hourglass, even the pair of readers that she never wore but held like a magnifying glass in denial of her need for glasses. And, of course, there was a picture. In a little plastic frame, my mother and I sat behind this very desk reading. And then, as if from someplace in the distant future, I was looking down at this very moment, looking down at grown Elbridge, who sat looking down at this picture of young Elbridge, young Elbridge who sat looking down at another picture of himself, and on into time, like a mirror held up to a mirror. So many alternate realities, endless possibilities, so many chances for mother to still be alive. I was fighting tears again when I heard Grace coming back.

She reemerged with two steaming mugs and handed me one that read "I HEART BOOKS" while she settled into her own chair.

"My empathy you have. My ears as well."

I nodded and sipped the too-hot tea.

"How's your arm?"

I gave her the so-so hand, clutching the mug to my chest with the other hand like a shield.

"How's your soul?"

I tried the hand again, but she shook her head, so I was forced to lower my defenses and join the conversation.

"I am currently trying to figure out how to just be," I said.

Grace sat impassively and took a first sip of her own tea, which I knew from prior experience meant, *I'm listening. Keep talking, boy.*

I sighed and tried to put what was formerly pure feeling into words. "I have never been comfortable with just me. Just sitting around and being a person in the world, occupying space but pointed nowhere."

She nodded and gave me a smile with no teeth.

"I've never really been Elbridge the friend, or Elbridge the student, or Elbridge the employee, and that never mattered because I only had to imagine myself as Elbridge, Clara's kid, and then Elbridge the hockey player. But now that it's gone—"

"And your mother is gone," Grace added.

I nodded. "I'm just plain old Elbridge, and I don't know really know who that is."

Grace took another sip, waiting for me to finish.

I scratched the back of my head and stared around the library, so familiar and yet wrong from this taller, older, duller vantage point.

"I can't even call myself Elbridge the son, because if I ever really knew my father, I sure as hell don't know him now. I feel embarrassed all the time, embarrassed to be back and embarrassed to have left, like I'm at home nowhere."

"And naked everywhere," Grace said.

I nodded again and felt better for getting it all out there to someone, especially when the someone listening was Grace.

"Where did all of this wisdom come from?" she asked.

"God only knows. Fishing, I guess? But I feel a little further out to sea every day. I've got some friends now, or at least *a* friend, and that helps. But I really don't feel like I know what I'm doing. Like every morning I wake up, and I'm playing a role in a play that I don't particularly care for, and no one will let me see the script. Does that make any sense at all?"

"Well of course you know that I know nothing," she said, an old remark. "But I can tell what they'd say." She gestured over her shoulder at the rows of shelves. "Most of them would be proud of you."

"Why?" I asked. "What's there to be proud of?"

She looked down into her mug. "I think I'd probably give Thoreau the floor."

"And what would he tell me?"

She looked up and stared at me with her unwavering gray eyes. "He'd say you're finding your own sun and moon and stars."

I was just getting ready to say something juvenile, "Gee, thanks!" for instance, when I remembered the House Bar, the windows, the universe unfurling like new shag.

"For peace comes dropping down slow," I said, still standing high above Lowland.

She nodded and reached for my free hand, giving it a squeeze, and I felt absolved. And then I immediately felt silly for needing absolution.

"Thanks for listening," I said. "I'm sorry I'm being such a whiner. Poor me, my shoulder hurts, my Mom's dead, I'm stuck here, boo hoo."

"Stop it." She sat up straight, not smiling anymore. "Catharsis isn't easy. Growth is painful. Wisdom is hard-won. Don't make light of progress or you will stop progressing." She paused, staring at me intently. "And I think you're just getting started."

I sat, pinned uncomfortably by Grace's eyes, and fought the urge to flail my feet around like a child.

She relaxed back into her seat. "I know one thing for certain. Your mother would be proud of you."

"And how could you possibly know that?"

"Well, for a start, you have yet to commit fratricide."

I smiled a thin smile she returned.

"Grace, how come she never told me about her skating?"

Grace looked down into her tea for answers, swirling the mug, but she found nothing hidden there and shook her head.

"There are some things she kept to herself. Which I was against, but then you know your mother. I think when you were born, she closed that chapter. It was easier to just put the skating, and some other things too, behind her."

"It would have helped, I think. To know. It would have explained why she was so—"

"Insistent?"

"I was going to say nuts."

"Earnest?"

"Insane."

"Dogged?"

"Banana. Pancakes."

We both smiled broadly then, and I felt my burden shift, like I'd handed Grace a piece of my big ol' rock and she'd slipped it quietly into her own pocket.

"I do need one more thing from you," I said.

"You mean aside from a new library card?" I swallowed and she narrowed her eyes at me. "I can tell that you've stopped reading. Your vocabulary is deplorable."

"Sorry. Yes, besides a library card. And some book recommendations."

"Anything," she said. "Always."

"Will you take a look at this?" I asked, and standing, pulled the now many-times folded scroll from my pocket.

Grace took the parchment and delicately unfolded it, tsk-tsk-tsking me for the wanton harm done to good paper. Then she became perfectly still as she read with what I knew was incredible speed.

"This is from the Duke?" she asked. "Did he deliver it personally?"

"No. It was his little lackey, that punk town crier."

She reread the document, taking a little more time to consume the detail of the calligraphy and the nuance of the language.

"It's well-written," she said finally, pushing her glasses up onto her forehead and rubbing her eyes. "But I have no more idea who could have penned this than you. So, what do you need from me?"

"I want to know if I should go?"

She laughed then, heartily, for the first time all day. She leaned back in her desk chair, which leaned with her, and put the back of one hand to her forehead like a silent-era starlet on a fainting couch.

"That's the richest thing I've ever heard. Elby, did you honestly come to ask a *librarian* if you should go to a *party*?"

I shrugged in embarrassment, unwilling to admit that I was asking her, as I'd so often done as I child, to fill in for my mother.

"Well, I think you should go. If for no other reason than posterity."

When I looked confused, she shook the scroll at me.

"Elby, this is the closest to capital H history we are ever likely to come by in Lowland. So, I say go. And take good notes."

I nodded, resigned.

"And one other thing," she said, and held up the bottom of the scroll. "It says Elbridge Corvallis *and his date* are invited . . ."

"You have plans for Saturday evening, Grace? Because I happen to know a fellow in need of a date. Not terribly good looking, you understand, but roundly kind to animals, small children, and the infirm."

"Ha! I'd love to, but it's bridge night at the library Saturday, and the old biddies really go at it without a chaperone. Just last month, Ernestine Nelson snatched Tandy Swift's wig right off her head after a bid dispute. If I left them unattended, there'd be bedlam."

I sighed. "Grace, do you happen to have a phone book?"

CHAPTER 14

Abbey stood on the sidewalk outside of the Knights of Columbus Hall looking like the answer to a question I never even considered asking. The spring breeze played with the hem of her dress and her hair, which was down but free of its usual plait. She waved as I approached, and I smiled back and walked the last twenty yards with my hands in the pockets of my only suit, trying not to look awkward despite the fact that we were standing on a sidewalk on Ash Avenue in formal attire preparing to enter a ball. It was just another ridiculous rung down the Duke's ladder to hell.

"Hey, Elby," she said as I closed the distance.

We stood and gave each other onceovers, unsure of whether to hug.

"This is where you say something canned like, 'Look how good you clean up!'" I said.

I said it because I was thinking of using this exact line about Abbey and realized how stupid it sounded. Also, I couldn't just keep standing there staring at her. She looked great, and I was little overawed by the presence of Abbey Winthers in formal attire. The dress was not-quite-black and ankle-length and allowed me to imagine Abbey in a whole new way, as if we just happened to run into each other on a street in New York City, two kids from back in the day now all grown up and cultured and long gone from Lowland.

Abbey smiled and I was envious of how she managed not to let her discomfort show.

"Well, you do," she said. "But I bet you wore a suit like that all the time, before."

"You'd think. But we mostly wore track suits."

She laughed. "I'll bet that was pretty nice, actually."

"It really was. Like a Catholic school uniform, except made of sweatpants."

"And hopefully fewer plaid skirts."

"You'd be surprised."

She laughed again and I liked the sound of it, liked how it felt to make her laugh.

"Where'd you get the suit then?" she asked.

"I had to buy it last year," I said. "Wish it didn't have to be black."

I saw her flinch with understanding. Then she took a step forward and put a hand on my arm.

"Nobody should have to buy their first suit for a funeral."

My smile left as my head went down. I looked past the suit and down to my shoes on the sidewalk, thinking of the last time I'd worn them, of the semi's blaring horn, and my father's silent grinning face above the steering wheel. I noticed the toe of my right shoe was still badly scuffed.

"I've got to be honest, though," she said, her hand still on my arm. "The jacket looks remarkable, given the circumstances."

"You know, it's funny, but I took it off and put it in the backseat that day so it wouldn't get wrinkled. I don't think I've ever been more right about anything in my whole life. They had to cut the other dress shirt right off my chest."

She squeezed my arm. "Is this the shoulder?"

"Yep," I said, wincing. "And your thumb's digging right into the scar."

"Oh, my god!" She withdrew her hand, scalded with embarrassment.

I looked up and met her eyes. Then I winked.

"It's the other arm, isn't it?"

I nodded and she punched me hard in the good shoulder. I imagined we looked like a pretty good couple, dressed to match and laughing together as the early April evening came on. Then Abbey's boyfriend stepped up on the sidewalk and slid his arm around her waist.

John looked at me and smiled, sticking out his free hand.

"Elbridge!" he said expansively. "Don't you clean up nice?"

.   . . .

I had the pleasure of childishly third wheeling into the hall behind John and Abbey like some kind of reverse tricycle. We got our seating assignments from my arch-nemesis, who was positioned behind a tasteful table with a white tablecloth and Union Jack bunting.

"May I have your names, sir and madam?" the little town crier said, smiling obsequiously.

"I'm John Newman." As the boy shuffled through the cards, John, still evidently feeling expressive, said, "Look how cute you are!" and tried to reach across the table to tweak the boy's hat.

The crier, I was proud to see, easily evaded the grope by sitting back in his chair and staring coldly at John.

"You're not on the list," he said, his smile turning vindictive.

"How about me, sir?" Abbey said seriously. "It's Abbey Winthers."

The boy rifled quickly through the cards and plucked out one near the back with a flourish.

"Ah, yes. Madam Winthers, welcome. I take it this is your—"

"Fiancé," John said at the same time Abbey said, "Plus one."

I felt the *fiancé* like a slap, and the *plus one* like an instant salve. My feelings continued to pendulum back and forth as the crier made a note on his ledger. The thought of Abbey marrying someone made me panic. I was extra panicky because it was some prick like John, and I flashed forward in time with cut scenes of their life: the tasteful wedding at Ash Avenue Methodist, 2.3 children, one house, two cars, three dogs. I was floored by the thought that I'd probably only see her again at the grocery store, chatting over our carts, hers stuffed with food for her family and mine holding a single jar of peanut butter. And then the weight swung the other direction, and I tried to remember who the hell was I to be upset? I was the one who left. *Swing.* She's too young to get married. *Swing.* I should have called. *Swing.* But she never called me. *Swing.* It was just one kiss, years ago on a darkened cul-de-sac, and it didn't mean anything. *Swing.* Unless it did. Yep, I'm an idiot.

I felt sweaty and uncomfortable and sick, though not as sick as last week when I called her from the library. Grace had handed me the white pages and excused herself to refill our teas. So, I looked for Abbey and couldn't find her, but did find her parents' number. It was weird, but as I dialed, my index finger seemed to remember the sequence, like a muscle memory of shape and flexion, so that as the phone rang, I had the same sudden onset of clammy nerves I had the last time I called. I was 15 going on 23.

"Hello?"

"Hi, Mrs. Winthers, you won't remember me, but this is—"

"Elbridge Corvallis!" She sounded delighted. "I wondered if you might call, sooner or later. I was sorry to hear about your mother. She was special."

"Thanks, Mrs. Winthers."

"Surely, it's Edith now."

"Edith. Right."

"You won't believe this, but Abbey is just here."

"Really?" I sounded too hopeful and perhaps a little letdown at the thought of Abbey still living with her parents.

"She comes by for dinner, Tuesdays. Hold on."

I felt relieved and guilty for judging her when here I was calling from a public library and living above a letch in exchange for lawn services and ogling.

Muffled shouting ensued, then Edith's voice returned to the receiver. "I hope you stick around, Elbridge. Abbey needs—"

"Thanks, Mom," Abbey cut in. "But I can take it from here."

"Okay, dears," Edith said. "Elbridge, you come by for dinner some evening. We've missed you." Then the receiver rattled, and it was just Abbey on the line.

"Well, isn't this very 1990?" she said.

"I'm honestly proud my voice didn't crack when your mom picked up."

"Hi, uh, Missus Win-*thurs*," Abbey squeaked.

I laughed, immediately at ease and amazed by the immediacy.

"So, you called me like a teenager. I can only assume you want to ask me to go watch the submarine races down by the river."

"Not quite, although I hear they're quite a sight. And I missed all those steamy parked cars my first go round here in the Low country."

"You didn't miss much. Lots of disappointment."

"Still, the anticipation is half the fun, right?"

"If you dated me back then," she said. "It was *all* anticipation."

"And now?"

"Less anticipation, same disappointment."

I laughed again and I swear I could hear her smile over the phone. I teetered on the edge of the boards, trying to decide whether I should hop on the ice or stay on the bench, and decided, as always, that I might as well skate.

"Well, speaking of dating, I know you're spoken for and all that, but I was hoping you might go to the Duke's ball with me?"

The line was quiet, so I panicked and added, "Platonically."

When it remained quiet, I desperately channeled Grace and tacked on, "For historical posterity?" My voice went up at the end. She was right: 1990, here we come. When it stayed quiet, I whispered, "Abbey?"

Then I heard her giggle. Actually *giggle*.

"I was waiting to see if you could come up with any more adjectives," she said.

"That was just cruel."

"I know," she said, still croaking with laughter. "But I'm not sorry." She stopped laughing then, letting the implications stretch.

"I—" I started, I think, to apologize for a half decade of total radio silence, but I never got the chance.

"I can't," Abbey said, cutting me off. "I got invited too, and I think John would cry if told him he wouldn't be able to wear his tuxedo again."

"I see."

"Sorry, Elby. Sorry about Susie, too, for that matter. She told me. You want to talk about it?"

"No, it's okay." What exactly was *okay*? I wasn't entirely sure.

"But I'll see you there?"

And see me she did. As that little imp handed me my seating card along with the jab, "And no plus one for you, Mr. Corvallis?" Of course he put us all at the same table.

. • .

To my surprise, our table was rounded out by my father and Bruce, whom I was very pleased to see again. They were chatting as we approached, and Bruce bobbed to his feet to give me a handshake. I introduced both Bruce and my father to Abbey and John, and we all settled in for the show.

Bruce began chatting with the couple, which left Robert and I to dust off our handy father-son scripts.

"Hello, Elbridge," he said. "Are you well?"

"Yeah, Dad. Doing fine. How are you?"

"Oh, aging, tired, etcetera."

"Mhmm. Need me to cut your grass next week?"

"That would be lovely. Especially as you still retain possession of my mower."

As usual, we were off to a great start, and I idly wondered how other fathers and sons got along. Probably, they had more in common than a single unifying allegiance to a dead woman and the fact that grass continued to grow.

"And where is our favorite physical therapist?" he asked. "I assumed she'd be clinging to your arm at such an auspicious—" He paused to wave a hand around the KC Hall, which was sixty yards long and twenty yards wide, full of folding chairs and tables covered with the same white table cloths and British bunting, and accented along the ceiling with thousands of red, white, and blue balloons held aloft by thin netting. There was a bar on one end and a stage with a podium on the other where tuxedoed quartet members tuned their instruments. The walls were beige and the floor tiles were beige and I'd be willing to bet my good right arm that if a sudden gust of wind swept away the cloud of balloons, we'd find a beige ceiling.

"Grace called it 'local history,'" I said, and my father raised his eyebrows, though whether this was because I had been talking to Grace or because she thought the Duke's ball was important, I didn't know. "Susie broke up with me."

Robert's face remained unchanged, and I bridled as the silence stretched.

"You didn't like Susie?" I asked.

"I don't recall voicing that opinion."

"But you're not upset we split?"

131

"I don't recall voicing that opinion either."

I sighed and dropped my head into my hands, rubbing my forehead and wondering, again, just what the hell I was doing here, sitting at a table with my father, at a fake duke's ball, at a Knights of Columbus in Lowland, PA. Then I felt a pat on my shoulder, and I raised my head to see Robert awkwardly swatting me with a limp hand. We looked at one another. He stopped patting but left his hand on my arm.

"Please don't say 'there, there,'" I begged.

"I would not dream of it. I will say, though, that I am truly sorry to see you here alone."

He didn't glance at Abbey, but I got the impression that he somehow intuited the situation on the other side of the table and the discomfort it was causing me. He gave my shoulder a squeeze, then released me.

"You know, I had to wait on your mother to make up her mind."

I leaned forward intently. "Really? Bruce told me that she was your student."

Robert glanced at Bruce, still animatedly chatting with the future Newmans, who wisely pretended not to feel the eyes burning into the side of his head. "And what else did my erstwhile colleague have to say?"

"He said you were kind of a punk."

Robert quirked his eyebrow and I searched my memory for the exact word.

"Firebrand?" I tried.

Robert smiled at Bruce. "That is accurate, I think."

"He also said that you got into some trouble for dating her, and that even though it was after she was your student, people still talked shit. But you got tenure anyway and wrote your book and stopped stirring the pot."

"Also fair, though admittedly thin on detail and context."

We watched one another warily, both standing on unfamiliar footing. I decided I could push a little.

"I talked to Lou Varney too," I said. "He showed me the trophy room."

Robert folded his hands and looked down at the table.

"Dad, how come she quit skating? Was it because of me?"

He sat quietly for a moment, searching for words. Then he sighed, resigned, and waved his hands around his head like he was clearing away deer flies.

"Not as such," he said, still not meeting my eye. "I am reminded of how little I have told you about us. That is my fault, and I apologize."

He finally looked up at me, and I nodded, not ready to forgive him, but also dying to know what was hiding in that great, gray head.

"It was a great combination of events," he said. "But the primary factor was undoubtedly my—"

And that's when the lights went out.

A single spotlight came on and shown down on the podium. After a gasp from the crowd at the change in atmosphere, a hush settled over the tables, which I noticed were all completely full. It made perfect sense that the single empty chair in the place was right next to me. Then the band kicked up while a singer began belting, "Gooooooood save our gracious queen, long live our noble queen, God save the queen."

I groaned and looked over at my father, who looked back at me and rolled his eyes. I smiled, considering the fact that I hadn't thought about my Dad-as-duke theory at all recently. Sure, the Abbey nonsense had left me distracted, but I couldn't say I was surprised to find him at my table. All of this noise and fuss was downright un-Robert, and if his apathy erased the question mark in my half-assed investigation, the appearance of the real duke at the podium punched in the period.

The man wasn't tall or short, fat or thin. His hair was brown and short, his face bland and smiling. He was perfectly nondescript, except for his red coat, which was bright and festooned with gold at the shoulders and cuffs, buttons that shimmered in the light, and a high collar that seemed to hold his chin up for him at an unnatural angle. Then he spoke, and any consideration of his physical features or wardrobe suddenly faded in the thunder of his voice.

"Be welcome, friends!" he said, and the hair on my head seemed to shift with the force of it. "I'm glad to see so many of the Queen's loyal subjects turn out for this auspicious event."

There were a few halfhearted catcalls, but the crowd seemed to be largely in awe of the presence at the podium.

"Her Royal Majesty has asked me personally to convey her regards, and to tell you that her heart is gladdened to see her sons and daughters, after losing their way these last few years, return to her bosom."

I looked to the entrance and saw the town crier snicker at *bosom*. And in the shadows behind the crier, I saw another two figures lurking out of sight. As my eyes adjusted to the gloom, I saw light twinkle off the uniform buttons and badges of two police officers.

"I know so very many of you, and I know too the plight so very many of you face every day. I want you to know that I hear you, and that I hear other things too. I hear the rattling of the chains which have locked up the mills. I hear the pounding of the nails into the boards over the closed storefronts. I hear cries as the children call out their hunger. And I hear the silence as Lowland goes quiet, slipping away to a ghost town, into history, into nothing at all."

I turned away from the police officers to see the serious faces of the crowd, some even nodding along. I couldn't believe they were buying this shit.

"Where are your leaders? Are they still listening? Is the mayor re-opening the mills? Are your congressmen putting gas in your tanks? Is the governor putting food on your table? No, NO, *NO!*" He pounded his fist on the podium with each *no*. Then his tone softened. "But what else can we do? This is the system, and we have to live in it, am I right?"

More heads nodded along now. When I looked, Robert's eyes were raised to the ceiling. I had no idea what he thought of all this, but I would pay a good chunk of my inconsiderable fortune for a peek inside his head.

WRONG!" the Duke yelled, pounding the podium once more. "We gave this brave new world a try and look what it has earned us. Slavery. Poverty. Poisoned land and poisoned water. Oh, you can vote, alright, but when your choice is between a fat cat and a dog that bites, that's no vote at all. The rich always get richer, and don't we know all about that here in Carnegie country?"

The catcalls had been replaced by a few shouts of ascent: "Yeah!" and "Hear, hear!" and even one "Amen!" from the back.

"But we have an alternative. We have a path to salvation. We must no longer toil within a system that uses us up and leaves us behind. Listen, now. Are *you* slurry?"

"No." The few responses were intermittent but sincere.

"They trample us underfoot then wipe us off on their golden doormats. I ask you, are *you* mud?"

"No!" The shouts were more coherent now, stronger.

"They burn you up and leave you in the grate. Are *you* ashes?"

"NO!" the crowd cried in unison, and I found I had to forcibly stop myself from shouting along. At our table, only John roared, pounding the table with his fist and stomping his feet, but we were one of the few pockets of quiet in the hall.

"But we are ashes, my friends!" the Duke cried. "We have always been ashes, and from ashes we shall rise anew! Because. We. Are. Ash. Avenue!"

The crowd went nuts. Hoots and cheers resounded around the KC Hall like a stadium in overtime. The Duke shook his fist above his head, basking in the noise. I watched my father's eyebrows rise in mild surprise as he peered around at the adulation.

Finally, as the cheers began to ebb, the Duke signaled for silence.

"I have seen a way back to providence. I can show you the way. But I need your support in this endeavor. No, I don't want your money. No, I don't even want your time. What I need is your support. I need your help this fall, when I seek the office of the Mayor of Lowland!"

When the crowd paused, uncertain of its footing, the lights suddenly came back on in a flash. The nets fell away, and thousands of balloons dropped slowly on the crowd. Then the Duke yelled, "The bar is open!" and the band kicked back up again with "God Save the Queen."

There was a roar as the crowd surged to their feet in applause. I turned to watch the police offers trying to wade through the mess of people and balloons towards the stage, but when I looked back up to the podium, the Duke was gone.

CHAPTER 15

Of course he made yard signs. The Duke's campaign support sprang up like mushrooms on the shady front lawns of the homes and churches on Ash Avenue. They were taped up in shop windows, restaurants, and gas stations. The signs seemed sprayed over every available surface, and I couldn't believe their sheer number and coverage, from eight-bedroom monsters to boarded-up businesses. As I drove down to the Horner for my morning skate, turning off of Ash onto Park, I even saw a sign tilting drunkenly in the parking lot of the Crow Bar. I decided that *this* is what mass hysteria looks like.

Thankfully, Lou Varney hadn't succumbed to the fever and the Horner was blessedly free of "VOTE DUKE" propaganda. I pulled into the parking lot as the sun was just beginning to peer over the tree line and stood for a bit, breathing in the cool April air, and listening to the trees sway and the gravel crunch softly under my feet while Golden Thunder's engine ticked as it cooled. I hadn't realized, but this routine had grown on me. I was feeling strong and healthy, and if my shoulder still hurt, it wasn't the searing omnipresent pain that it had been the previous year. I was enjoying my work with the Dillon Bros., getting a little more competent every day at a job that was rewarding more often than it was awful. Strenuous and dirty? My god yes, but never boring.

The wind brought me the smell of pine and damp river and I was reminded of so many other mornings spent trundling through this parking lot lugging my stone-heavy bag, my mother just steps behind. Now I was alone, but not quite lonely, and that seemed alright.

The dark lobby always seemed eerie in the morning. Without the wafting rattle of the popcorn machine and the blinging arcade games and the running, laughing children, it felt a little sad. I dumped my bag and poked my head into the trophy room, keeping the lights off as I approached Clara's case to stand before her picture. Her hard eyes were level with my own and the same half smile played across her lips as she stood perpetually poised to start the race. Her suit said *USA*, and I thought of the mountains you had to climb to get into that stratosphere. She had to be the best in her town, then her district, then her state, then her region, then the entire goddamn country before they let her put on those three simple letters. I'd probably never get the chance, but I was glad she got to and sad she never got to do more while she wore them. What else had Robert been about to say before the Duke cut the lights? What was the "great combination of events" 23 years ago?

"Why didn't you keep going?" I asked her, but she just stood there, silent and poised, still ready to fly after all these years, grinning her little grin.

"What should I do about hockey?"

"What should I do about Abbey?"

"What should I do about Dad?"

"What should I *do*?"

"I miss you, Mom."

•. •.•. ·

If the lobby was unnaturally eerie when quiet, the ice was like church. The humming coolers sounded like the murmuring hush that falls over the congregation just before the choir gets the show underway. The overhead lights made the surface of the ice shine, but with the accompanying lamps in the stands and lobby still off, the light seemed to bounce and reflect until it seemed like I was skating on stained glass, or the dully glowing surface of the moon. The cold air was crisp and sharp in my lungs, clean and yet untainted by Zamboni propane and the sweat of a hundred other bodies. As my legs and heart and mind came awake under the strain, I felt whole again. I wondered if this was what it was like for Clara. Was heaven one unending perfect moment on a clean sheet of ice? Or was dead just dead?

I put myself through the paces and my mother and the Duke and even death gradually faded from my mind. I limbered up with a few laps, stretched, then did some footwork drills before getting the pucks out. I worked the half wall, got some reps from behind the net and the slot, then moved to some full-ice puck movement and dump-in retrieval drills. Everything I did was designed for a full team practice, and at first, I'd felt silly trying to alter the drills to be workable solo. But after a year, I'd streamlined what I could and dropped what I couldn't until the procession of activities felt natural if a little unorthodox, like a yoga routine for a one-armed man. I noticed my shot was also getting harder thanks to all the empty ice time. Before, practice was a lot of waiting: waiting for the coach to start the drill, for my turn to run a drill, for the goalie to get square. But since my injury I'd just been firing puck after puck at an empty cage. I couldn't really take a slap shot anymore thanks to my limited range of motion, but my wrist shot wasn't impeded by my shoulder, and to be honest, I'd rarely had an occasion to take a slapper anyway. It was hard to tell in a vacuum, but both my accuracy and speed seemed to be better than when I left the Bull Elk.

I finished with suicides. There was something fatalistic about finishing every practice with a sprint to the death, but it seemed even more appropriate now than when I was a kid. When I finished the last sprint, I dropped to a knee and sucked wind. I felt terrible and fantastic in the contrasting way that only hockey made me feel: exhaustion and elation, excitement and fear, anticipation and dread, love and hate. I heard the Zamboni doors open on the other end of the ice, and I stood to clear out of the way so that Lou could get the ice resurfaced for the next group. I stepped off the sheet and was headed down the long hallway behind the bleachers to my locker room when an old-timer in equipment straight out of 1978 stopped me.

"Hey, you're the Corvallis kid, right?" he asked.

"That's me."

"Want a little more ice time?"

"Ehhh." I was thinking about a nice hot shower and maybe crawling back into bed for a little while before work.

"I hate to bother you, because I just caught the tail-end of your insane death march out there, but we had a couple of guys call in sick this morning. We could really use you."

He looked earnest and his smile was wide under the ancient Cooper helmet. He was missing one of the canine teeth on the right side of his mouth and the tip of his tongue poked through the hole when he smiled.

"I haven't played a real game in a while," I hedged.

"Yeah, that's just what I told the fellas back in the locker room. I said, 'Now listen, I don't think this kid's Silver Foxes material!' But they insisted I ask you, so here I am, hat in hand."

I couldn't help but smile. "Alright."

"You got a dark jersey?"

I looked down at my own plain white practice jersey. "This is all I got."

"That's okay. We'll figure something out. Get some water and we'll see you out there." He extended an ancient leather glove to me. "I'm Bob, by the by, Bob Williams."

"Elbridge," I said, and bumped his fist.

* • ● •

When I returned from the locker room, it was to 20 or so Silver Foxes standing around in a circle at center ice in a smattering of white and black jerseys. All of their sticks were lying in the middle of the circle, and they chatted amiably as I approached. When I joined the circle, their heads all turned to face me, and I noticed everyone was smiling. I even recognized a few of the faces, some from around town and some gliding back from the past, though I couldn't come up with any names.

"Foxes, this here is Elbridge Corvallis," Bob said. "He's joining us today purely on a conditioning stint before returning to the minors, so don't go too hard on him."

There were chuckles and groans, and someone said, "Hurry it up already, my feet are frickin' freezin'."

"Elbridge," Bob said, gesturing toward the pile of hockey sticks. "Would you like to do the honors?"

This wasn't my first pick-up game, so I knew the drill. I skated into the circle and started tossing sticks at random to either side of the red line that divided the rink in half, making sure that each side had one of the goalie sticks. When I was done, all the Foxes went to retrieve their sticks, then began trading jerseys until each side held an even number of players all wearing the same generally colored sweater. The white side was short one man, and so I joined their squad as they skated towards their bench to drop off water bottles and argue over who got to start, or more likely, who got to sit down first.

I was glad to see Bob amongst the white jerseys, and he grabbed me by the arm as I made to step onto the bench.

"Oh no," he said. "You're playing with me. Center okay?"

It was my usual position, so I nodded and headed for the faceoff circle where I squared off against a man who had to be 75 years old. His knees bent in toward each other and he leaned hard on his old wood stick so that he looked like a fragile tripod. When I skated up to him, he gave me a grim nod.

"Don't hurt me, please," he said. "My old lady's a battleax and she'll come for you and everyone you love."

I laughed and promised and then we were underway.

While it was absolutely nothing like playing with the Bull Elk, there was a general rhythm to the game that you found at every level of play, a kind of tidal effect, and while the back-and-forth action between the nets operated at a different pace, the motion was ultimately the same. I found I was actually a little nervous, and I knew it wasn't because I was afraid of any of the Foxes. Then I realized this was the first time I'd played a real game, or even shared an ice surface with another warm body, since the week my mother died.

I skated to the bench without really touching the puck and an old guy in Kelly green hockey pants slid not-so-smoothly over the boards to take my place. I hunkered down on the bench, and as always, mentally reviewed the previous shift: Took the face-off easily from the old man; played well positionally; could have engaged once or twice on defense but still a little timid about the shoulder. I berated myself for that hesitancy while listening for the ghost of Coach LeDeux to start yelling at me. When Green Pants came huffing back to the bench waving for me to switch, I realized Le Deux's cutting voice wasn't coming, and would never come again unless I wanted it to. I smiled as I vaulted the boards. Is this what having fun feels like?

Bob was playing on my right wing, and he was still pretty savvy. He played a real heads-up style so that he was always looking around and ready to make these terrific little bumper passes where the puck came onto his stick and was off again in another direction before the defense could react. He was quiet and effective and maximized my foot speed with his little passes and before long we were circling in the offensive zone.

We cycled around the net, working the puck around and quickly exhausting the already winded black Foxes. Bob reminded me a great deal of an old Bull Elk teammate, Johnny Brock, except thirty years longer in the tooth. They both knew where I would be before I got there, so there was always a pass waiting when I arrived. I marveled at how quickly some players can gel like that, and I wondered if it was an innate ability or a learned skill, if it had something to do with the chemistry of playing style or just luck of the draw? Whatever the reason, I made a pass from the corner to Bob behind the net and went directly to the front slot as 20 years of rough-handed coaches had taught me to do. When I got there, a puck was waiting.

From behind the net, Bob yelled, "Shoot!"

And so, I followed instructions and let instinct take over. I caught the pass and turned, took one short stride toward the net, and rose up through the release, gathering power from my left foot and trunk and chest and shoulders and funneling it into my arms, all guided by a delicate flick of the wrist, and released. It felt incredible, like the culmination of all the solo practice and drilling condensed into one pure act of economical motion. I can't really tell you how good it felt, after all this time, to just let her rip at a goalie, other than to say it was incredible. I also can't really tell you how bad I felt literally one second after I let the shot go.

I saw the poor old goalie's eyes widen as the puck hurdled straight for his head. In a very unprofessional display for a netminder, he dropped to try to get out of the way, but it was too late. A shot humming at 80 miles an hour from less than 20 feet away doesn't provide much time for evasion. I closed my eyes at the moment before impact, thinking for sure that I'd just killed a Silver Fox. And then I heard the ping.

When I opened my eyes, the goalie was lying supine in the blue paint of the crease, and the rest of the Foxes were staring up into the rafters of the old rink. Then they all turned to stare at me. Apparently, I'd missed the goalie's head and struck the crossbar of the net behind him. The puck was soaring with such velocity that it had ricocheted up into the ceiling insulation, lost to time or building demolition.

Bob skated over and stood next to me in the ensuing silence. "Maybe," he said, looking at the goalie lying still as a corpse. "Take a little pepper off next time?"

I skated over to the goalie to apologize and promised to quit shooting for the rest of the game. The poor guy, still looking a little wild around the eyes, managed a smile and a nod as I dusted ice off the back of his jersey. Both teams then gathered around to offer their comments and advice: "You got outta the way there quicker than you dodged Nam," and "Jesus, Bill, maybe you oughta buy a lotto on the way home," or my favorite "He could at least a bought you a drink first." And then, true to the game, everyone gave him a tap on the pads and play resumed like nothing had happened.

Skating on my left wing, and in stark contrast with Bob, was a fairly young and very overweight Silver Fox. I'd played with guys like this all my life, black holes, where the puck goes in and never comes out, but it had been a while since I played with one so lacking in the usually associated individual talent. Every time I got the puck, he yelled, "Pass!" and so I gave it to him. Then he'd shoot and miss. I'd retrieve it from behind the net and, sure enough, the call would come from the same general area. "Pass!" So, I did, again. And he missed, again.

When I went to retrieve it a third time from the corner, I was unsurprised to find him standing in the high slot, stick in the air, screaming, "Pass!" at eleven. I fed him again on a perfect little saucer and this time he really went for it. He opted for a one-timer, his stick slicing down to shoot the puck without trapping it first, and I watched with pure joy as the puck sailed past his stick and between his legs. His stick followed through a full second too late, slapping nothing but ice. But with the force and momentum of his girth behind the attempt, he couldn't halt the extreme follow-through. He tried to get his feet reset, but they were no match for the mountain of inertia that lifted him up off the ice and then deposited him back on it, right on his ass.

It's poor form to laugh at a teammate, so I tried to stifle my joy. Then I noticed that play had completely stopped, again, and that members of both teams were doubled over in hysterical laughter. The goalie I had nearly killed was down again, dropped in the crease and shaking with mirth. Bob had taken a knee to rest and laugh simultaneously. I skated over to the poor guy and looked down at him through his helmet cage to see tears on his face.

"You alright, bud?" I asked. I was concerned, because the most painful impacts were always the hits in open ice, and double that when you don't see them coming. Then I noticed he was rocking slowly from side-to-side, laughing so hard that I expected to see the ice turning yellow underneath him.

I extended him a hand and he took it, rising slowly to his feet. When he was finally fully upright, he gave me a pat on the shoulder.

"Good pass," he said.

       •   • ● •

The locker room air was palpably thick with the familiar scents of sweat and old gear in an insufficiently ventilated environment. The Foxes stripped off equipment that you could find hanging in the Hockey Hall of Fame, real leather and steel buckles, and given the smell, I'd bet at least one of the goalie's pads might actually have been stuffed with horsehair. The chatter, the feel of the old wood benches and other humans brushing against my shoulders all made everything else seem far away. The equipment may have been from a bygone era, but the atmosphere was the same. Maybe a little more griping about joint pain and a little less talk about dates for Friday night, but I felt like I'd walked in on a different family's Thanksgiving meal, and they'd just slid me out a chair.

Bill sat next to me as we began the process of de-arming. "Thanks again for subbing out there," he said. "We do our best, but time's a cruel old bitch."

"Honestly, I was pretty surprised," I admitted. "You can still move, and you're not the only one."

"Oh, there's a few of us who played college and minors. Randy over there even had his cup of coffee with the big boys."

Randy, of the Kelly-green pants, looked up at us from laboriously unlacing his skates. "WHL," he said. "Didn't even last six full games."

"Well, the whole league didn't last much longer," Bob said to general laughter. "Most of us figured it out early enough and came on back to work the mills or start a business or just be close to the folks. That's what's important at the end of the day."

I must have looked skeptical because Bob nodded and patted my still-padded knee.

"I know, I know," he said. "Old man talkin' crazy, but you'll see it too. Ask Gordie or Mario or Gretzky, and I bet they'd all scratch their names right off the side of that cup with their own fingernails if it was a choice between hockey immortality and their first-born child. It's all just bucket after bucket of blood and sweat and tears to play in slightly bigger arenas."

Randy popped back up from untying his skates like a prairie dog. "Aw, screw you, Bob. You're just jealous that the kid could still do it and you already blew your load. I say go for it."

Bob smiled. "That's as may be, but go for it or no, you know where all roads lead don't you, young gun?"

I shook my head. "Lowland?"

The Silver Foxes hooted with laughter at that one. Randy's head bobbed in and out of his oversized shoulder pads like a turtle and Bob leaned back to chuckle up into the exposed pipes that threaded the ceiling of the locker room.

I laughed along with the old codgers as someone tossed me a cold yellow Coors from a Styrofoam cooler. I opened the can and sat back, letting the chatter wash over me. It was true, some of the fellas could barely stand up and others looked ready to go for another hour, some learned to skate last year, and some had been playing since FDR sat in the big chair, and yet here we all were, happily tired and shooting the bull.

Bob leaned over and gave my knee another thump. "I've played with a lot of guys, Elbridge. And I thank you for holding back on us dinosaurs, because I know what you can do." He looked me in the eye, and his gray brows knitted together in concentration. "I been coming early to watch you skate Fridays before we drag our old bones out there. I see how you move. I see you work. I can tell you're smart. And Randy's right, if you want to make it back, I'm not sure there's anything out there that could stop you."

"And what if—" I choked a little on words I'd never been able to say out loud. "What if I don't want to make it back?"

"That's what I was trying to tell you. No matter where we start or where we end, the ice is still gonna be here. And so will your teammates, whoever they may be. And so will the suds." He gestured around with his can. "Elbridge, all roads eventually lead to beer league."

CHAPTER 16

"So, I'm standing with a wet mattress in the parking lot like a boner," Rob said and smiling, rubbed the back of his head, spreading sawdust liberally through his buzzed hair. "And goddamn if she doesn't drive right past me."

"You're joking," I said. "The poet? From the House Bar?"

Rob nodded and ran the board through the planer again. The smell of freshly shaved wood filled the old living room, and I found that I'd come to love the aroma. It smelled old and slow and natural, like what work must have smelled like before the mills came and then went, minus all the horse dung.

"Alice, queen of beauty, dream of dreams, saw me soaked to the bone trying to get the mattress out of my truck and failing. I don't know if you've ever tried to move a wet mattress, but they're pretty damn heavy, and apparently if they're caught in a thunderstorm, they just keep getting heavier. But the problem is they don't *look* any heavier, so here comes Alice and I'm basically buried under this mattress with no hope of escape because it's gradually filling with rain."

"Did she say anything?" I asked.

"She said, 'Need some help, Fish Man?'"

"Woof."

"Yeah, and I couldn't say yes, because it's pouring, and it just looks like a silly little mattress. So I say, 'No, I'm good, thanks.' And she says, 'You sure?' And I laugh and say, 'You just run on back up the mountain' or something stupid like that. And you've got to remember this whole time I'm trapped in the truck beneath my mattress, being slowly buried alive."

146

We laughed and passed the board back and forth as it became increasingly level. The Dillon Bros. had been hired to put a new floor on the main level of a house toward the north end of Ash Avenue, just before the homes petered out and the road wound up into the forested hills towards Low U. For a while there was nothing but the slap of the board on our palms and the whine of the planer and distant birdsong trickling in through the four windows left open to help ventilate the sawdust filled room.

"Did she say anything else?" I finally asked.

Rob nodded solemnly. "She said, 'Good luck with that, bud.' And then she drove away and left me to die. A slow crushing death by mattress. Farewell, light to my candle."

"So, really more like an ash tray holding your cremated heart?"

"Alas, tis true. But well said, young Corvallis."

"We are exactly the same age, Rob."

"In years, perhaps, but not in mileage."

I flopped my bad arm around like a wounded duck and quacked piteously.

"Okay, yes, you might have me in physical mileage, but in spiritual mileage, I'm basically ancient."

I thought about mentioning my own presence in the lovelorn aisle of the romance department, but I preferred not to talk about Abbey with Rob, or with my father, or with you, really, but that's how storytelling goes. I still hadn't seen her since the Duke's ball, and I was frankly too scared to call. If I never asked, then I didn't have to find out if she was actually engaged. Better to keep the cat in the bag.

Then Ron's walkie-talkie beeped. He leaned over to turn off the planer as Ron squawked, "Rob, it's Ron. Over."

"Ron," Rob said, holding the walkie to his lips and speaking very slowly. "If it's Bill Watkins dragging his fat apologetic ass in late again, I want you to repeat after me. Are you ready?"

"But, Rob," Ron said, whining just a little.

"Ron. I said, are you ready?"

Ron's sigh came through crystal clear. "Go ahead. Over."

"You tell Bill Watkins to Fuck. Right. Off."

"Are you finished? Over."

"Yes. Did you tell him?"

"It's not Bill," Ron said. "There's a call in for Elby. Over."

"Oh, well why didn't you say so? He's standing right here." Rob turned the walkie toward me and held down the button.

"Hi, Ron," I said, waiving for no reason.

"Well, hello there, Elby. We really should go for a drink one of these evenings. Over."

"Definitely." I really did like Ron, though I didn't see him much outside of the office, and I was rarely there unless I was picking up my paycheck or we were carpooling for a job. He was the kind of guy who would check his stapler for staples before trying to use it. He regularly cleaned the office microwave. His work boots were spotless. In other words, Ron was careful, clean, and a bit of a dandy, but the perfect complement to Rob, who could best be summed up by the bumper sticker on his rusted truck, which read, "It's not abandoned. I'm just fishing."

"I hear you're in lady trouble, and you know I'm a good listener—"

"Ron," Rob, still holding the radio, cut his brother off. "You said there was a call for Corvallis?"

"Oh, yes," Rob said. "Sorry, Elby. Your father called. He said it was an emergency and that you should come, and these are his exact words, and I know because I wrote them down, 'with all possible haste.'"

Rob beat me to it and took the question right from my mouth, "What's wrong?"

There was a pause on Ron's end, and then he spoke cautiously into the silence. "He said it was something about a moat."

Rob looked at me incredulously and I looked at the walkie-talkie hopefully, waiting for the laugh that would turn the whole thing into a joke.

"Over," Ron said.

. . .

The north end of Ash Avenue is the kind of place where everyone drives a respectable car at a respectable speed. So, I fit at least half the bill as I made my way south towards downtown, because Golden

Thunder could not exceed 15 m.p.h. The reason was not the engine, which could be relied upon to go at least triple that, given a straight line. The trouble was the brakes, which could not be relied upon for anything. At all. I found that, with the help of gravity, friction, and a low initial speed, I could get where I needed to be, if not quickly, then at least in one piece. But I hadn't traveled Lowland north to south in a while, and as I made my way past the courthouse and Carl's Hardware and Jumbo's Diner, my speed gradually picked up pace until I was tipping the speedometer at nearly 36. My knuckles started to sweat. The s-curve was coming.

There'd been a game in Lowland since they built the s-curve over the sometimes trickling, sometimes raging creek, which I had never played because I'd never owned a car. The game went like this: High school kids would hurdle through the s-, trying to top each other's speed, all while blasting their stereos and remaining both on-road and intact. I entered the first turn at what had to be a record-low pace, and you are welcome to call it disillusionment or fatalism or cognizance of my own mortality, but I was surer than any teenager who'd ever entered the gauntlet that I would not survive.

I leaned like a bobsledder through the serpentine, stomping on the breaks ineffectually. The car bucked continuously, shuddering as one caliper would catch and then let go before another would grab and release. I swerved perilously close to one guardrail, then another, before coming shallowly out of the first turn and swerved well into the left lane, praying that a logging truck wouldn't come blowing through to end my suffering. I closed my eyes just for a second, remembering my father, the screaming wheels, the blare of a semi's horn, the cold leather of the door handle, my uncomfortable black tie, crooked and still too tight.

And then I was through and coasting down onto south Ash Avenue, my speed gradually slowing with my heart rate. I passed the Winthers' residence and tried to play it cool while also scoping out their driveway for a sign of Abbey's green Blazer, but it wasn't there. I was glad, because Golden Thunder was huffing a little more than usual and I, too, was sweating heavily. I probably had enough on my plate. *Moat?* What the hell did that mean?

When I pulled up in front of my father's house on the southernmost tip of Ash Avenue, I used the curb and my once golden rims to grind to a halt in an incredible display of noise and smoke and poverty. And sitting there, parked in my father's driveway like an omen from hell, was an enormous yellow excavator. There was a man sitting on the treads, his legs dangling, puffing on a cigarette. No one else was in sight, so I went to greet the devil with a sigh.

As I approached, he nodded at me, but didn't put out his cigarette or climb down, so that when I reached him my face was perfectly level with his crotch.

"Nice ride," he said.

"Thanks," I said. "It's new."

He snorted and smoke curled out from each nostril. "This your place?" he asked, gesturing towards the house with his head.

"Nope."

He nodded again. "Old guy told me to get lost when I rang the bell. Told me some jagoff would be here to set me straight. You my jagoff?"

I shrugged, in no particular hurry to get my ass kicked again. "Aren't we all somebody's jagoff?"

"Hmm." He stared down at me, then flicked his cigarette into the yard and slid off the tread to land heavily on the concrete. He extended his hand. "Donnie."

I shook it firmly. "Elbridge."

"That's some kind of name."

"It's the old guy's fault."

"Figures."

"So, what's going on? I heard something about a moat?"

Donnie shook his head. "Craziest goddamn job, and of course it gets screwy right away. Somebody called and ordered a moat dug. Right here. Mailed in the specs. Paid in cash. So, I show up this morning and the old guy says, 'What moat? I din't order no moats.'"

I tried to picture my father saying, "*I din't order no moats.*" It made me smile.

"Glad yinz think it's funny," he said. "Cuz I sure don't. Donnie gets a job. Donnie does a job."

"Well, I'm sure I can straighten this out. You got paid, right?"

Donnie nodded sourly.

"Can you just leave this here?" I nodded at the excavator. "No one uses the driveway."

Donnie lit another cigarette and shrugged. "I was waiting on a call from the city anyway to clear underground power and sewer. But the customer likes a show, so I always get the Big Dog here dropped off to show a little face n'at." He patted the machine affectionately.

"Alright then. Who should I call with an answer?" If I was hoping for a business card, it wasn't coming.

"I told you." He narrowed his eyes at me through the cigarette smoke. "I'm Donnie."

"Right. I'll be in touch."

He shrugged and said, "Whatever." Then he gave Big Dog an affectionate squeeze before walking off up the driveway, and I could have sworn I heard him say, "Jagoff."

• • •

I tried the doorbell, then the front and back doors, but they were all locked and no one was answering. I went to the garage, but it was locked too. I pressed my ear to the door, but I couldn't hear any snorting or stamping. I'm not sure what I would have done if I heard a neigh. Call the cops? Skip town? Set it all on fire? I was mad now and it was all my father's fault. Again. He'd made a mess and then called me away from work to clean it up for him while he either cowered or escaped. I wasn't in the mood today to let it slide, so I set about breaking into my childhood home.

All the windows on the first floor resisted my efforts to pry them up, so I was forced to take more desperate measures, namely, climbing a tree. In my defense, it was an old sycamore with thick branches and good handholds, or I wouldn't even have attempted it. I also knew about the scalability of this particular tree because I'd used it before to escape and return under the cover of night to avoid the sharp ears of Clara Corvallis. She was the lightest of sleepers, and thanks to the great age of the house, the stairs that went directly past her bedroom were unbelievably creaky.

I ascended slowly and carefully, my shoulder aching from the unfamiliar positions I was asking of it. The leaf cover was more substantial than I remembered, but I guess we were both a little older and fuller for the intervening years. As I climbed, I began to enjoy the nostalgia: the rough bark under my hands, the leaves tickling my face, the expanding view of the yard and the roofs of Ash Avenue running north, the ripe smell of May. Despite myself, I was losing focus on why I was mad at my father. Then the branch I was standing on snapped.

I gasped as all my weight suddenly transferred to my hands, arms, and shoulders, one of which screamed in agony, but I held on desperately because the fall would hurt worse. I tried not to look down and increase my panic, but I was in considerable pain and my hands began to sweat alarmingly. Going back down was out, and I could try to keep going up, but I didn't think my shoulder could withstand the motion of rotating all my body weight up onto the branch. I peered through the branches and found that I was almost level with the roof, but about six feet away from the overhang. I had no choice but to swing for it.

So, grunting, I started pumping my feet, angling upwards. My eyes blurred with the pain as each swing increased the arc and the subsequent pressure on my shoulder, but I swung on until my lungs burnt from the panting. When I felt my hands begin to slip, I decided it was now or never. With one last effort, I pumped my legs like a child on a swing set, trying to achieve the impossible dream and make it all the way over the top. I let go.

I landed on the shingles with a momentum that ripped the skin off my palms and tore the knees out of my jeans and left me wedged under the eave, panting, bleeding, alive. I lay there for a while, looking up at the clouds, considering the great messiness of life. This was the exact same spot where I used to lie and read, gazing up through the tree, wishing I were elsewhere. Now, a decade older, I said a prayer of thanks to be right where I was.

Eventually I decided to get up and try the window, if for no other reason than it might save me from having to get back into the goddamn tree. I tested my shoulder, which felt no worse than I expected it to, but the window was stuck. I knew, though, there was a difference between stuck and locked. I knew this because I'd broken the lock years ago, and unless Robert had developed a sudden interest in home repair, it was likely still a matter of pressure and persistence. I placed my flayed palms flat on the glass, spreading my fingers wide and my hands shoulder-length apart to maximize the contact. Then I pressed inward and up, jiggling from side to side like I was shaking cereal out into a bowl. At first, nothing happened, but I could hear the crack of the wood unsticking from the white pane, and then it slid up, a centimeter at a time, until there was enough room to get my fingers between the sill and sash, and suddenly I was traveling through time.

I stepped back into my old bedroom, and the first thing that hit me was the smell. It had been cleaned in here, very recently, and the lemony aroma was almost overpowering after the fresh summer air. I looked around, and though everything was smaller than I remembered, it was all precisely as I had left it after my last visit before Mom died. No one had redecorated, so Jaromir Jagr still glowered down at me from the wall. I pulled open a few drawers to see my old socks, underwear, and t-shirts all folded and ready to wear. They didn't smell musty, which made me think that they might have been washed, or at least aired out. My bookshelf was still in one corner, and when I ran a finger down the spines of my favorites, it came away dust free. I was suddenly very tired and considered lying down on the bed for a spell, but I shook it off and tried to focus on why I was here.

I opened the bedroom door and listened.

"Robert!" I walked down the hallway, calling his name, but it was all quiet on the southern front.

I put my head in a few doors but didn't uncover anything of interest. The house felt like a shrine to a life that no longer existed, one with a father and a mother and a son living semi-happily under one roof, now more than a decade in the rearview. My parents' bedroom was empty, and I say parents' because I found Clara's bathrobe still hanging from the back of the bedroom door. Her pictures still hung on the walls. A pair of her shoes were lying, likely were she last discarded them, under a chair in a corner.

I felt some empathy for Robert then as I pulled the door shut. I wasn't ready to deal with all the emotions still tied to her, so it was understandable why Dad, more than a year on, was still dragging his feet about getting the cardboard boxes out for Clara's belongings. But when I tried to imagine sleeping in that shrine to her memory, all I could picture was myself unfurling a sleeping bag in front of her trophy case at the Horner. The image made me shiver.

At the end of the hallway, the door to Robert's office was shut. When I tried the handle, I found it was locked and was immediately suspicious. I returned to my own bedroom for a paperclip, which I found on the ill-used desk wedged into one corner, then returned to the study. I kneeled in the hallway, unbending the clip and finagling the tip into the small hole on the front of the knob. The muscle memory came back to me from childhood, where no room was safe from me and my junior lockpicking skills, and I found the pin in no time, exerting the gentle pressure necessary to pop the lock.

On the other side of the door, a wave of funk and book musk hit me with such force that I fanned my hand in front of my face to clear the miasma. It was what I imagined an Egyptian tomb smelled like when they rolled the great stone doors open after so many years—minus the corpse, thankfully. I checked the corners to see if my father was lurking anywhere, dead or alive, but it seemed like he had chosen the flight option rather than face Donnie and his excavator. I sighed and walked over to the desk, thinking of the time and skin wasted in climbing the sycamore, and looked down at the pad of stationery squared in the middle of the hardwood. Then I noticed the top of the page, which was embossed with gothic script in a letterhead that read, "From the desk of the Duke of Ash Avenue."

CHAPTER 17

I finally started reading again. It was a slog to get through *Elbridge Gerry: A Definitive History*, but since then the rusty dam gates creaked open and I flowed back into the rocking chair in the dust-dancing light of the bay window. Thanks to my new library card and Grace's gift for recommendations, I was happily contemplating the fate of someone other than myself. It was nice to take a break from narcissism, if you know what I mean. And it was nice, too, to relax in a chair on a Tuesday afternoon and transform Robert Corvallis, the maybe Duke, into Someday Elbridge's problem.

Then, of course, the phone rang.

"Elbridge, we need to talk." My chest did a little involuntary palpating as I leaned against the awful mustard countertop and Abbey's exasperated voice sighed into my ear.

"Sure," I said. "What's up?" I tried not to sound eager, because I wasn't exactly eager, and I tried not to sound afraid, because I wasn't exactly afraid either, but definitely somewhere well north of normal.

"It's about the moat," she said, and I exhaled in relieved remorse.

"Please, not you, too. Can't we talk about anything other than my father?" *Like, say, your engagement? Or my complicated feelings? Or this lovely May weather?*

"Sorry," she said. "Official business."

"Should I call my lawyer?"

"No, but your father might consider it."

I laughed, but I was the only one. "Wait, seriously?"

"Elby, your dad can't have a moat. It's against the law."

155

"Abbey, are you telling me there's a Lowland ordinance that specifically forbids the construction and maintenance of a moat? Because I know there are some funny blue laws round here, but this feels extra ridiculous."

"Of course not. And we're not talking about buying beer on Sundays. There are some serious risks he's taking adding an open body of water to a residential street, the least of which is flooding, and it only goes up from there. Like, for instance, has he considered the incredible drowning liability an unfenced moat presents to children, dogs, drunks, and the elderly?"

I had failed to consider this, or the moat in general, since my run-in with Donnie last week. It was easy to stay in my own little closed loop: skate, work, sleep. Simple enough to straddle the boards, to gently look towards my own future and then live each day accordingly. And the Duke? Robert? Lowland? Straddle, straddle, straddle.

"You're going to have to talk to him, Elby." She sounded a little less reproachful, and I got the impression that she was attempting to avoid conflict. Perhaps she was even making this call to prevent her boss from making a sterner call, in the way a parent gently takes a glass ornament from a child's hands to prevent the inevitable. "It's got to stop."

"Agreed. I'll talk to him."

"Thanks." She sighed in relief, and I wondered at the response. Did she think that I would take my father's side in this incredible clusterfuck? As far as I was concerned, Donnie could be digging Robert's grave, and so long as the yinzer didn't stick him in it, I couldn't care less.

"Anything else you need to talk about?" I asked.

"Not at this very moment."

"Rain check then."

"Yep," she said. "This weekend looks like rain, though."

"Would you say that Friday evening looks the rainiest?"

"Yeah. I can swing by to help you get the gutters cleaned out."

I couldn't tell if that was meant as a metaphor for my life, or if there was someone on her end snooping and she was being oblique, or if Miss Mary actually expected me to clean the gutters out. I decided it wasn't great for me that it could be all three.

My book lost its luster after the call, so I went for a run. The warm-then-cool spring air reminded me of past evenings, playing freeze tag in the backyard with the other kids from the neighborhood while the sound of the Low High marching band rose up from the football field like steam, drifting out and filtering down over Ash Avenue. I'd say that those were better days, but at that time Clara's cancer must have already begun blooming in the meadows of her endocrine system, and Robert, well, probably even then he was nursing whatever grudge had led him down the path to potential Dukedom.

I left Golden Thunder where it belonged, ground into the curb, and kicked my dirty workout sneakers south towards town. I ran past all the shabby elegant homes, looking like old men who once owned the most expensive tuxedos money could buy, but now looked thin at the elbows, frayed at the cuffs, all baggy and out of fashion. The trees, on the other hand, didn't give an acorn for fashion, and were thick and full and towering even amongst the grand old gents. I heard a ruckus up in an oak, and when I jogged closer, I saw the branches shivering. As I passed underneath on the sidewalk, I couldn't help myself and whooped.

Hundreds of starlings burst from the treetop and strung out over Ash Avenue like a ragged scarf caught in the wind, curling in on itself and unfurling, again and again, before finally touching back down in a new tree further up the road. I marveled at the synchronicity and wondered if there was a message there? You know, something about birds and patterns, motion and rest, maybe about finding your flock? Then I realized that, no, I was just a fool looking for symbolism on a sidewalk, and that somewhere Excavator Donnie was calling me a jagoff.

I kept running, on through the downtown and around the S-curve, then past three or four houses I'd worked on over the last six months. I felt some pride in seeing them restored, even if they didn't look all that different from the outside, and I wondered where that feeling came from after being gone for so long. You've been paying attention, right? Maybe you can fill me in later. Anyways, I jogged past the Winthers and saw Abbey's Blazer parked in the driveway, but I didn't stop. We had our meeting on the books, and we probably both needed the time in between to get our shit figured out. I didn't know what I was going to say to her. What could I say? I wondered how other adults dealt with their lives, if they were always this sloppy? When I looked up, I was standing in front of my father's house. *Home again, home again, jiggety-jig.*

There were lights on, but I was giving Robert a wide berth after he'd summoned me to deal with Donnie, whose excavator was still parked in the driveway. So I walked around back, grinning at the thought of Robert and his inevitable face-off with the owner of the Big Dog. When I entered the backyard, I also reentered all those old summer nights: the smell of someone grilling and someone else fighting the oncoming dark on a riding mower, the feeling of a little hand slapping lightly in my palm, the quiet voice in my ear whispering, *freeze.* The neighbor's had put a new fence in, attached to the old one that ran along the back of Dad's property. The old fence, built by my mother to keep the tag-playing children from tumbling into the Allegheny River by way of the ravine, was made from waist-high unpainted wood, grown crooked and shabby now in the dying light. The new fence, by comparison, was head high and white plastic and straight as a pin, and clearly built to distinguish between the well-kept grounds to the north and my father's yard. The grass wasn't knee-high yet thanks to the shade trees, but it was definitely going wild.

I rested my elbows against the back fence and listened to the river as it flowed past below. Once, apparently, the mill had been so loud day and night that you couldn't hear the river at all. But for as long as I could remember, I'd slept with my window open to catch the breeze that ushered in the sound of flowing water all through the night. That same breeze, or the breeze's great grandchild, lifted the hair off my neck and made me shiver pleasantly. Then the fence wobbled.

More memories then, of my mother, of sweating on a hot day to help her put the fence in, of digging hole after hole for the assembled pilings. We had worked from each side, starting early in the summer and working a few hours, a few evenings a week, gradually nearing each other in the middle of the yard. We'd look up every so often and wave at each other, my mother frequently coming to my end to check my work, having me re-dig, add more nails, straighten or shift. It was hot and frustrating work, but Mom tried to make it fun, singing, telling jokes, pretending to cut her fingers off.

And then, after a month of labor, we finally met in the middle to drive in the last post. That's when she proposed the idea. To dig this hole a little deeper, to put something we treasured at the bottom, to promise each other we'd wait an impossible amount of time—five years!—to dig the post back up and share our treasure.

I examined the fencepost, giving it an experimental shove. I reflected that it was clever of my mother to choose an impediment that would prevent me from cheating until I was strong enough to cheat. And by then of course, I wouldn't remember the promise. Well, the joke was on her, because I did remember, even if I was ten years late to the party.

I tried rocking the post from side to side, which caused a little more motion. I stopped to clear some of the grass away from the perimeter and was surprised at the tenacity of the little creeping tendrils. Once the roots were pulled, I entered my blocking stance and gave it my best *hut one, hut two,* and really leaned into it. The fence dipped, buckled, then uprooted with a sucking sound. As I peered into the dark little hole, I tried not to think about tombs: Jesus, mummies, mothers.

I knelt, stuck my hand in, and pulled out a little Tupperware tub. Once unsealed, the tub revealed a jewelry box I had completely forgotten about until I saw it, whereupon I remembered everything: the deep green wood, the silver edging, the four tiny, clawed feet, the little song it used to play which my mother let me listen to while she got ready for work in the mornings. The box trembled in my hands, the silver shiny if a little tarnished, and when I lifted the lid, music.

The improbable song tinkled out across the lawn like a requiem, carrying the memories of a rainstorm, pancakes on a griddle, a rotary phone ringing, but most of all, my mother, humming and brushing her hair, putting on her earrings, smiling at me through the mirror. I sat down in the grass and cried.

· · • ·

I'm not sure how long I sat there in the yard listening to the music box play, but eventually another noise penetrated the song and its accompanying memories: laughter. At first, I thought it was my mind playing tricks, but it was a braying, unfamiliar laugh, and for the second time that evening I looked toward the house. While the kitchen lights were off, the adjacent room in the southwest corner of the house was alight and throwing shadows into the now dark yard. That was the dining room. And unless my father's seldom-used laugh had changed, he had company.

I snapped the lid on the music box shut, put it carefully back in the Tupperware container, and cradled the tub in my arms like a baby, listening. I could hear voices, clinking glassware, and . . . jazz music? I rose and, still gripping the music box tightly, wandered in a daze toward the square of light at the opposite end of the yard. It felt like a space-walk, and with the memory of the jingling music box mixing with the disembodied laughter ahead, I felt I was stepping straight out of my body and into the light.

The glow felt warm when I entered it, and though the evening wasn't cold, I was oddly calm. My hands were painted an angelic yellow as they reached up for the sill of the window. I had to pull myself up to see in, but whether it was the light or my state of mind or divine intervention, my shoulder didn't protest at the effort.

I can see you don't believe me here, and I don't care. Call me an unreliable narrator all you want, but here is what I saw when I lifted my-self, pain-free, to the window: laid out before me like some renaissance tableau was the Duke of Ash Avenue hosting a dinner party.

Robert sat resplendently at the head of the table in a crisp, red mili-tary uniform, festooned with buttons and ribbons, epaulets at the shoul-ders and sashed across the chest. He was laughing with the man to his right, who was unfamiliar to me, and as surprising as it was to see Robert laughing, it was more shocking to see the source of the braying laughter slap my father on the back. Robert Corvallis, engaged in backslapping! I decided I'd had a stroke.

The feeling was heightened as I took in the rest of the faces around the table, including Bruce and Grace and a few other people I recognized faintly as the parents of children I used to know. Sitting at the far end of the table from my father and closest to me, Dick Newport had a note-book in front of him and was scribbling away as my father held forth.

All fourteen of the dining room chairs were occupied, and I could see small conversations going here and there, though everyone occasionally turned to listen to Robert as he made some rejoinder. There was much sympathetic nodding, and the company seemed generally at ease despite the presence of a red-coated lunatic. The meal was clearly over, given the scattered cutlery and saucy emptied plates, but the wine was still going around, and no one was reaching for their jacket. Two things struck me then: my father was the Duke of Ash Avenue, and he could host an exceptional dinner party. I considered knocking on the glass, but what the hell for? So, I eased myself down and left the Duke's house behind.

I felt empty by the time I walked home, and given the order of the evening's events, not entirely surprised when the phone rang again before I could sit down. I snatched the receiver from the wall and answered without a shred of my usual trepidation.

"Hello?"

"Elbridge, it's Coach LeDeux."

"Hey, Coach. What can I help you with?"

"I'm going to be in your neck of the woods this weekend."

"Welcome to Western PA," I said. "Make sure you try a pierogi."

"Ha!" His laugh was a short bark, like someone choking on a peanut, and it made me smile because I'd never heard it before. "Listen, I hear you've been skating."

"Yes, sir." I wondered absently how he could possibly hear my steel blades scratching all the way from Minnesota.

"Well, if it's alright with you, I'd like to come see for myself."

"Sure thing, Coach."

"Where you training?" he asked.

"Horner Memorial. It's in Lowland, on Ash Avenue. Like everything else in town. If you're coming from the north, you can't miss it."

"I'll find it," LeDeux said confidently. "Let's call it Saturday, nine. You got a partner or two to work drills with?"

"Of course." If it weren't for my unnatural calm, I might have been rattled by the question. I'd been skating alone for more than a year, but I didn't want to slice my own foot off before I even got the chance to skate. Then I remembered the Silver Foxes, and I wondered what Bob Williams had going on this weekend.

"Fine, fine," LeDeux said. "We'll see you Saturday. And Elbridge?"

I paused in the act of lifting the phone away from my face, already thinking about how I could track Bob down.

"Yeah, Coach?"

"We missed you this year."

"Thanks, Coach."

He hung up, and I was left holding the receiver in one hand and my little music box in the other. I still felt like I was floating in a becalmed sea as I sat at the borrowed card table and opened the music box again. The lilting little song came out again and filled my kitchen with memories of my mother. Looking inside, I found a tin soldier that I recognized as part of a revolutionary war set I'd treasured. The man was seated on a horse, and with his tricorn and white curls, he was undoubtedly George Washington. I smiled to think of the little general lying buried in state in the backyard of the only man to oppose him in 200 years.

Beneath the soldier, I found a sheet of paper, rolled and bound with string. When I pulled it out, the paper was thick and yellowed with age. Unlike with the previous scroll, which I still wish I'd never opened, I slid the binding off immediately. As I saw my mother's neat handwriting spread out on the small scrap of paper, my heart beat with pleasure. It was a poem, written in her lovely cursive, and underneath, a little afterward, which I read while the music from her jewelry box warmed the kitchen.

"I went to find the pot of gold
That's waiting where the rainbow ends.
I searched and searched and searched and searched
And searched and searched, and then—
There it was, deep in the grass,
Under an old and twisty bough.
It's mine, it's mine, it's mine at last. . . .
What do I search for now?"

"This is always the best part, Elby. Now you can search wherever you want for whatever you like so long as you never quit searching. Love, Mom."

CHAPTER 18

Campus was closing down for the season; I could tell by the robes. They flapped and fluttered around the newly minted graduates like hero capes, and though I had no real interest in more formal education—especially my father's brand of dusty learning—I was a little envious. They were all so happy. So accomplished with their jaunty little hats and ironclad optimism. So full.

With my try-out just two days away, I should have been feeling optimistic too. I had a very real chance to get my life back, meaning this would be my last trip to Low U, and perhaps any college, for the rest of my life. By the time the campus was up and running again in the fall, I'd be back in Red Lake, Minnesota, lacing up my skates for real. Admittedly, Red Lake wasn't *that* much larger or more interesting than Lowland, but it did have a top-notch ice arena and a hell of lot less baggage.

But as I weaved my way through the smiling knots of families and friends, trying to stay out of the backgrounds of pictures, I couldn't help but think how these grads, these *kids*, weren't that much younger than me. I might have been standing here myself but for the grace of—whom? Clara, for pushing me into hockey for love or freedom or to recover some of her own failed athletic dreams? Robert, incidentally, in my frantic desire to become anything other than another version of his closeted familial absence? Lowland itself, maybe, and the Rons and Robs and Donnies who started pulling the plow so early they already seemed wrung out? I had the strangest feeling that my left eye was looking at my own graduation, less one mother but otherwise equally sure of the future and my footing in it on this bright summer day, while my right eye continued to see the quad as it always was: sepia-toned and useless to me. It gave me a headache.

The brass handle of Bruce's building felt especially cool and calming under my hand as I finally escaped the courtyard into the dark, quiet hall. This time around, I had no trouble finding my way up the right set of stairs to Bruce's office, and I grimaced at my growing knowledge of campus despite my best efforts. When he called the day before to invite me up for this visit, Bruce had been intentionally coy, only offering "something I might like to see." So, when I knocked on the door, I did so hesitantly, my capacity for further surprises exhausted after yesterday's events.

"Come in, come in. Hello, hello." He smiled and patted my arm and then the arm of the tired armchair tucked in the corner. Bruce's office looked the same as it did from my previous visit, lamp-lit and smelling not unpleasantly of books and coffee and his slightly aggressive cologne. He had on a different sweater vest than the one he'd worn at my father's dinner party, and both vests were different from the one he'd worn the first time I'd met him. I wondered where you bought sweater vests in Lowland. Maybe that was one of the perks of tenure, the dean offered the use of his private tweed-and-wool man.

"Hello, Bruce," I said, taking the offered chair and trying not to slump as I imagined his students doing. I crossed my legs awkwardly, and then sat there regretting the decision as my hip, still tight from the morning skate, creaked ominously.

"Was that your bones?" he asked, peering at me in alarm.

"No," I said. "It must have been the chair."

I was dying to ask him about the dinner party, but I was curious to see if he'd offer the admission on his own terms. I settled for a neutral, wait-and-see strategy. "So, what's up?"

He shook his head as if to clear water from his ears. "Well, two things. First, I wanted you to see these." He swiveled his chair towards a filing cabinet and rattled around inside before swiveling back with a folder that he offered to me with a gentle hand.

I opened it to find photocopied press clippings, all labeled with the *Lowland Lantern* masthead.

"I had the dragon in the university archives dig these up," Bruce said, leaning in so that he could peer over the edge of the folder. His bald spot caught the golden light from his desk lamp, and he grinned sheepishly. "To tell you the truth, I'm quite afraid of her. She really is an unpleasant woman. Why be an archivist if you don't like to retrieve materials from the archives?"

I looked at the first story, dated September 1966 with the headline "Professor Stages Walkout." Underneath was a black and white photo of a young man in a dark coat, sitting with his knees drawn up underneath what I recognized as the big oak in the quad. He wore thick glasses and a narrow tie. Behind him sat rows of students, some holding signs or raising fists blurred by the camera's focus on the figure in the foreground. I looked closer, and underneath the glasses and the mop of hair, I recognized Robert Corvallis. My eyebrows raised in surprise.

"Aha!" Bruce chuckled with delight. "I knew you didn't believe me about your father qua firebrand."

I shook my head as I rifled through the pages with my thumb. I truly did not believe it, and yet here was the proof. It was impossible for me to imagine that timid man leading rallies and fomenting campus rebellion. As a kid, I wasn't even allowed to get a dog, not because of the usual non-starters like responsibility or allergies you usually offer to children, but because Robert required "crystalline quiet" to work. His words, *crystalline quiet*, stuck with me and festered so that even now I liked to have the radio on while I read or the windows open while I slept. But here he was, under my hand, holding a bullhorn for Christ's sake, and I wondered where that Robert had gone. And at the same time, I realized that wherever he'd gone, he'd finally come back.

"Why didn't you tell me?" I asked with my head still sunk in the folder.

"I did!" Bruce said, affronted. "The last time you were here."

"Not about this." I closed the folder with a snap and waved it at him. "Why didn't you tell me about Robert *qua* Duke." I jabbed his *qua* back at him like a needle.

"I'm not—I don't know what you're—hmm." He leaned back in his chair and swiveled away, pretending to tidy papers on his organized desk.

"I saw you," I said. "At the dinner party."

The silence stretched out like summer break. Bruce gulped a few times and looked up at the ceiling, but the drop tiles weren't giving anything away. He turned to stare out the window at the happy clumps of graduates, the green afternoon, the big oak tree. Finally, he spoke without turning back.

"It wasn't my place to say. It's still not my place. But your father is working towards something, Elbridge."

"Yeah, a mental breakdown. Or are you another one of these *Duke for Mayor* fools? I thought you had more brains."

I was pissed at this reasonable old man. For taking my father's side. For enabling him. For acting out of character when all I needed was a little rationality.

He sighed and turned back from the window. His eyebrows were drawn down and he looked forlorn or resigned or some other emotion no one can actually read off of another person's face despite what all the novels say.

"What he's doing," Bruce said, then stopped, working some words around like mouthwash. "It's not about himself."

I rolled my eyes. "It's always about Robert."

"That's what I was trying to show you." He gestured to the folder. "It's not. Or it wasn't. And I can't say how things were for you and your mother at home. I would never presume so much. But I can say that this Robert, Robert the Duke, and the Robert that you're holding there are one in the same. They are agents of change. And just like then, this town is crying for it."

He paused to look down at his hands, feeling the knuckles of his right with his left. "When the mills started shutting down, he tried to get some aid from the state, applied for grants, did some groundbreaking sociological work. When they packed everyone off for Vietnam, he stood up or sat down, whatever was called for or least expected. When civil rights were either just words or the big black boogieman, your father was one the movement's few champions in these Allegheny hollers. And he got attention. People threw bricks through his windows and black sedans followed him around. They threatened to fire him at least a dozen times.

But he never backed down, and that all meant something then. It meant something to the town, and it meant something to me."

"And now?" I asked.

"Take a look around, Elbridge. Would you say things are getting better in Lowland?"

I thought of Ash Avenue and its shuttered store fronts, of the chain link and padlocks across the mills, of the men sitting around tired of waiting for a phone call to end the furlough and tired of fish floating dead in the river and tired of the Crow Bar soaking up their dollars and just plain tired. I shook my head.

"Can't you see why everyone likes to read Newport's stories about people like you and your mother? Can't you see why they go in so earnestly for all this Duke mystique? Everyone's just looking for a rope."

"Seems like just enough to hang themselves with if they elect my father mayor."

"And that," he said, tapping the folder, "is where you're wrong. You should really be talking to him about all this. But, for the sake of argument, let's say if, even then, you still don't trust your father's motivations, I hope that you might trust Grace's. And mine."

I sighed and rubbed my face. It was too much to process at the moment, and I needed a little time alone to sort through all the loose change. Then I remembered what Bruce said when I first walked in. "Oh, Jesus, what's the second thing?"

"I'm so glad you asked," Bruce said, and smiling, reached for the phone.

• •● •

The campus library was an imposing presence on the otherwise idyllic college quad. It brooded behind the oak tree like a limestone falcon, narrow and stoop-shouldered. As I trailed Bruce towards the big double doors, I was oddly reluctant to enter. Compared to this menacing figure of higher learning, Mom's library was a quaint country affair, and I immediately felt I didn't belong. I had the suspicion that, upon entering, some uniformed authority would stride over purposefully and demand to see my ID, so obvious was my unsuitability for entry. But, after Bruce entered and turned to find me lingering, he smiled and came back outside. We stood side by side, craning our necks upward like inverted gargoyles, taking it all in.

"It won't bite," he said.

"I know."

"I understand you're something of a reader yourself."

"Hearsay. Slander."

"You know the fiction section alone has ten thousand titles."

I side-eyed him skeptically, but he continued to smile placidly up at the gleaming white stone façade.

"Speaking of libraries, what do you think of Grace?" he asked.

"Well, she's wonderful." I turned to face him. "You know she worked with my mother?"

He nodded but kept his face turned upwards, hands clasped behind him as the sun warmed our backs.

"She's the best, like a second mom, especially since—"

Bruce nodded again, encouragingly.

"She's smart and kind and funny, but then, you'd know all of this already since you sat right next to her at my father's little soirée."

"Yes," he said, and I caught him eyeing me subtly. "What I meant to say was, what do you think of Grace and *me*?"

I laughed then, a little hysterically, which caused Bruce to frown and several families taking pictures of their graduates to glance at us in alarm. Realizing I might have caused offense, I patted him on the arm.

"I'm sorry," I said, getting control of myself. "It's only funny because it seems so obvious now that you've said it. I can't believe I didn't think of it sooner."

He smiled a big kid grin. "Well, you've had a lot on your mind." He rubbed my back softly. "Shall we go in? I don't want to be late for our meeting."

He led me through the lobby, gracefully pausing to allow me to gape at the big open atrium and the three floors of shelves that flanked it on all four sides. It was like a cathedral for books, and I'd never seen anything so simultaneously alluring and terrifying.

"There will be time for ogling later." Bruce nudged me toward a stairwell off the lobby, where I reluctantly followed him down into a very unlovely sub-basement. If the floors above were full of light and whispers and the aroma of well-ventilated pages, the basement was its evil twin. Low ceilings and narrow hallways marched off in three directions, all lit by humming, underwhelming fluorescents. The smell of books was stronger here, compacted, somehow less healthy, as if the sheer weight of the volumes above was pressing down on it, tripling the slowly decaying paper odor like a pressure cooker.

Bruce stepped up to study the room numbers indicated on a wall placard. "To be honest, I've never been down here before. It is a little, hmm—"

"Awful?" I supplied.

"Ambient," Bruce suggested, then got his bearings and turned left.

We walked halfway down a hall, which must have run the length of the building above, before Bruce turned and knocked on a non-descript brown door. An older man with neatly parted gray hair and an even neater gray suit answered, took us both in with a glance, and smiled thinly.

"Thank you, Dr. Bartlett, for conveying our friend here." He extended his hand to Bruce, who shook it warmly.

"My pleasure, Dave." Bruce broke the handshake and gave me a pat on the shoulder. "I'll just leave you to it. Elbridge, I imagine I'll be seeing you tomorrow. I've got a little surprise in store. Come and see."

Before I could ask the five or six obvious questions, like *What's happening tomorrow?* or *Where the hell am I and why are you abandoning me?* Bruce was already back at the stairwell.

The man, Dave apparently, pushed the door wide and gestured for me to enter. The room was not quite a classroom and not quite an office. It had a chalkboard on one wall and enough chairs to host a class with low capacity and generous ideas about personal space. There was also a desk, green steel, a filing cabinet, blue steel, and an overhead projector, gray plastic.

"Please, Mr. Corvallis, take the desk," Dave said, and plunked himself down in the middle of the first row of chairs. He kicked his legs out, crossed his arms in a way my father would have described as pure petulance, and watched me walk awkwardly to the rolling desk chair (yellow steel, an amazing alloy rainbow, you have to agree). I sat and the chair screamed in protest. I shot to my feet, but Dave only smiled and waved me back down to another, smaller scream as I eased my way into it more gently the second time.

"What's this all—" I started, but Dave's hand shot up. I paused, waiting, but Dave calmly kept his hand in the air, looking me straight in the eye.

"Uh, yes?"

Dave, hand still raised, looked left then right, questioningly pointing his free hand at his smart gold tie.

"Yes," I sighed, already weary of a game I didn't even know I'd started playing. "You, there in the front."

"What do we do to break through a neutral zone trap?"

I hear you: A hockey question? In the basement of a library? I was astounded too. So astounded that I felt like crying. Then I decided he was messing with me, and all of my dislocated college anxiety and misfit discomfort fell away, and I decided, okay then, *let's fucking play.*

"Two options. You can try the dump and chase, and with a blue line-anchored trap, it will work just fine. Pucks in deep, get on your horses, first man into the corner, second blocks the outlet, third to the net front. But if they're setting their line high, then gaining the red line and avoiding icing is going to be a challenge. So, I'd go for a neutral zone drop that gets the defense moving backwards and pins them in on one side, then reversing the play to a defenseman coming up with speed."

I wasn't surprised to see his hand shoot back up.

"Lemme guess," I said, smug. "You're confused?"

"No," he said, lowering his hand. "I'd like to know what the defenseman's options are at that point."

I looked around distractedly for a minute, trying to get a feel for the situation I was in, before remembering the blackboard behind me. I stood and found some chalk in the tray before turning to face the class. "May I?"

"By all means."

"At that point, he can do three things." I quickly drew the oval for the rink, two nets, and five lines, and filled out the X's and O's.

"He can leg it, because he'll have speed and a pretty clear sheet to work with." I drew a hard arrow toward the net from the lone X at the back of the play.

"Or, and this is useful if we're not working with the world's quickest D-men, he can make a cross-ice pass to a winger we leave here." I erased one of the forward X's and moved it over, then drew a dotted line to simulate the pass. "This obviously has the advantage of being quicker than skating it up, but if he misses the pass were back to icing."

"And what if they get wise and cover him?" Dave asked.

"I'm glad you asked that, because this is my favorite iteration." I erased and redrew an O to cover the forward X. "You can see that we've got a lot more confusion here now in the middle of the ice, and that we're not being successful loading one side. So, what do we do? We have our defenseman advance towards the far wall." I erased the lone back X and moved it to the left side of the board.

"Now look. If he skates cross-ice, he's going to draw at least two men, one to forecheck and one to cover center ice." I moved two O's correspondingly, then shifted another X back down. "If this forward slides down, we have an easy cross-ice pass, and now we've got numbers and a lane for either the dump and chase or to maintain possession into the zone with a pass here or here or here." I ticked off the options, set the chalk down, and stood staring at the mess I'd made. And the only thing I could think about was how much fun it was to draw on the blackboard again, like I was back in sixth grade and hockey was still fun and Mom was still alive.

I dusted my hands off and turned to face Dave, who sat studying the board for a minute. Then he rose smoothly and walked over to stand opposite the front desk.

"My name is David Barker," he said, still looking at the board over my head. "I'm the athletic director here at Lowland University. I wanted you to see what your office would look like before I offered you a job."

CHAPTER 18

"I told him hell no."

"But what did you actually say?" Rob asked.

"I'd have to sleep on it."

"Pussy."

I stared down into my coffee, which I held in two hands and tried to draw strength from like it was some kind of battery. Jumbo's Diner was crowded this morning as people got ready to muddle through the last day before the weekend. On the other side of the table, Rob just grinned. This was good news for him. This was a heavy weight on the *Elby is staying* scale.

"Do you get an office at least?" he asked.

I nodded. "A shithole in the basement of the library. Apparently, they're out of space at the student rec center."

"Does it pay, though? That's the big one."

"Some," I admitted. "Not much. They're still a club team, but the AD seems pretty serious about making the jump to varsity. I guess that's why he tracked me down."

"And why he doesn't have to ask some committee's permission to offer the job to your broken, uneducated ass." He thumped the ketchup bottle with a slap like a steak hitting a butcher's block. Ketchup flew out over his eggs in a thick stream. "I know you don't need to hear this from me, but I'm going to say it anyway. Your job with Dillon Bros. isn't going anywhere. In fact, I'm betting you could do both pretty easily. Leastways until the team makes the jump to the big leagues."

I nodded again. I was grateful, I really was, but have you ever been grateful for a thing and at the same didn't want any part of it? I had my tryout in the morning, and it was tough to think about anything else with that great big sun shining 24 hours away. I was grateful for the interruption when Deb came by with a warmer and leaned in to chat as she topped off our mugs.

"Yinz going down to the courthouse?" she asked.

"What for?" Rob wanted to know.

Deb jerked her chin towards the diner's big front window, and through the painted-on breakfast specials, we could see folks moving in ones and twos north up the sidewalk towards the center of town.

"What's going on?" I asked.

"The signatures," she said, raising her eyebrows significantly so that they arced above her red cat-eye lenses. "Today's due day."

"Due day for what?" Rob asked. He looked at me, but I could only shrug back.

"Been living in the river? The Duke? Running for mayor? Today's the day he has to get his 2,000 signatures to get on the ballot for November."

I still hadn't talked to my father since I'd uncovered his big secret, intending to put the whole mess on ice until after my tryout. Now though, I felt a little sinking in my guts as I remembered the Duke's gala and his big announcement. That Duke, who wasn't my father (I still hadn't worked that one out), had called for the support of the people just before the balloons dropped and the cops waded into the chaos. Now, I guessed, was the accounting of support.

"Well," Rob said. "Did he get 'em?"

It was Deb's turn to shrug. "I signed."

When we both turned to regard her, she lifted her chin defensively. "What? We need a little shake-up round here."

"And the, uh, British stuff?" I asked, genuinely curious.

"Aw." She waved her order pad around her head dismissively. "He's just blowing smoke, n'at. I don't think we need any more Queens. I *do* think we need something to change. Before everything gives."

We all nodded quietly at that one, and I stared out the window as people continued to trickle toward the courthouse like pilgrims to a shrine. And though it surprised me, I realized what it was I saw on their eager, strained faces: hope.

* * *

In the end, it was the horse that got him. If he'd just walked to the polling station, even in his redcoat uniform, he might have escaped the notice of the police officers who loitered near the entrance to the gym with their hands resting on their gun belts. But when you ride through a high school parking lot on a gelding, you're going to draw the heat.

After parting ways with Rob, who had real work to do, I joined the crowd heading up towards the town square. We walked past the movie theater, an open bar, a closed bar, and an office supply store that I thought was probably secretly a bar that couldn't afford the liquor license, then through the little park that separated Ash Avenue from the courthouse. There I stood on the edge of the crowd that had gathered in front of the courthouse steps.

I heard the murmur rising before I saw him, because I was too busy fixating on my nemesis, the goddamn town crier, who was standing on top of the brick stairs (all five of them) and haranguing the crowd to put their names down in support of the Duke. I wondered why he wasn't in school but realized that with the middle school and high school both adjacent to the courthouse, he'd probably slipped over the fence during recess to do some casual political canvassing. Honestly, the little bastard probably had the brightest future of the whole lot of us.

"Elby!"

I looked around but couldn't locate the source of the voice in the crowd which had the rowdy quality of fans waiting for a concert to start.

"Ellllbbyyy!"

Turning in a complete circle, I finally found Grace's pale sickle of a face peering over the shoulders of two good old boys, who standing with their arms crossed and eyes steadily scanning the crowd, looked like nothing other than her personal security detail. I watched her tap each man on his outside shoulder, and when they both turned in opposite directions, she slid smoothly between them, a wicked smile on her benign face.

I smiled back at her as she enfolded me in a firm, willowy hug. She was wearing a shawl, which I thought was perfectly librarian of her. Her hair smelled like tea and gardenias.

"Did you see?" she asked excitedly. When I shook my head, she pointed back over the heads of her confused entourage, who were still trying to figure out which one had tapped the other with mixed results. "It's him."

And so it was. The Duke came clopping across the parking lot resplendent in red wool and gold brocade, his tricorn perched jauntily, his chin tipped up in what Dick Newport would later describe as a "cant of noble bearing and posture." And despite everything, I had to agree. He looked pretty damn regal. Tall, broad of shoulder, chin a firm cleft, and hands strong and competent on the reigns. He looked, frankly, too tall, broad, and regal.

"Grace," I said. "I don't think that's him. That's not Dad. It might be the Duke from the gala, though. It's hard to tell, but I think they look the same."

"I know," she said, her eyes wide as she found my hand and gripped it tightly. "Isn't it all so wonderfully strange?"

"Who—what?" I started, but Grace raised her free hand to her lips, shushing me.

"I have my suspicions," she said. "But your father has never been particularly forthcoming with the particulars."

"Why didn't you tell me before that he—" I started again but was re-shushed.

"Watch. For posterity."

And watch we did as the Duke, or a Duke, approached the crowd. The murmuring turned into a hum as people began to notice the rider, and turning as one, a general cheering broke out. More people picked up the refrain as the Duke edged his horse up to the front of the crowd and lifted his hand in acknowledgement. I heard the usual "Duke! Duke! Duke!" break out, as well as the newer and more distinct "Ash AVE! Ash AVE!" that had cropped up since the gala. There was even one old coot in the middle who raised his rattling scarecrow of a fist and hollered, "FOR QUEEN AND COUNTRY!"

I wasn't surprised any longer by the gullibility of folks, but I was a little alarmed by a new, swelling feeling that grew in my chest. I felt it come not from the sight of the Duke, impressive as he was right then, but by the feeling of goodwill and optimism that gathered up and ran through the crowd at the sight of him. People turned their faces toward him and smiled or hooted despite themselves, like some ancient culture watching as the sun finally reemerges after an eclipse. And that's when the cops tackled him.

Well, not tackled, exactly. More like pulled him from the saddle, which involved a lot of pushing and pulling from several directions at once. If this Duke, whoever he was, appeared to be a confident horseman as he crossed the parking lot, his skills were not up to the challenge of fending off three uniformed officers while corralling a spooked horse. The beast reared, and as its hooves kicked out towards the faces of the nearest onlookers, the Duke toppled to the ground.

Grace gasped, and I stepped forward to help the downed man, then stepped back from the horse's ferocity. Eyeing the hooves, I wondered if they were the same feet that nearly caved in my head on the floor of my father's garage a year ago. The horse's eyes rolled, and it spun in a tight circle as the officers piled onto the downed redcoat, then spying a gap, it whinnied and headed for daylight and the park beyond.

The crowd swelled forward as the Duke fell, then swelled back as the horse lashed out, flowed as the policemen piled on, then ebbed as they came up with the man in handcuffs. One officer was saying something to the man, presumably his Miranda rights, while the rest cleared a path towards a squad car that was waiting on the square between the courthouse and the park. First, one boo, then several, then hundreds came flying towards the officers who seemed to belatedly realize how outnumbered and on the wrong side of popular opinion they were. And that's when things would have gotten ugly if a big yellow school bus didn't come screeching to a halt between the officers and the crowd.

The bus read "Lowland University" in big block letters on the side, and beneath, where it used to say, "Home of the Patriots," someone had taped up a cardboard sign that read, "Home of the DUKES." The crowd, right on the edge of violence a moment before, took a collective step back from the big humming engine. When the bus doors slid open to disgorge an army of college students chanting "DUKES! DUKES! DUKES!" the crowd of locals released a long-held breath and cheered.

I watched in amazement as the students, still piling off the bus, shook hands and slapped backs and mingled with the locals like we were all at some weird, ragtag kegger. As the trickle of students finally stopped, the bus driver emerged, ducking the frame to stand like a giant on the top step. He stood with his hands on hips, smiling and watching the show, then he caught sight of us and waved. Grace laughed and my mouth dropped open as Bruce Bartlett came down the steps to wade in our direction. His latest sweater vest looked dashing in the late morning light.

• • ● •

Abbey sat in the bay window holding a Rolling Rock which was the only thing sweating in the cool evening breeze. She wore jean shorts and had one bare leg braced against the sill while the other dangled out over the mostly dead front lawn, staring down Ash Avenue like it might be hiding her future. I stared at her profile, backlit by a streetlight, and wondered the same thing.

"What?" she asked when she caught me gawping from my rocking chair.

"I was thinking about the roof," I said.

She smiled. "Which one?"

"All of them, I guess. Why did we like them so much?"

"Change of perspective," she said and turned back to the window, though she took her smile back with her.

I was surprised when she actually showed up, at 9:30 p.m. and toting a six-pack, but Abbey had always been like that. Just when you least expected her, she'd be there, and it wasn't until after she left that you realized she arrived exactly when you needed her the most. I'd initially declined the beer, thinking of my try-out in the morning, but as usual she was right, and I found my muscles relaxing and my tension easing away with every fresh breeze.

"Floor looks good," she said without looking at it. "This all the original hardwood?"

"Yeah, but it's mostly smoke and mirrors. If you move the couch, it's just joists underneath."

"Ugh, don't tell me that, Elby. I'll have to report you and get this place condemned. I'm already having enough trouble with your father as it is. You know that crazy old bastard actually filled that goddamn moat with water?"

"Definitely don't ask about the wiring then," I said, quick to change the subject before the ghost of Robert Corvallis did to this conversation what the real Robert did to all the conversations he was involved in. "I have a good enough handle on carpentry now to do a passable fix, but Mary won't pay me for the labor or the materials, and I'm just not that nice. Plus, it's sturdy enough for my use."

"So, you're saying you haven't had sex on it?"

I coughed on a sip of beer, which she ignored.

"Or are you saying you have had sex on it and yet it still stands? You strike me as a gentle lover."

"I, um, when did you cut your hair?" I asked, transparent as the evening. Her hair *was* lovely, though. It was short and dark and framed her face just right and I liked how it looked a little like a robin's wings in the exact moment before it lifts off. Of course, I didn't say any of that. What I did say was, "It's nice."

"My mom still cuts it. Grown-ass woman and mommy still cuts my hair. I ought to be embarrassed, but I'm not."

"How come?"

"Like you said." She turned to face me again and gave her head a little shake, which, if anything, amplified the bird effect. "It's *nice*."

Well, what do you say to that? Nothing, it turns out, because Abbey was out of the sill and moving past me towards the kitchen. For a wild second I thought she might be leaving, and I lurched out of my chair and prepared a host of reasons, ranging from stupid to sad, to delay her departure. It turned out she wasn't leaving, though. Instead, she paused by the stairs that ran up to the third floor.

"I did say I'd help you with the gutters," she said. "This place even got a roof?"

⁘ ⁘ ⁘

"That's Sagittarius," she said.

"It's not."

"And that's Taurus."

"That's not even a real constellation."

"And that one over there is the milkmaid," she said. I could hear the smile in her breath. "You can tell by her pail."

"Her pale what?" I asked.

"Then there's the dippers, of course, but what few people realize is that they are actually connected, and together they form the Great Ewer."

"That's like an udder, right?"

"I always thought you were smart and just hid it well," she said. "Turns out you're just a big dummy after all."

I laughed, and despite the jokes at my expense, lying on the still-warm shingles with Abbey, I couldn't think of a place I'd rather be. So, of course I did my best to fuck it up.

"What about John?" I asked.

"What about him?"

"You picked out a wedding dress yet? Got a venue? Will there be cake? I love cake."

She sighed and covered her eyes with a ropey arm. "First of all, I don't owe you anything, especially an explanation."

"Agreed."

"You blow back into town and you don't call, so I think, *fuck 'em.* Then your mom dies, god love her, and I think, *aw poor boy.* Then you get in the crash—I actually visited you in the hospital even though you were a gomer, by the way—and I think, *aw double poor boy.* Then you get better, but you still don't call, even though you're right here for months, and you're too good for everyone and 'boo-hoo I'm hurt' and 'boo-hoo I'm lonely' and 'waaah I don't want to be here,' and I'm right back to *fuck 'em.* Meanwhile, I've got a life, I've got ambitions, I've got John, everything is just fine. So why, I ask myself, do I keep coming back, night after night, to a broken promise from a stupid boy on a dark street half a decade ago?"

I turned my head to stare at her while she looked up at the stars.

"Don't say sorry. We were both too dumb back then to know any better."

"And now?" I asked.

"We're still dumb," she said and turned to look at me. "I broke it off with John."

I opened my mouth and then closed it, so elated that I was unsure if I would start singing instead if I tried to speak.

"No, it wasn't because of you. My dad hated him too."

"Rick Winthers is a good man. Wise and strong and handsome."

She finally turned to look at me. "He's not sure about you either, smart ass. And neither am I."

"Abbey, I—"

"Have the biggest day of your life tomorrow." Her face was hidden in shadow, but her voice was scratchy with emotion. "Honestly, I don't know whether to wish you luck or pray you get hit by a bus."

"Thanks," I said, my own voice surprisingly also full of confused emotion. "I think."

"Elby, I'm not going to tell you that if you leave, I won't be waiting when you come back. I'm not going to say I'll come with you to some godforsaken corn belt. I'm not going to tell you it's me or hockey, because no one knows what's going to happen tomorrow, or Sunday, or on the fourth Sunday of Advent. So, why don't you just go out there tomorrow and do your best. Then we'll see."

"All roads to beer league," I said.

When Abbey opened her mouth to ask what that meant, I kissed her. I could tell that she was smiling.

CHAPTER 20

You probably think you know how this goes: He wakes up and she's gone. Or he wakes up and she's there but he's late for the tryout. Maybe you're a practical thinker and you're assuming Golden Thunder doesn't have gas or his skates have been stolen or LeDeux doesn't show. Or maybe you're a sentimentalist and you think the sight of her lying there, the sun having fluttered in and nestled in her disheveled hair, convinces him that he doesn't need to prove anything because he's got everything he needs right here.

Wrong. Wrong wrong wrong. First, let's get real. She climbed off the roof and went home. Second, I not only set my alarm clock, but I had the oven timer going too, and I even borrowed a clock-radio from Miss Mary which cost me one awkward, gropey waist hug because she'd been dipping into the slivovitz again. Then I didn't need any of them because who sleeps late when your life dangles by a skate lace?

Golden Thunder had gas and didn't complain about taking me to the Horner, where I arrived an hour and a half early to find Lou Varney had already unlocked the place. My skates were in the bag and sharp as knives. And just as the nerves were starting to get the best of me while I sat in the locker room by myself, contemplating the "EAT PUSSY!!!" graffiti and counting the seconds, Bob Williams came in to shoot the shit and tie his own skates and run over the game plan and tell me, in no uncertain terms, that none of this mattered anyway because hockey was a fool's game played by thugs, coached by idiots, and refereed by morons who wore striped pajamas and were wrong for a living. By the time Lou Varney popped his head in, I was fully dressed and laughing hard as Bob rolled on the padded floor of the locker room moaning sexually. You had to be there, I guess.

"Elby," Lou said. "Your coach is here."

I liked the sound of that, *my coach*. I nodded and, Bob in tow, followed Lou down the long hallway behind the bleachers.

"There's one more thing." Lou stopped as he reached the door separating the cold ice from the hot lobby. "I don't know what to tell them."

"Tell who, Lou?" I asked, but he was already stepping through the door into the lobby.

He swept his arm to the front doors. "Them," he said. And there, waiting outside of the glass, was the whole goddamn town.

Okay, not the whole town, but there was a pretty good-sized mob spilling out across the gravel parking lot. I saw Rob and Ron Dillon towards the front, as well as Dick Newport smoking a cigarette in his trench coat, and a number of other faces I half-recognized from a job or the Crow Bar or from the murkier outskirts of my distant, primary Lowland memories. As we followed Lou through the lobby and toward the trophy room, Rob saw me and gave me a quick thumbs up while his brother waved with the exaggerated, two-handed motion of a groupie on the wrong side of a velvet rope.

In the trophy room I found Martin LeDeux, back to the door, examining Clara's trophy case. He hadn't changed so far as I could tell, still ramrod straight and not tall so much as imposing. He wore the classic, forest green Bull Elk sweatsuit and still sported the signature laurel crown of gray hair, his bald spot shining in the one overhead light.

He nodded as I entered, then turned back to the case.

"Corvallis."

"Coach."

"Your mother?"

"Yep."

"Pretty."

"Couldn't say, Coach."

"Course not."

We stood, side-by-side, staring at my mother's blown-up speed skating picture. She was half-smiling, determined, mean. I was queasy, loose-boweled, spiraling.

"You look fit," he said.

"Thanks."

"You ready?"

You ever heard a more loaded question? Because I still haven't.

"Yep." I adjusted a strap on my shoulder pads through my practice jersey.

"Well, let's get to it."

I nodded and turned to follow Coach. As we made to leave the trophy room, Lou stopped us with a hand.

"The, uh, the folks out there?" he asked. "What do you want me to do?"

LeDeux never looked at me. The man simply made decisions; no consultation required. It was one of the great mysteries of the league why he even bothered to hire assistant coaches. He pulled the door open, passing through the lobby towards the rink door, and called back over his shoulder, "Let 'em watch."

I followed, and Bob, whom I'd forgotten amidst the panic of judgment day, whispered loud enough that LeDeux had to hear too, "Spooky fellah, ain't he?"

And suddenly I was grinning again, walking back onto the same sheet of ice I'd learned to skate on, with nothing in front me but a blank sheet of paper, ready to write something new.

• • • :

This is going to sound vain, but the only person I wanted to see in the stands wasn't there and that stung my pride before I'd even gotten started. I tried not to look at the crowd, but between drills, when I was sucking wind or when LeDeux was explaining something to me that I already knew how to do, I would sneak peeks into the gradually filling bleachers, but I never saw her face. I see, now, how it might actually *be vain*, at least a little bit, but she'd never seen me play, and I wanted her to see what I did best.

So instead, I worked for everybody else: LeDeux and Bob, Rob and Ron, Dick and all the Lowlanders who were curious to see just what made me so damn special. So I sweated, and the heat came up off my shoulders and my friction-warm stick blade on the hard carved ice surface and rose out through the big recirculatory fans and over Lowland so that even the people who weren't there got a taste. Susie and the rest of the sadist physical therapists, Miss Mary and Grace and Bruce and my father, the Duke of Ash Avenue, they all pulled up from what they were doing and turned their faces north towards the Horner. And without realizing it, they gave it back to me. And I took it all, their energy and their hope and their pride, but I took their disappointments as well, along with their shame and their longing, because they were all mine too. They always had been, even if I'd never realized it. I took it all, and I funneled into the only thing on earth that I could do, and I did it well, for me and for them. Or at least that's what I like to think happened.

As I worked my way through the footwork drills, loose, determined, confident, I thought that my face might finally look something like my mother's did in that picture I so envied. And like the Clara hanging in the trophy room, I smiled just a little, imagining her skating beside me, pacing me through the turns, pushing me to go just a little bit faster, try a little bit harder. I wanted there to be no doubt when her ghost came to me that night as I tried to sleep.

"Did you do your best?" she'd ask.

"Yes, Mom."

"Then that's all I can ask."

By the time we got around to some shooting drills, I could feel that LeDeux was impressed, though of course he didn't say anything. He and Bob were feeding me one-timers from either side of the net, and I was rattling them off just like I'd done to the poor Silver Fox goalie I nearly decapitated. If anything, I was shooting even harder. My shoulder felt good, and I stayed in the rhythm I'd developed over so many mornings alone in the Horner. Stay loose, don't overextend, draw from the core and not the shoulder.

Bob was magic, perfect, and his passes were tape-to-tape every time. LeDeux gave me some knucklers, but you could tell his heart wasn't really in messing with me. The crowd had to be partly feeding LeDeux's good will. They cheered every time I hit a goalpost and remained respectable otherwise, it being the morning still and the odds of a fight breaking out during a tryout pretty unlikely. I hoped Lou was selling some popcorn, maybe convincing folks to stick around after and rent some skates to take their own turn around the rink. It would be the very least I could do to begin paying him back for all the ice time he'd donated to my rehabilitation cause. I felt grateful for the crowd's support, for Bob's stellar passes, for LeDeux's willingness to give me a second chance. I was just wondering what LeDeux had in mind next, *C'mon, gimme what you got*, when he called for slapshots.

"What?" I asked. My stomach sinking into my heels.

"Slapshots, Corvallis," he barked. "One-timers. Blueline."

The crowd hooted when he called for slapshots. Who doesn't want to see somebody hit some clappers? Me. *ME!* My shoulder was going to come completely apart, and everybody would be right there to watch it happen in real time. There would probably be hooting.

I lined up on the blue line while LeDeux and Bob gathered pucks into separate corners. God bless Bob, who took more time to gather 20 pucks than anyone that savvy could possibly take without indicting himself. I stood on the blue line, bent over, stick across my knees, watching Saint Bob batting pucks slowly and clumsily into a corner, wondering what the hell I was going to do next, when the one person I wanted to see finally showed up.

"ELBY! ELBY! ELBY!" Abbey screamed, banging on the glass closest to the lobby entrance. We were on the other end of the ice, and at first I didn't notice, and then (yes, okay, vanity for sure) I thought she was just really excited for me. But as she continued to scream and pound and the crowd started to murmur, I pulled up from the blue line and signaled to LeDeux that I needed to go see what was up. He raised his eyes to the ceiling, conveying, "You're fuckin kidding me, right?" without saying a word.

By the time I reached the other end of the rink, Lou had helped Abbey get the door open and she was standing with one foot on the ice as if she were about to charge out onto the rink to me.

"Elby!" she cried, and I saw that there were tears in her eyes. "Oh, God. It's your father. He's got a gun!"

"Abbey, what do you mean he's got a gun?" I asked, reaching my gloved hands out to stabilize her. So far as I knew, no person in Lowland, an admittedly gun-happy town, was less likely to own a firearm than Robert Corvallis.

"He's got a rifle, Elby, and he barricaded himself inside the house. The cops are there, and they can't get him to calm down. God, I'm so sorry. This is all my fault."

"It's not your fault," I said, feeling ignorant and helpless.

"It *is*," she said. "It was all the stupid fucking moat. He wouldn't fill it in, and then you couldn't get him to fill it in, and I told my boss to just leave it alone, but then he got frustrated and called the cops this morning and they *all* showed up and now your dad is threatening to shoot anyone who crosses the water. The cops are getting really nervous, Elby. I think they're going to kill him."

So that's how I found myself plowing down Ash Avenue behind the wheel of Golden Thunder still in full hockey gear. Have you ever tried to drive a car in full hockey gear? I can't not recommend it highly enough. The skates alone make the whole endeavor a liability, like pushing the pedals wearing very sharp, short stilts. At least I was able to get my gloves off and shucked into the passenger seat while I headed south from the Horner towards town. I flew past the Crow Bar, which already had a few cars in the parking lot at 9:52 a.m., it being a Saturday and all. I buzzed past my apartment where Miss Mary, watering the grass in her nightgown, waved the hose at me. And then I was into downtown proper, whipping between the stores on my left and the park on my right.

If I had been in my right mind, I would have realized that it was time to slow down. Outside of the potential to run down a pedestrian, I should I have slowed down because there is always one habitual squad car parked at the park's entrance to nab speeders. Had I remembered the squad car, or if it had actually been sitting there, I would have leaned on the brakes and either slowed down in time or pulled over to get my ticket. But I forgot the squad car, urging myself to greater speed, and the omission nearly cost me my life.

Past the park then, past the courthouse and Jumbo's and Carl's Hardware, and suddenly I was south of downtown proper with nothing between me and my childhood home but straight road and neighborhood. And that was when I remembered the s-curve.

It loomed up from the other side of a slight rise in the road like some monster anaconda, ready to eat me whole. I slammed on the brakes and Golden Thunder declined to respond. Not even a shudder. If anything, the car gathered speed as we slid down the small hill towards the double bend in the road. I tried again, stomping one skate then both over and over onto the brake pedal. Nothing. The *click* as I fastened my seatbelt sounded a lot like prayer.

Now, of the many regrets that I have had about leaving Lowland as a teenager, getting more practice on the s-curve had never been particularly high on that list until that moment. Other Lowlanders my age had experience with the s-curve, gained from being 16 and powering through it with the gut-sure confidence that only comes from having no conception of the very real possibility of their own demise. Me? I left town before I had the chance to be the kid with all the confidence and none of the common sense, and I returned too late, harnessed with the perfect clarity of how fragile I actually am. I was sweating fat drops in the hot car, had never stopped sweating from the tryout, in fact. I thought about LeDeux's face as I hollered across the ice.

"Gotta go, Coach."

"Corvallis!" he'd cried.

"Thanks for everything."

I'd said it with finality, and I meant it earnestly. He'd always been kind in his gruff, Saskatchewan way, and the second chance he'd offered me was beyond anything I deserved or had a right to expect. And what did I do with it? Blew it right out my ass.

The wheels screeched as I went into the first turn and felt the car rock as if it was considering rolling out from underneath me like a horse with an itch on its back. My gloves tumbled from the passenger seat and the change in the cupholder rattled in time with the hood and the trunk. There was a grinding screech as the left side of the car made contact with the inside of the first turn, and sparks flew up past my window. Absurdly, I wondered if that would buff out. Then suddenly I was headed into turn two, under positioned, over accelerated, doomed.

But let's dispense with the suspense. You already know I lived because I'm telling this stupid story. I entered the curve going 78 and I left going

71 without any paint remaining on the side panels. I know because I checked the speedometer, like a sailor checking his knots just before the boat capsizes. This is still an s-curve record, both for speed of entry and exit. I know because I still check occasionally with the bartender at the Crow Bar, who keeps an honest-to-god ledger in a little blue notebook where he also tracks bar tabs and sports bets.

What comes next is lost to me in what I have to assume is the same way that soldiers can't recall the minutes and even hours leading up to the instant when the grenade goes off at their feet. With no way to slow down, I pointed my car south, pulled into the middle of the road, and began honking my horn to ward off oncoming traffic. I couldn't see the end of the street yet, but I could see the flashing lights of the squad cars that had barricaded Ash Avenue to clear the road and yard of pedestrians, or potential casualties. My mouth went dry.

I was going to run into a squad car doing 60 and there was nothing I could do about it. As I neared, all that I have are impressions of memory that may be false. One officer turned to look behind him, then several, who all began to clear out of the way, holstering their drawn pistols or just running with their guns in their hands, willing to take a chance on getting picked off by the nutjob with the rifle if it meant avoiding being mowed down by an Oldsmobile Cutlass Supreme. As the house lurched into view, I still believe that I saw the window above the front door thrown open and a little gray head sticking out in surprise. Then I focused on the squad cars, veering around the first and then splitting the gap between two others, my speed still high, and wondering what was next. When a brave officer began backing his squad car straight toward me, I was faced with two alternatives. Turn left and potentially hit the fleeing officers or turn right and destroy my childhood home, likely taking out my father, the Duke of Ash Avenue, in the process. The trolly problem really isn't as much of a philosophical quandary as everyone makes it out to be.

But as I made my decision and turned towards the house, I felt my wheels lift off the ground and looked out the window in puzzlement to find that I was airborne. I forgot about the fucking moat.

CHAPTER 21

"God, I hate this place."

There was no one to hear me though, just the miserable little TV and the white plastic bed and the teal hospital gown and a vase of flowers that all appointed the now depressingly familiar St. Anthony critical care suite. The flowers, though? Those were new.

"If it makes you feel better, I hate it as well."

When I tried to turn my head to identify the speaker, my neck failed to respond, only creaked in protest. The rest of the system check went well though: my limbs worked, shoulder no sorer than usual, toes and fingers wiggleable. Panicking a little, I tried harder to work my neck, but it wouldn't budge. I started to pant, moving my shoulders left and right. It felt like some invisible hand held my chin tipped up. Tears came with the memory of the wreck, of the water rushing up to meet me, of the smack of Golden Thunder's grill hitting the moat and the second smack of my head striking the steering wheel.

And just like that, I saw both versions of my life collapse. No one needed a paralyzed hockey player or carpenter, a coach or a boyfriend, a son or a friend. All that work, and it ended in a moat in Lowland, PA. I started sobbing.

Then my father was there, standing at my bedside, wrapping me in the first hug of our lives.

"It's okay, Elbridge," he said. "It's okay."

"No no no no no no," I sobbed, moaning into his thin shoulder.

"It's *okay*," he said. "Really."

"NO!" I shouted, pushing him off me with all my strength, my neck aching in protest.

Robert was propelled across the room, staggering into a beeping piece of machinery. He disentangled himself and stared at me like I was a rabid animal he was trying to stick a shot into, then cautiously came back to my bedside. He extended his arms slowly to either side of my head and reached behind my neck. For a second, as he bent closer to my face, I thought that he might kiss my forehead or strangle the life out of me. With Robert, it could go either way. Then I heard the rasp of Velcro, and he straightened, holding up a neck brace and smiling.

"Now try."

Slowly, I turned my head, first right, then left, all the way to each shoulder. Then I cried harder, descending into full-on relief.

Robert let me cry for a while, retrieving the chair he had been occupying from the corner and moving it to my bedside. Then he sat so I could look at him without moving my head. Eventually my shoulder-shaking sobs dwindled to a trickle, then stopped altogether.

"So," he said. "You have been held asleep for medical purposes—to reduce the brain swelling, or so I've been told—for about 48 hours. I imagine that you have questions."

A hundred thousand things bubbled up, and I let the quickest one that made it to my lips tumble out. "How come you're not in jail?"

"I have been released on my recognizance." He held his hands together as if they were still manacled, then pulled them apart slowly. "It may surprise you to hear that this is not the first time I have been required to post bail."

"Actually, I'm less than shocked."

"Oh?" Robert quirked one gray eyebrow. "With whom have you been whispering?"

"Bruce. He even showed me some old campus newspapers. He seemed very proud of you."

Robert winced. "That must have cost him. He truly is terrified of that archivist."

"You think the gun charge will hurt your mayoral ambitions?" I asked.

"Elbridge, we live in Western Pennsylvania. I think it would behoove me to include the mug shot on my campaign poster. Besides, it was an antique and unloaded black powder musket. People no longer possess any sense for symbolism."

"So, you're going to do it?" I asked. "Run for mayor?"

"I never imagined so. Or at least one part of me never imagined so."

"But?"

"But I have been talking with some people, people I trust."

I thought here of Bruce and Grace and Dick Newport, imagining a town run by a council of citizens like that with my father at their head.

"I think you should do it," I said. "Can't get worse, right?"

Robert smiled. "Your unbridled support, as always, means so much to me."

"I mean it though. I'm not saying it right, and it took me a long time to realize, but I do see it now. You could do something for Lowland. Put it back into gear. Give it something to be proud of again." I scratched my head. "Maybe something other than the Duke, though?"

"Thank you, Elbridge." He actually looked pleased with me for the first time in my living memory. "And yes, I believe that the Duke has served his purpose."

"How are you actually going to get on the ballot if all the signatures were for the Duke?"

"I have considered this. It will mean some litigation, which will force some culpability on my part to at least some of the Duke's pettier transgressions. And between these most recent firearms charges and whatever equine, aviation, and sedition charges they can level against me, I dare say I will be busy."

"Maybe you can find a lawyer who will give you a four-for-the-price-of-one deal?"

"As to that, I have been studying in my spare time."

"Dad," I pleaded, rolling my eyes.

"I passed the Pennsylvania bar exam in December," he said with a small, satisfied smile. "Frankly, I fail to see what all the fuss is about."

"You know some people build model airplanes when they retire."

He snorted to let me know what he thought about *some people*. "Maintainers."

"I have to ask you, who was the other guy? The one at the gala and the courthouse who they arrested?"

"An actor from Pittsburgh. Poor man, he got a little too into the role, I think. That appearance at the courthouse was not my doing. He showed up of his own accord."

"Where'd he get the horse?"

"From the same stable where I acquired him, I suspect. You know you can rent horses by the hour?"

"About the whole Duke thing," I said, then stopped, unsure how to ask the one question that still bothered me the most.

"Yes, the time for clarity has come." He crossed his legs, and folded his hands into his lap, making himself look thinner, smaller, contrite. "I have a condition, Elbridge. One with which I was diagnosed shortly before you were born, and only then because your mother demanded I seek treatment. You see, my personality is prone to . . . waves, shall we call them? When the tide is in, I am prone to manic, often illogical decision-making. My powers of observation, my lateral thinking, even my charisma is heightened, while my reservations and self-preservation instincts become extinct. In short, I am both the best and worst version of myself. Then the tide recedes, and I sink into profound bouts of depression, regret, and torpor."

I nodded, thinking of the gregarious Duke alongside tepid Robert.

"Your mother tolerated the swings until she became pregnant," Robert said. "Then she offered me an ultimatum."

"Get help or I walk?" I asked.

"Precisely. So, I got help. A slew of medical doctors said I had this or that. Psychosis, manic-depression, cyclothymic disorder, hyper-euphoria, bipolarism. Different hats for the same head, I believe. And I have been living in a drug-induced fog ever since. That is, until your mother got sick."

"Oh."

"Yes. *Oh*. And now I have much for which to answer."

"What's next then?"

We were interrupted by Dr. Shafar, who knocked briefly before entering as all doctors do.

"Ah," he said, removing his round spectacles and wiping them on his lab coat. "I see our patient is finally awake."

"Yes," Robert said. "I was just telling him about our new treatment strategy." He said "treatment strategy" with the healthy skepticism I expected of my father, but he smiled all the same.

"Excellent. Elbridge, your father has been on the wrong drugs for a long time. Medical science, pharmaceuticals in particular, have come a long way since 1974. I think this new regimen will anchor him right in the middle of a considerably less misty ocean."

As I watched the two men grin at one another, I had the impression that, given the chance to dine together, they would either have the most meaningful conversation of their lives or somebody would get stabbed with a fork.

"But let's return to the patient at hand," Dr. Shafar said, patting my foot through the thin hospital blanket. "Once again, Elbridge, I must say that you're a medical wonder to have come out of such a crash with simple whiplash, severe as it was. Of course, cranial hemorrhaging *seems* scary, but once we got the brain swelling under control, it was just a matter of time."

Dr. Shafar didn't use the word "coma," for which I was grateful, but I still didn't understand the sequence of events. I remembered the breakneck speed, the launch, the water, then nothing at all. It seemed, by rights, I ought to be dead. I was starting to feel a little ragged, and one of the machines I was hooked up to chimed alarmingly.

Dr. Shafar silenced the monitor with a button. "We should let you rest."

"If you would," my father said. "Please show him the helmet first?"

"Ah, of course," the doctor said and left the room. He returned a moment later carrying what I recognized as my hockey helmet. He held it out to me with both hands as if he were offering me communion.

I took the familiar black plastic in my hands that shook with emotion. This helmet had endured three years' worth of blocked shots, high sticks, cross checks, and plexiglass collisions with hardly a scratch. Now, it was split from forehead to spine by an inch-wide crack.

"Like an overripe cherry, right?" Dr. Shafar said happily. "If we could only get everyone to wear one of these bad boys while they're driving, I'd have less work to do!"

As I held the helmet, I thought about the old advertisements with the scrambled eggs: "This is your brain on drugs." Then I remembered that the rest of my equipment had gone into the moat as well, and I panicked. With Golden Thunder drowned, it was all that I owned. My second skin. I couldn't afford to replace it, wouldn't be able to replace it even if I had the money. You can't just buy more skin.

"The rest—" I began, then stopped to swallow. "The rest of my equipment. Did it . . . ?"

"Oh yes," Dr. Shafar said. "It's fine. Wet, of course, but when we hung it in here to dry, we got complaints from all the nurses because it smelled so bad. 'Like an old dead dog stuffed with older, deader dogs,' one said. Quite the image. Anyway, I'll check, but I think we put it in the custodian's closet."

I smiled in relief and slumped back into my pillows.

"Yes, sleep," Dr. Shafar said. "If you're feeling up to it, I think your father could take you home in the morning."

"Thanks, doc," I said, already closing my eyes.

As I drifted off, I heard the door shut, then my father began to sing a little song to himself that came back to me from the deep, dark, rocking fault lines of infancy.

"All hail the tinfoil crown,"
A dark nursery, maybe?
"How beaten smooth its wings,"
A nightlight shaped like a moon.
"How lightly rests the tinfoil crown,"
The wind tapping the roof with the big sycamore's branches.
"Upon the brow of kings."

· · ● ·

"You have three new messages," the answering machine said. "First new message."

I had made it up the stairs under my own power, thought it wasn't a graceful ascent, and Dad kept a hand on my back the whole way. Apparently, I had headaches and dizziness to look forward to for the foreseeable future. When I finally got the door unlocked, the bright sunlight coming through the bay window hurt my eyes. I felt a little maudlin, and Dr. Shafar said my mood might be affected as well.

"The brain is a big baby," he'd said. "It pouts when you spank it."

Robert continued up the second set of stairs to my bedroom to drop off what clothes and sundries I'd used during my stay at the hospital and to give me time alone with my messages.

"I hope you got the flowers," the answering machine chirped out Grace's voice, answering one more mystery. "Bruce and I figured no one had ever given you any, and everyone should get flowers at least once."

"Bruce and I" made me smile, headache be damned.

"Come by the library when you're feeling up to reading again. I've got some things put aside for you that I think you'll like. Or just come by for tea. We've got plenty to talk about." She said the last part with a grin in her voice and I wondered if she was in love. What a world, right?

"Feel better soon. Hello to Robert for us."

"Next new message."

"Hey, Elby," Abbey said.

Leaning against the wall, I rested my head against the ancient drywall and closed my eyes. Her voice, even this tinny version, made my shoulders relax.

"I swung by the hospital, but you were still sleeping off your little fender bender. Why is it every time I come to visit you in the hospital, you're in a coma? The Ash Ave. grapevine says maybe you're coming home today? I hope that's true. Anyways, my mom wants you to come by for dinner this week, so call me."

Did she just say dinner at the Winthers? *Well, hot toddy.*

"And just so you know, my dad still doesn't like you."

Okay, *lukewarm toddy.*

"Next new message."

"Corvallis, it's LeDeux."

I sank into a chair at the folding table at the sound of the voice, but I prevented my head from slumping down to its pliable brown surface. I told myself there were always other teams, other tryouts, other chances.

"That's some town you got there."

And what if I didn't want to leave? What if I was tired of the fight? What if I wanted to coach and raise houses and kids and begonias for Christ's sake? And I was ready for what came next because screw you,

LeDeux, and screw your league, and screw everyone who thinks I'm washed up, because if this is what washed up felt like then call me Mr. Clean.

"I'm gonna take a flyer on you, Corvallis. Good skating. See you in September."

"End of new messages."

I'm not sure how long I sat in the folding chair before my father came tentatively into the kitchen and took the other seat.

"Good news?" he asked.

"Well," I said, honestly unsure how to answer the question. "Grace and Bruce say hello. And I've been invited to the Winthers for dinner."

Robert raised his eyebrows and tried to hide a little smile by rubbing his chin. "That all sounds like pretty good news to me." He paused and lowered his hand, serious again. "And the hockey?"

"They offered me a roster spot for next season."

"Elbridge, that is wonderful news." He reached across the table to grab my hand. "If anyone has earned their redemption, it must be you."

When I failed to respond, he shook my hand. "Why are you sad? Is this not precisely why you have been working so hard?"

"I don't know anymore. I thought so, but this last year, being back here again, I just feel like everything has changed. Like I've changed."

We sat in silence for a minute, wrapped in our thoughts, though he held on to my hand.

"I cannot tell you what do, any more than your mother can." He squeezed when he said "mother." "But the man that they fished out of a drowning Oldsmobile is not the same boy who came home for a funeral."

We smiled at each other, and he squeezed my hand one last time before letting it go to fish in his pockets. He came up holding a set of keys, which he dropped onto the table.

"I have two things for you. One is your mother's car, and the other is my blessing. And though I suspect you really only need the former, take them both with you when you go."

"But where should I go?"

"I don't care, son, so long as you make an educated decision."

Teachers, huh? Go figure.

As he rose to leave, I got to my own unsteady feet and gave him a hug.

"You have any plans on Sunday, Dad?"

He shook his head.

"Why don't you come by," I said. "I'll make gazpacho."

Lou Varney was just locking the door when I pulled up to the Horner. He didn't recognize me at first in Mom's old Jeep, but he waved at me as I made my way gingerly across the evening parking lot.

"Good to see you up," Lou said, clapping me too firmly on the shoulder so that I swayed, forcing him to turn the pat into a bracing hand.

"Sorry," I said, finding my balance. "The doc says I should be better soon. I was wondering—"

Before I could finish, Lou pulled the ring of keys from the lock and twisted one off. He handed it to me, then turned to go.

"Past time you had one anyway," he called over his shoulder. "Just lock up when you're done. Ice is yours in the morning if you want it."

"Thanks, Lou," I called as he settled into his beat-up pickup.

He waved out the window as he drove south, and I watched as the truck, headlights off, made its way down Ash Avenue towards town. The road unfurled like a ribbon in front of him, his grill pointed towards Lowland and the pink sky beyond.

Yanking the old door open, I walked across the dark lobby and flicked the lights on in the trophy room. My mother was still waiting for me, same hood, same half-smile. It could have been a trick of the pastel sunset coming in through the window, but when I approached her picture, she looked a little proud. I didn't ask her what to do this time. I didn't break down in laughter or tears. I just looked, one last time.

"Goodbye, Mom."

Then I turned out the lights.

ACKNOWLEDGMENTS

My thanks to my inspirators, George Athan Billias, Miguel de Cervantes, and Homer. Billias' book *Elbridge Gerry: Founding Father and Republican Statesman* was the model for Robert Corvallis' fictional work, and it remains the foremost authoritative source on the life and times of Elbridge's factual namesake. As far as Cervantes and Homer go, I think all writers owe each some small debt of gratitude, though the Corvallis men owe perhaps a greater measure than usual.

My thanks to my editor, Sarah Chapman at Catamount Press, for the keen eye and gorgeous cover, and my writing groups, the Pittsburgh yinzers and the Grand Rapids Writing Tribe, who all read draft after draft of these chapters and to whom I'm eternally grateful.

My thanks to the Good Hart Artist Residency. Without their beneficence with a well-timed stay in the closing days of drafting this novel, I doubt it would have ever made it over the hill. Thank you to Sue, Bill, and Joanne, who advance creative work every day through selflessness and generosity.

Finally, first and last, my thanks to my family, without whom none of this is worth a damn. Claire, you have my heart for letting me shut the door in the evenings. Dad, Kelsey, David, Kay, and Paul, thanks for picking up the balls I dropped in the decade of writing this thing. Mac and Cully, my joy incarnate, you inspire me every day just by being incorrigibly you. And to my mother, for whom this book is dedicated. Your love and support are deep as the sea.

ABOUT THE AUTHOR

Garrett Stack is an author and poet writing from the Middle West. He holds degrees from Indiana University, San Diego State University, and Carnegie Mellon University. His poetry and short fiction can be found in many literary journals and magazines as well as on his website www.garrettstack.com. *The Duke of Ash Avenue* is his first novel.